His eyebrows rose  disarmed one of his t against the one remainir with the sword, but he advantage by ducking un kicking the other male in the rear before pressing his sword against his opponent's throat, ending the match.

Dracula whistled involuntarily. Despite himself, he was impressed.

The vampire pulled his hood away from his face and shook his hair free, long red tendrils escaping down his back. Dracula's heart gave a start as he realized it wasn't a male at all, but a *female*. A *beautiful* female. And she had the longest, most beautiful shade of red hair he had ever seen.

Praise for Sydney Winward

"Bloodborn's action-packed ending will thrill paranormal fans looking for a mix of old myths and new twists!"

~Tricia Hill, InD'tale Magazine
~*~

"I definitely suggest reading this book if you love vampire stories and great characters."

~Linda Tonis at Paranormal Romance Guild
~*~

"This is an intense story line that holds your attention as you get caught up in the fierce twists and turns and hot chemistry. Lots of excitement. A thrilling must read, every page will have you enthralled and panting for more."

~Tayra S, Reviewer

~*~

"The world-building Sydney Winward develops over the course of the series so far is brilliant and adds to the reader's enjoyment."

~N.N. Light

~*~

"Unique, perfectly paced and completely ship-worthy."
~Georgette, Reviewer

Bloodscourge

by

Sydney Winward

The Bloodborn Series, Book 3

Bloodscourge

Cover Art by *Abigail Owen*

The Wild Rose Press, Inc.
PO Box 708
Adams Basin, NY 14410-0708
Visit us at www.thewildrosepress.com

Publishing History
First Black Rose Edition, 2021
Trade Paperback ISBN 978-1-5092-3507-0
Digital ISBN 978-1-5092-3508-7

The Bloodborn Series, Book 3
Published in the United States of America

Dedication

To all the fictional characters who make my mind
a fun place to hang out.

Chapter 1

Fog slowly crept across the ocean. Elisabeta Trelles put one hand in front of her. Mist curled around her fingers, smooth and cold. Not completely unlike the silky slippers she wore with her trousers and loose shirt. The soft material hugged her feet, but even the luxurious feel of them couldn't push the images of their most recent pillage away. Men and women's faces burned in her memory, eyes cold and empty.

Guilt churned within her stomach, but she quickly pushed it away. They did what needed to be done to survive.

The *Scarlet Dawn* cut swiftly through the water with hardly a sound, one of the fastest ships money could buy. She had lived most of the past few years on this ship with her brother, Miles. They were always moving and only docked for short periods of time. They had too many enemies to keep to one place for long.

A deep noise echoed across the expanse of sea, and her eyes darted upward. It rang out again, slow and ominous. A fog bell.

"Now the real fun begins!" Miles jumped down from the rigging, took a spyglass from his pocket, and looked into it as if it could cut through the dense fog. Every ten seconds, the bell chimed through the night, telling others of its location in the fog.

"We pilfered enough from the last ship," she dared

to say, fingering her red hair as she stared in the direction of the sound. "We should leave this one be."

Miles raised an eyebrow at her.

The look sent an eerie chill down her spine, one that spoke of dire consequences should she refuse his order. Every time she looked at her brother, she saw an exact replica of herself. Red hair that blazed like fire. Green eyes like calm forest trees. Freckles from too many days spent under the sun.

According to the sister at the orphanage, their father had been a noble, their mother a servant. When their mother learned she was with child, she ran in hopes of hiding her growing belly. However, she wasn't with just one child, but with three. Miles had been born first. Elisabeta second. And their mother died giving birth to the third, who died with the cord around her neck. They had been on their own most of their lives. At nineteen years old, they were already veterans of the swindling and pillaging trade and, unfortunately, they were good at it.

He clicked his tongue and patted her cheek, a fiery threat burning in his eyes. "Such a pretty face. It would be too easy to marry you off. I keep you under my wing out of the goodness of my heart. Now, what did you say about pillaging the ship?"

She swallowed against the fear of being separated from him. All their lives, it had been just the two of them. She didn't know who she was without him, and despite despising her brother, she loved him too. They were family. He was all she had.

"I said it would be an easy target," she replied lamely, pushing down the defiance wanting to rise within her.

"Good girl. Now put out the lanterns."

She snuffed out each lantern on the ship. The rest of the crew worked quietly, giving no indication their ship was on the prowl for its next target. The fog bell continuously chimed from the other ship, growing louder as they approached. She waited for the inevitable. Screams of fear. Blood spilling on the deck of the ship. Over time, she had become numb to the killing.

In moments, the other ship noticed them and ceased their bell, but it was already too late. Their crew shouted and scrambled on deck, attempting to turn, and outrun *The Scarlet Dawn*, without success.

Miles's crew released a chorus of battle cries and hopped aboard the second ship. The clamor of steel on steel filled the foggy air. She turned away to watch the water sloshing against the sturdy wood, but nothing blocked out the screams of fear and death. She frowned when she felt nothing for their fear. For their pain. Too many years living on the streets stripped bare a person's empathy.

Minutes passed and the fighting died down. She turned her attention away from the lapping waves and walked across the plank of wood leading to the second ship. As she had expected, the blood of dead sailors pooled on the deck, seeping into the wood. She stepped over fallen bodies and entered the captain's cabin. Miles held a knife to the captain's throat as the man lay on the table, bent awkwardly backward.

"T-t-this is all of my cargo, I-I-I swear!" the captain stuttered, his eyes wide with fear.

"Unless it's been a slow year, I don't believe you," Miles spat.

Elisabeta glanced around the cabin, her eyebrows furrowing when she located only a few rolled carpets. The captain would likely have more carpets below deck, but from Miles's unsatisfactory frown, she doubted it.

Force clearly wasn't getting them anywhere. A woman's gentle touch would likely work better. There was a reason Miles liked to take her on raids. Her assets worked well in their favor.

She took Miles's wrist and he allowed her to pull the knife away from the man's throat—all part of the act.

"What is your ship doing out in the middle of the night in a fog like this?" she asked softly, making sure to appear unthreatening.

The captain rubbed his neck where the knife had rested moments before, and then he lifted his gaze. He stared at her with his jaw agape, and she shifted uncomfortably under his scrutiny.

"We're in the trade business," he finally answered after an impatient nudge from Miles. "It takes a few days to reach Blackwater. We sell rugs, but our wares are few. I swear, Miss."

"Miles…" she whispered, glancing at the anxious captain. "He has nothing. At least leave one survivor."

Miles didn't heed her plea as he pressed the knife against the captain's throat once more. "I leave no survivors."

"W-w-wait!" he cried. "I-I-I don't have anything, but I will trade a secret of riches for my life."

The grip on Miles's knife slackened, his interest piqued. "Go on."

"I know the location of a petrified dragon egg."

Her heart gave a start. The dragons had been extinct for centuries, but the leftover petrified eggs were worth a fortune. They could buy a castle with the coin. Perhaps even a country! They would no longer have to pillage. They would no longer have to kill. Their lives could improve drastically.

"Where?" Miles demanded.

The captain uttered one word, but the word sent icy fear through her blood. "Vampires."

"The vampires have it?" Miles asked thoughtfully. "Are you certain?"

"Yes," the man nodded. "The key to the treasury is safeguarded by the captain of the vampire army. But he's a brute. It won't be easy to get past him."

By the look on Miles's face, he seemed to be contemplating the feat. She'd heard of the vampire city of Ichor Knell before. Thousands of vampires lived within, and it was one of the most dangerous places for a human.

Her brother grinned and turned his head to look her over. Against her better judgement, she began to tremble. This was suicide.

He paced back and forth, back and forth in the small captain quarters. "I can make an elixir to mask your human scent. The vampires will think you are one of their own."

"Me?" she squeaked. "No, no, no. I can't go there. It won't work."

Miles glared at her. With a commanding, no-nonsense tone, he said, "You will enter the city smelling like a vampire. You will convince them you are a vampire, and you will make friends in the right places. And whoever this captain is, you will seduce him and steal the key to the treasury."

Her blood turned to ice, freezing her from the inside out. She wanted to flee, but her legs wouldn't obey her. She wanted to argue, but her tongue wouldn't move. Miles had never asked her to do anything like this before. She couldn't do it. She wouldn't.

The ship's captain spoke, still looking terrified out of his wits as he eyed the knife in Miles's hand. "There is one problem with your plan—vampires mate for life."

A flash of heat burst through her, thawing out the ice that had previously occupied every inch of her. If she thought killing was cruel, this cinched it.

Her eyebrows furrowed as she envisioned the life she wanted for herself, a life without bloodshed. She wanted the dragon egg. It could give them a new life. They wouldn't have to pirate any longer. They could be nobles. They could buy anything their hearts desired. However, doubt pricked at her mind. Would Miles stop swindling, even with the egg?

"It's a risk I'm willing to take," her brother said casually as he flipped his knife in his hand. Addressing the captain, he said, "Is there anything else we should know?"

He shook his head. "That's all I—"

Miles slashed the man across the throat. She looked away and tried to block out the sickening gurgling noises escaping him before all became still.

"He knew too much," Miles said with a shrug as he cleaned his knife, his eyes flashing dangerously. "We will sail straight to Ironfell, which is closest to Ichor Knell. From there, I will see you as close to the vampire city as I am able. You will report back to me often. But you better do this right, or I will—"

"No."

The word from her mouth surprised her. She had never disobeyed her brother before. *Never*.

"No?" He arched an eyebrow and approached her slowly, backing her into the wall and glaring at her until she could no longer hold his gaze. Instead, she fixed her attention on the freckled hand he had struck her with far too many times before. "I can easily find someone else more willing to take your place. If you are no longer useful to me…"

She shook her head and swallowed the lump in her throat. Miles was all she had, and should he choose to discard her… "I will do as you ask."

"Then you will go to Ichor Knell and be useful to me. Understand?"

Defiance burned bright within her, but she found herself nodding in agreement. She would follow orders. She would procure the dragon egg. And then they could start a new life.

"Good girl," he said with a grin, patting her cheek. A blaze of anger burst through her at his touch, but she forced her expression to remain blank. "Let's get you outfitted with a handful of weapons. I believe you have a brute to impress."

Chapter 2

"You like that?" Dracula Ardelean shouted as he held a vampire male upside down over the bridge, shaking him as if trying to make coins fall out of his pockets. The male dangled precariously, his head only a foot from the raging water below.

"Don't drop me!" he pleaded. "I will do better. I swear!"

He rolled his eyes and allowed the male's ankles to slip from his fingers, momentarily followed by a splash as the river's current swept the vampire away.

A sigh carried on the wind from the other side of the practice field—which he picked up easily with his heightened vampire hearing. He glanced over to find Nicolae Covaci sitting on the fence post, a bored look on his pale face. His long blond hair amplified the paleness of his skin. His crystal blue eyes appeared both gentle and piercing at the same time.

"Must you torture your recruits?" Nicolae asked, drumming his fingers against the fence as Dracula moved closer. "No one will return if you continue this behavior."

Turning his attention to his dearest friend, he glared. Nicolae was one of the few people who didn't shrink under his gaze. He had known him all thirty-five years of his life; Nicolae was only a couple months younger than him, though vampires lived indefinitely, and they both looked to be in their late twenties. "If they're too cowardly to face me, they don't deserve a spot among my army."

"Shah Jorin's army," Nicolae corrected. "You are not Shah, nor will you ever be."

He rolled his eyes again. Being the shah was the last thing he wanted. "I could do a far better job than that halfwit of a vampire. Ichor Knell is in chaos."

As if to prove his point, the mourning bell tolled slowly, five chimes for each death from the following day. Thirty chimes total. Six deaths. Three more than the previous day.

Someone had smuggled iron weapons—one of the few things able to kill a vampire—into Ichor Knell right under the shah's nose, and somehow, the church got a hold of them. Ever since, chaos ensued. Corruption leaked through the foundation of the church like an oozing, puss-filled wound.

Those who didn't follow their teachings ended up getting buried six feet beneath the ground, an iron stake through their heart. Dracula certainly didn't want to meddle. He was just one lone vampire who currently had no death wish.

"You should take care when speaking of our shah," Nicolae cautioned. "You never know who is listening."

"You worry too much."

He twirled his sword in the air, eyeing the next batch of fearful recruits on the training grounds. They all huddled together like cowards, watching him with wide eyes. "You!" he called, pointing to a male far too scrawny to hold a sword correctly. "Come fight me. Show me how much you want to join the army."

The vampire swallowed audibly, trembling as he

raised his weapon and cautiously approached. He had valor, Dracula had to give him that.

"Take a swing," he said, watching the recruit's sloppy footwork as he lunged. He easily sidestepped and tripped him, pushing him right over the bridge and into the water below. He, too, got swept away by the current. "You lazy buffoon. Don't bother coming back!"

"Is he doing it again?" a voice quietly asked beside Nicolae, and he turned his head to find Lucian Dragomir skulking about. He usually hid himself away in the safety of his home, rarely showing himself in public. He was ten years younger than Dracula and was a stark contrast to Nicolae. Whereas Nicolae had blond hair and blue eyes, Lucian had shoulder-length black hair and violet eyes. He always bared his fangs instead of keeping them retracted, too, as if he *wanted* to be an outcast in society.

Nicolae nodded. "He won't let anyone sign on at this rate."

He didn't get the chance to listen in further when one of the recruits charged at him, releasing a war cry. He turned just in time to block an attack. The strength behind the attack was weak, the vampire only an adolescent. The older a vampire, the stronger they were, but he believed age meant very little.

There were vampires in Ichor Knell who were centuries older than him, yet he could most likely best them in a skirmish. Strength was not as important as skill. And he would teach these new recruits a thing or two as soon as he found some worthy of his time.

The recruit who had attacked him stared wide-eyed. Dracula's tall, bulky frame cast a shadow over the fear in his expression. His uncertainty annoyed him. With two heavy swings, he sent the young male's sword flying out of his hands, and before he could scramble away, he ran him right through.

The vampire screeched and fell backward. He clutched his side and released several long, pained whines.

Pathetic.

As the vampire clutched his bloody side, the hole started to knit closed as if the wound hadn't happened in the first place. Blood still soaked his clothing, but in a few minutes, there would be no trace of a scar.

The entire training field hushed, all eyes watching the display. Horror seeped from many in the crowd. Others looked like they might faint. And a select few wore hardened expressions. These were the ones he wanted in his army.

He walked slowly from one end of the training field to the other, making sure all eyes were on him.

"Fighting is not a game!" he shouted to all the recruits near enough to hear. "If I choose you for my army, it's because you have what it takes to keep the citizens of Ichor Knell safe. If you want an easy wage where you get to sit around all day and do nothing, this is not the job for you. You will get hurt. You will train harder than you have ever trained before. But if you are a coward, then leave! Get out of my sight."

Unsurprisingly, some vampires scrambled away. Half of the remaining stared with fearful uncertainty in their eyes, and the other half stood proudly with chests puffed out. This would be enough to start with. With the chaos erupting in Ichor Knell, they needed more soldiers who knew how to fight.

He hefted his sword onto his shoulder, wary of nicking himself. "Congratulations," he said, his eyes as hard as stone. "You've made the cut. You will report here bright and early in the morning at the crack of dawn. If you are late, you will polish swords until your hands bleed."

The sun never shined in Ichor Knell, as permanent dark clouds protected the city and its inhabitants from receiving a nasty burn from the sunlight. But even Ichor Knell had a morning, afternoon, and night.

As a dismissal, he pressed his fist over his heart, the new recruits doing the same before taking their leave. He watched them go, his mind already spinning with exercises for tomorrow. The first phase of training would be brutal, but it would also weed out more recruits unworthy of this position.

Lucian and Nicolae snickered by the fence. He huffed in annoyance as he finally turned his attention to his friends. "What are you two laughing at?"

Nicolae spoke in the Old Language, saying something about fierce brutality. Dracula sighed wearily, sheathing his sword, and leaning casually against the fence nearest them, rough and worn from soldiers draping weapons and armor over the wood.

"No one speaks the Old Language anymore, Nicolae," he said.

"I have to keep the language alive somehow. Between Madeleine and I, we have our work cut out for us."

"Speaking of Madeleine..." Lucian cut in, nodding his head in the other direction.

Dracula turned to see Nicolae's mate, Madeleine, waddling slowly toward them, her large round belly clearly making it difficult to navigate the training grounds. Like Nicolae, her blonde hair reached her waist, but she wasn't just a vampire. She was an elf. Or at least used to be before Nicolae had turned her. Her long, pointed ears stood out almost as much as her large belly.

But Madeleine wasn't alone.

Ilona accompanied her, a curly-haired brunette with light brown eyes and pale pink lips. His friends had tried to convince him to court her time and again. They were persistent—he had to give them that.

He frowned and turned away, watching the dark clouds hanging over Ichor Knell instead of the two approaching females. He didn't know whether his disinterest in Ilona stemmed from not wanting to settle down yet or from the fact she just didn't…match him. Her vampire transformation was a bobcat. His was a bat. She had light brown hair and a timid demeanor, he had dark brown hair and he was uninhibited. Her beauty mattered little. It only got one so far. Besides, they never had *anything* to talk about.

"You look lovely today, dear," Nicolae said, suddenly at Madeleine's side and looking at her with more love in his eyes than Dracula had ever seen anyone look at another person before. "How are you feeling? How is the baby?"

"Both well," she smiled.

"You two are breeding like rabbits," Dracula grumbled as he stared at her near-to-bursting belly. "How can two vampires be so fertile?"

Something in vampire blood made them less fertile than humans and elves. Sometimes it took decades, even centuries, for two vampires to conceive.

"It must be my elven blood," she replied, breathing heavily at the exertion from walking across the field. "Baby number six attests to as much."

Six children in fifteen years… It was unheard of in vampire culture.

He finally dragged his attention to Ilona. She smiled timidly at him, a dimple making an appearance on her cheek. He didn't return her smile, but he had enough manners to reach for her hand and kiss her fingers. Again, the contact just didn't *feel* right. It frustrated him.

He wanted to find a connection with her, especially because she was a dear friend of Nicolae and Madeleine, but it just wasn't there. No matter how hard he searched for it, any sliver of fondness for the female evaded him. No spark. No excitement. No twitterpation.

"Hello, Vlad," she said. His eye twitched at the greeting.

That was another thing she did. She called him Vlad. Although it may be his first name, it was also his father's name, a human he despised more than anything in the world. Which was why he chose to be addressed by his second name, Dracula.

"Ilona."

An awkward silence followed. He never knew what to talk about with her. Conversation didn't come naturally in her presence.

"Walk with me?" she asked.

He scratched his head, overcome with uncertainty. He had never been alone with her before, and he wasn't sure he wanted to. Still, he obliged and allowed her to slip her arm through his. Sweat still clung to his skin from recruitment exercises, but she didn't seem to mind. They walked beneath the boughs of a tree with emerald jewels for leaves, and he suspected the others were watching them. He felt their eyes on his back, but he didn't turn around.

She turned to face him. Again, he felt nothing. Nothing at all. No spark. No excitement. She wasn't meant to be his mate. Why did no one else understand?

"I fancy you," she said, a blush rising to her cheeks. She spoke to him more boldly than she ever had before. That was different. Yet, his heart raced with panic at her confession. What was he supposed to do? He wasn't particularly fond of her, but he wished he was. Courting her would seal their group of friends more soundly.

"Thank you..." he said slowly, and thankfully, she didn't seem to notice his hesitancy.

"Please accept this."

She handed him a yellow and blue handkerchief, a token of her desire to court him. He reluctantly took it. He noticed her laundry-like scent in the fibers of the cloth. Again, emptiness washed over him as he gazed back into her light brown eyes. Could something develop over time if he gave this a chance?

He wasn't sure what to say. But he didn't need to say anything as she stood on her tiptoes and kissed his cheek before hurrying away with a deep blush on her face. He stared at the handkerchief, unsure of what to do with it. It was impractical and just took up space. Such a small cloth couldn't even wipe dirt from his forehead.

His frown deepened as he returned to the others, who had most certainly been spying on the exchange judging by their knowing grins. Madeleine's face beamed, her smile unrestrained.

"So?" she asked.

"So...what?"

"Will you give her your handkerchief in return? Will you court her?"

"Bah!" he said and drew his sword, resting it on his shoulder. "I have no time for courting. I have new recruits to train. She will just have to court someone else."

Madeleine took his free hand, her eyes wide as if she might start crying at any moment. The silver elven sheen in her eyes worsened the effect, creating a guilty pit in his stomach.

"But she's in love with you," she said, her chin quivering. "You would break her heart?"

He groaned, but when he tried to look away, she tugged harder on his hand, forcing him to meet her watery gaze. Elves were capable of feats of magic, and for a moment, he swore she was doing something to churn the emotions inside him. Her magic had been stripped from her upon transitioning into a vampire, but still, he wondered.

"I feel nothing for her," he said, shooting a glance toward Nicolae, silently pleading for help, but he only shrugged. "We are not compatible."

"But you can be!" she insisted. She took a step closer to him, her manipulative tears continuing to pool in her eyes. "You haven't given it much of a chance. It couldn't hurt to at least try. It's not like I'm asking you to become her mate. But a little courting never hurt anybody."

He groaned again. Courting was the last thing he wanted to do right now, but her words did hold a sliver of truth to them. He wouldn't truly know unless he tried.

Prying his hand away, he stalked toward the soldier barracks, agitation in each step. "I'll think about it."

He hoped his words were enough to satisfy the vampire-elf. Yet, as he entered his room in the barracks and shut the door behind him, her words gnawed at him. It couldn't hurt to at least try. Besides, he wasn't courting anyone at the moment anyway.

His disheveled room stared back at him, littered with more weapons than he could count, discarded clothing on the floor that didn't quite make it to the dresser, and a meager bed he never got around to making. Nicolae always said he was a slob, but why take the time for tidiness when he could be on the training grounds with a sword in his hand?

Crossing the room, he dug deep within his drawer and located a handkerchief he had created years ago, the black cloth wadded up and wrinkled to the point of being hardly recognizable. First, he would press the cloth to restore it from its slovenly shape. Second, he would think about giving it to Ilona. Once he gave it to her, there would be no coming back.

"Females," he muttered under his breath. They made life more complicated than it needed to be. Unfortunately, it was the price every male had to pay eventually. Perhaps his time to pay it was now.

Chapter 3

Freedom.

Elisabeta never realized how oppressed she was under her brother's thumb until she escaped his presence for a short time. He no longer rained his dominance upon her, and for the first time in a couple years, she breathed easier.

She took a deep breath of the cloudy vampire air, tasting freedom on its wing—a stark contrast to the confining salty sea air. For a moment, it didn't matter she entered vampire lands. It didn't matter at any moment she might become a vampire's dinner. What *did* matter was the new adventure waiting before her, one she could experience without Miles.

"I am a lunatic," she whispered to herself as she walked along the path leading to the vampire city, her knuckles white from clutching her dagger with a vice-like grip. She had already passed several people who she assumed were vampires, but none looked at her as if she was a human. Miles's elixir worked. They thought she was a vampire.

Getting her blood sucked dry wasn't what worried her most. Rather, the moral dilemma before her knotted her stomach. How could she ruin a vampire's life because of Miles's greed—and her own? As a human, she may be able to walk away after seducing the vampire, but he wouldn't be so lucky. He'd be tied to her forever. A thief. And he'd never be able to take another mate.

She shook the thought away and continued forward with purposeful strides. This vampire was a brute. He likely deserved what she had in store for him. At least she told herself as much. It helped ease her guilt, if only slightly.

A *gasp* of wonder escaped her as she rounded the bend and took in the city of Ichor Knell in full view. The black castle spiraled upward into the swirling black clouds, more ominous than she imagined the vampire land to be. Her anxiety grew as she trekked down the slope leading into the city, and she pulled her hood tighter over her hair, making sure to conceal the lower half of her face so only her eyes showed. If she was going to catch this brute's eye, she wanted to use every asset she had at the right time.

The city was just like any other to the extent of having a working class and a noble class. From what she observed, nobles lived in the wealthy sect of Ichor Knell, and the working class lived everywhere else. The smell of clothing dye hit her hard as she passed vampire females dunking cloth into large, colored bins. The dyestuffs stained their hands as they worked, but they were so engrossed in their gossiping they didn't notice her walk by.

She grimaced and stepped carefully to avoid soiling her boots. What a messy job. Dyeing clothing would be the last thing she wanted to do.

Homes and businesses littered the city from blacksmiths to logging to dressmakers. The civilized state of the city surprised her. They weren't barbarians as she had been led to believe. In fact, she remembered passing a school on her way in. Vampires were far from barbaric.

Her footsteps ceased, discomfort growing within her. There were two things she hadn't noticed on her way in. Brothels—which made sense considering vampires mated for life—and pubs.

"Oh no," she whispered, now overly aware of her grumbling stomach. What was she supposed to eat? And how was she to hide food under vampires' supposedly excellent sense of smell? She couldn't drink human blood like vampires. Would she have to hunt for her food? In the dead of night?

She anxiously pinched the bridge of her nose. Making herself smell like a vampire was one thing. Surviving was another.

The clanking of metal brought her out of her thoughts. Her heart pounded harder than it had ever pounded before. She followed the sound, and sure enough, the path led her to what looked like training grounds. Dozens of vampire males skirmished one against another, practicing footwork, striking, and blocking. She grimaced when one vampire sliced through another's arm. The vampire yelped and dropped his sword. Her eyes widened as the wound started to heal immediately, and within moments, it closed up like it hadn't been there in the first place. Vampires could heal that quickly?

She shuddered. They might assume she healed quickly too and wouldn't take care around her. She had to be careful, otherwise a wound that might be a nuisance to a vampire could kill her as a human.

Taking a deep breath, she scanned the soldiers for their leader. The captain. This so-called brute she needed to trick to obtain a key to the treasury. However, she frowned when she realized locating him was no easy feat. Everyone dressed in a similar attire with boots, trousers, shirts, and leather armor. One thing they didn't wear were helmets. But which one was the captain?

She searched for the burliest, ugliest vampire she could find, with thinning hair and rotting teeth. That was how she imagined him. Yet, as she scanned the soldiers, only a few matched the description. Could one of them be the captain?

Determination sparked inside of her as she drew her own sword. If she couldn't locate the captain, she would make him come to her.

Chapter 4

Dracula watched the training soldiers with a careful eye. Often, when one of them made a grave fighting error, he corrected them. But as far as first days went, it was going better than he had expected. Still, disappointment surged through him over his unskilled recruits this year. Starting from scratch was time-consuming.

He subconsciously fingered the black handkerchief in his pocket. After practice, he planned to seek out Ilona and present it to her. Despite not having any feelings for her he hoped something might come of his efforts. Besides, no other females interested him anyway.

"He looks like he might have potential," Nicolae said beside him, nodding his head toward a male who dodged his opponent's attacks with ease.

With a huff, he turned to his friend. "Don't you have something better to do than dally at the training grounds? As long as you're here, you might as well pick up a sword."

"No fighting for me, thank you very much. I prefer the quiet solitude my books offer. Besides, Shah Jorin has no use for his advisors right now."

A frown came unbidden to his face. The church recently became more involved in the government, and one by one, Jorin's advisors were either sacked or pushed aside. The only solace he found was knowing Jorin still paid Nicolae for a job he wasn't currently doing. Madeleine and the children needed to be taken care of somehow other than from Madeleine's meager pay as a launderer. He worried for them often. Times already weren't easy for vampires in Ichor Knell, but with five children and one on the way?

"Did Jorin lower your wage again?" he asked, his frown now a permanent fixture upon his face.

"Yes, and with Madeleine working less due to her condition, it makes it more and more difficult to feed the children. The church increased the cost of blood and hunting to feed my large family is proving to be a difficult task." Nicolae sighed, his shoulders sagging with the heavy burden of caring for his family. "It would be easier if children fed as infrequent as adults. But my littlest needs to feed every few days. When the baby is born, he or she will need to feed every few hours."

Digging into his pocket, he produced a few marks of his own. He had been saving for a dagger, but there were more important things than weapons. "Here," he said, handing the coins to Nicolae. "You need it more than I do."

"You can't keep doing this, Dracula," Nicolae insisted, trying to hand the coins back, but he refused to take them.

"You and Madeleine are like family. Family looks out for each other. Besides, at least I can hunt if I need to. You have a family to watch over."

His friend's eyes became suspiciously moist as he nodded and pocketed the coins. "Thank you. I will repay you for your kindness someday."

He waved away his thanks, grumbling incoherently under his breath. Praise and gratitude both discomforted him. He didn't give the coins for gratitude. He gave them because it was right.

A commotion in the very center of the training grounds pulled his attention away from Nicolae. His eyebrows knit together as he carefully watched the disturbance. Three vampires fought in a growing circle, and from the looks of it, one of them was winning.

He narrowed his eyes and leaned closer as he carefully watched their movements. The winning vampire moved with nimble agility, whirling quickly to fight two at once, and blocking just as quickly to prevent injury. But he wondered why the newcomer covered his face and head, as if he didn't want people to know his identity. One thing was certain—he didn't belong to Dracula's army.

"Dracula, you must be impressed," Nicolae commented as he, too, watched the display.

"Hardly."

Yet, his gaze remained fixed to the vampire, watching him move fluidly like water moving around rocks in a stream. He skillfully nicked the other vampires as if he had trained for years. His opponents couldn't get a single hit on him.

His eyebrows rose in surprise as the vampire disarmed one of his two opponents and faced off against the one remaining. He didn't just use his skill with the sword, but he used his short height to his advantage by ducking underneath a powerful swing and kicking the other male in the rear before pressing his sword against his opponent's throat, ending the match.

Dracula whistled involuntarily. Despite himself, he

was impressed.

The vampire pulled his hood away from his face and shook his hair free, long red tendrils escaping down his back. Dracula's heart gave a start as he realized it wasn't a male at all, but a *female*. A *beautiful* female. And she had the longest, most beautiful shade of red hair he had ever seen.

"Now are you impressed?" Nicolae teased, but he ignored him. Before he could comprehend his actions, he drew his own sword and started toward the center of the field. She didn't see him coming, as she faced away from him. Everyone hastily scrambled out of his way, watching warily as if wondering what he would do to a female vampire on his field.

He pressed the point of his sword toward her back, though not close enough to draw blood. "Never turn your back to the enemy."

She spun around. Her eyes widened for a moment as they raked over him before a smirk appeared on her lips. "Am I turning my back to the enemy? Or am I simply trying to lure the enemy into a false sense of security?"

He returned her smirk with an amused half-grin of his own. He liked this fiery female. But how well would she do when faced against him in combat?

Dracula struck first to test the waters, and the female easily deflected the blow with a perfectly executed block. He attacked again and again, and each time, she blocked it with ease. But then she started returning his blows, her hair wild as they fought.

A surge of excitement coursed through him. The female was dangerous. He couldn't resist danger.

She delivered an overhead blow, and he blocked it,

having far too much fun with this little game. She was a young vampire—there was little power behind her attacks. But she was fast, and she was skilled. Every once in a blue moon, someone would impress him, and this was that someone.

Unfortunately, he couldn't fight her for too long—he had training to complete.

Dipping into his strength reserves, he attacked with fierceness in each blow and by the way she struggled to keep up, he knew he was winning.

With one last strong blow, her sword flew out of her hands. Not giving her a chance to recover, he swept her feet right from under her with the flat end of his sword. He hovered the tip of his weapon over her heart, watching as her chest rose up and down with each heavy breath. She stared up at him with wide eyes as if she thought he would run her through. As a vampire, she would heal quickly. But he had no desire to hurt her. Unlike most of the other recruits, she had earned his respect.

He held out a hand to help her up. She took it, and the moment their fingers met, a spark traveled from his fingertips, up his arm, and flipped his stomach over. He snatched his hand away in surprise, even as the spark continued to crackle through his heart like lightning. He regarded her curiously.

"What's your name?" he asked, his gaze raking over her soft jaw, her red lips, and along the freckles dotting the bridge of her nose. Fire and mystery filled the depths of her green eyes.

"Elisabeta."

A half-grin pulled on his lips, and he hefted his sword onto his shoulder. He hoped to see more of her in the near future. "Dracula," he replied before turning and sauntering to the other side of the training field.

He twirled his sword in his hand and scanned the recruits skirmishing one against another. One recruit in particular stood on the sidelines. He watched the fighting with wide eyes, yet he possessed an air of determination. The male obviously wanted to learn how to fight, but he didn't know where to start.

Whistling to get the male's attention, he summoned him with a motion of his head.

"Yes, Captain?" he asked on his toes as if itching to fight.

"Name?"

"Brander, Captain."

"You have no partner. You will practice with me."

Brander swallowed hard, staring back at him with wide eyes. "Will you impale me?"

He grinned wickedly. "I haven't decided yet. But then again, you have not given me a reason to impale you. Try not to disappoint me."

They began skirmishing with one another, though he toned down his swordplay for Brander's benefit. They traded blows, and as the other vampire became more confident, so did his footwork and attacks. The recruit attacked fiercely and quickly, at least until he misstepped. He took the opportunity to grab Brander's wrist with one hand and place his other hand on his shoulder. He violently wrenched Brander's arm backward until he screeched and dropped his sword.

"You left yourself open," he said casually as if he didn't currently have the power to break the vampire's arm. "If you expose yourself, you give your opponent the opportunity to kill you. The trick is to waste as little time and energy as possible on one opponent so you can quickly move to the next."

"A-a-are you expecting us to get attacked?"

He shoved Brander forward and frowned as the vampire scrambled to pick up his weapon. His gaze drifted toward the mourning bell that stood tall and foreboding in the middle of Ichor Knell. It hadn't pealed yet, but he felt sure it would sometime today.

Something big was on its way, and he wanted to be ready.

"Get back into stance," he instructed, ignoring Brander's question. He raised his sword but made the mistake of glancing back toward the field where he had fought Elisabeta. He found her watching him, her red hair blowing lightly with the breeze as she leaned casually on the fence. An unexpected surge of nerves burst through him, making him feel hot around the neck. He never experienced these feelings around Ilona.

He quickly looked away and growled when he found himself no longer able to pay attention to the skirmish. That had never happened before. His impeccable focus was unmatched no matter the circumstance, and now of all times a female got under his skin?

Releasing a deep breath, he sheathed his sword. "On second thought, we've been practicing all day." He turned and raised his voice so the entirety of the recruits could hear him. All fighting ceased immediately. "You are worn. You are tired. But take heart you will get stronger! Very few of you have impressed me today. And I would be humiliated to be seen with you on the battlefield. Change my mind. Be here again tomorrow at the crack of dawn."

Murmuring started as soon as he finished his speech, but he didn't care what they said to one another. Coddling wasn't his style. Tough love, perhaps, but not coddling.

Some recruits stayed longer to practice. Others returned to the armory to deposit their practice weapons and armor. He moved toward the armory to make sure his new recruits stored their armor in the right place rather than leaving it in a heap on the ground like the day before. He had been very close to impaling yet another vampire for it.

However, not a single piece of armor was out of place on the racks as he entered.

"Captain?" a recruit with sandy-blond hair asked, approaching hesitantly. The male's eyes gleamed red, which indicated his thirst. "I need to hunt. I might miss tomorrow's practice."

"How inconvenient," he replied, rolling his eyes. "Go feed. You're allowed one feeding per month."

The male saluted him before scrambling away.

He turned. And froze.

The vampire named Elisabeta walked into the armory, her red hair standing out like a beacon in the night. He ducked behind a rack of shields, his heart pounding fiercely. Even amidst the stench of sweaty vampires, he picked up her scent. She smelled like wildflowers—something nonexistent in Ichor Knell due to a lack of sunlight.

Subconsciously, he dug his hand into his pocket and shoved his black handkerchief down. He couldn't give it to Ilona with Elisabeta's scent driving him mad.

Her scent became stronger as she wandered closer, clearly looking for something—or someone—and as she drew nearer, he edged further away. The spark he had felt after their skirmish made him believe it would be dangerous to get close to her. Not because he was afraid of courting someone he fancied, but because he *wanted* to flirt with the exciting spark. He *wanted* to see what kind of danger the spark might put him in. *That* was what he found dangerous and exhilarating.

The mourning bell tolled, startling him out of his thoughts enough to knock a shield to the floor. He flinched as it clattered loudly on the ground, all eyes darting in his direction.

So much for escaping unnoticed.

He cursed his luck as Elisabeta spotted him and made her way toward him. He busied himself with righting the shield, pretending not to notice her approach. Where did she hail from anyway? She had a lilt to her words, but he couldn't place its origin.

"You're the captain, I presume?" she asked.

Finally, he turned to her and instantly became annoyed by the excitement churning in his stomach. She was beautiful. Green eyes. Red hair. And he loved the freckles on the bridge of her nose. This near to her, he noticed something he hadn't before. Her lips curved upward ever so slightly as if they were naturally shaped that way.

He leaned his shoulder against the wall, watching her carefully. He didn't know a thing about her except she was the best swordswoman he had ever known. Still, she couldn't be trusted.

"Depends on who's asking," he said, giving her his best intimidating stare. "If you're from the church, then scram."

"Then it's a good thing I'm not from the church."

She cocked her head to the side, a curious glint in her eye. "You must be an old vampire for how skilled you are with the sword. Two hundred? Three hundred?"

He snorted in amusement. "A vampire soldier never lives to be that old. It would be much more probable to die from an iron wound. I am thirty-five."

Her eyebrows rose in surprise. "That is young for a vampire, especially one to be commanding an army."

"It is." He leaned in close to her and heard her breath hitch as he smelled her neck, his breath on her skin. He couldn't help himself from flirting with danger. It was too fun. "And you..." he said in a murmur, inhaling her scent once more just to make sure, "are just barely of age. Eighteen?"

"Nineteen."

Pulling away from her, he regarded her once again. She was a complete mystery. Only nineteen? And she could handle the sword with an expert hand? Not to mention she was a female. Females didn't fight. They sat around with their needlework, or if they were poor, they did laundry. Just like Ilona and Madeleine.

His fingers itched to touch her again, to feel the electrifying spark between them. He wanted to continue flirting with danger.

What a horribly delicious idea.

"I want to join your army," she said suddenly. His playful side vanished in the blink of an eye. For a moment, he thought she was jesting. At least until he noticed the serious look in her expression.

"Absolutely not. I don't know where you're from, but here, females don't join armies. You would be better off doing laundry."

"But I came all this way."

"Then you came all this way to do laundry. Get out of my sight."

He started to turn away, but to his surprise, she grasped onto his hand, a spark shooting up his arm once again. His heart raced. His stomach turned. And it only worsened when she didn't let go.

"But why not? I am highly capable of joining your army. I am better than most of your recruits."

He snatched his hand away, towering above her as he glared. To his annoyance, she didn't flinch. "It isn't about skill. In Ichor Knell, it's about survival. Females cannot join the army because it's a hazardous job. They are better suited to rearing children and keeping our population alive."

Her eyebrows furrowed. "But vampires mate for life. If their male mate dies, they cannot bear any more children. But I suppose if they have a child every one or two years—"

"Every two years?" He paused, looking at her strangely. She smelled like a vampire, yet she didn't know about vampire fertility? Perhaps she grew up with a human parent, or with relatives who didn't explain to her how often vampires could conceive. Her ignorance made his desire to flirt flee right out the window. "Vampires aren't very fertile, which likely has to do with our long lives. It can take decades, sometimes centuries, to conceive a single child."

Unless one possessed elven blood like Madeleine.

The rosy heat of embarrassment entered her cheeks. A small pang of remorse tapped on his heart. And why were they speaking of mating habits? He hardly knew her. Nicolae, ever the proper one, would be ashamed of him.

"Out of my sight," he said with a wave of his hand. "I don't want to see you on my training grounds again. Find some female's work. Find a mate. And make babies to your heart's content."

The time to flirt with danger had passed. He had embarrassed her. He had shamed himself. And he had let his loose lips do talking he hadn't meant to do. His bloody lips! How many times had they gotten him in trouble?

Too many times to count.

A flash of determination seemed to replace her embarrassment, and although she said nothing more, she strode out of the armory. He watched with a cautious eye. He wasn't sure he liked the little flash. He got the distinct impression he would see her again. And soon.

Chapter 5

Elisabeta had messed up.

She had him for a minute! And then her lack of knowledge of vampire culture had turned him off. She wasn't ready to be thrown into the jaws of seduction. She had to learn more about the culture before trying again.

A frown pursed her lips as she flipped through her brother's notes about vampires in the dismal, colorless apartment she had rented. When she had gone looking for a brute of a captain, she had expected to find a surly, bulky, hideous vampire. What she hadn't expected to find was a very handsome, very tall, very…everything…male.

She swooned at the thought of him. He had the most intense dark eyes. The most intense dark hair. And the way he had looked at her as if piercing her very soul with his gaze… She could hardly breathe.

"Heaven help me," she whispered to herself.

To try and distract herself from thoughts of Dracula, she continued flipping through Miles's notes. He hadn't included much information about vampires. Instead, he focused mainly on the art of seduction. For example, *fake an injury to make the male come to your aid.* She blushed from her head to her toes. Not only did she not know *how* to seduce, but she couldn't come to terms with the immorality of her quest. This wasn't right, but she held onto the hope of finding another way to obtain the key from Dracula.

First, she needed to learn more about vampire culture. And fast.

She slammed the notebook shut and pushed herself out of her chair. Staying in her apartment all day wouldn't help her. Instead, she needed to find work, and dare she think it, perhaps she could do laundry. She'd never done honest work before, so if Dracula thought doing laundry suited her, she would take his word for it. Besides, immersing herself in the culture would help her learn more before she confronted him again.

Braiding her long red hair down her back, she set off into the city, dodging peddlers, pickpocketing several wealthy looking nobles out of sheer habit, and moving through the bustling crowd toward the place she remembered females dying fabrics. Surely someone could point her in the right direction from there.

She spotted another easy pickpocketing target, a female with her attention on one of the glass windows displaying a beautiful red dress. She looked to be thoroughly distracted, she wore her coin purse on her belt, and she situated herself in a bustling crowd where Elisabeta wouldn't get caught. Was she asking to lose her money?

Moving closer with her eyes forward and not on her target, she didn't miss a step as she slipped a coin purse from the female's belt and continued on her way, no one the wiser. Again, too easy.

She threw one of her pickpocketed coins in the air and caught it repeatedly. This was enough coin to pay her rent for at least another month. Hopefully, she wouldn't have to stay that long. Being near this many vampires made her anxious, though she tried her best not to show it.

At last, she reached her destination, watching as females dunked vats of cloth into the large bins and stirred them around with wooden paddles. This was close enough to laundry, right? Dracula couldn't fault her for choosing it. After all, there was not a male in sight. Dyeing clothing seemed to be female's work.

An important looking female supervised the dyeing process closely, her eyes missing no detail. She was plump, with a stern expression permanently etched onto her face, and eyebrows that looked closer to one instead of two. A mole stood out above her lip and made her look even sterner than she would without it.

"Excuse me," Elisabeta said as she approached the female, who regarded her with immediate suspicion. "I am looking for work."

The female stood with her hands on her hips, surveying her up and down. "You have no dresses in your closet?"

She glanced down at her outfit and frowned. She had always worn a shirt and trousers, especially on Miles's ship. The outfit hid her curves and made her stand out less than a dress. Besides, trousers were easier to move in than skirts. Easier to fight in too.

"You find something wrong with my outfit?"

With a huff and a roll of her eyes, the female dropped her hands from her hips. "Wear whatever you want. It's not like anyone will see you anyway. Come along. I have no work for you in dyeing clothing, but I do have something inside." She motioned with a crook of her finger and Elisabeta followed. Rows of bins were lined up in the large room, each with females kneeling beside them and dunking already dyed clothing into the water.

"My name is Madame Glover, and you will report directly to me at the end of your shift. We not only dye clothing, but we launder nobles' clothing as well. Here we have those washing the clothing with soapwort, others twisting the clothing to remove excess water and beating them dry. You will be stationed here." She led her to a wash bin surrounded by two other females who glanced up with curious eyes. "As you can clearly see, Madeleine is with child and under no circumstance will she get up to refill the bin with hot water. That will be your job when the water starts getting cold. And this here is…"

"Ilona," the other female said with a slight dip of her head.

"I'm sure you can help get our newcomer started?" Madame Glover asked. Ilona nodded. "Good. I will be off."

Madame Glover left and Elisabeta knelt, not sure where to start. On board the ship, a servant washed their clothing for them.

"Beautiful hair," Madeleine murmured as she reached for Elisabeta's braid and trailed it through her fingers. "I've never seen red hair before."

"Never?"

Madeleine shook her head. "It's not common in Ichor Knell. Where are you from?"

A dangerous question, but it was one she'd rehearsed. "Northbury," she answered, which was the truth. Elisabeta and Miles had been born there, but they hadn't stayed. "It's extremely snowy and cold, and not at all a pleasant place to live."

Ilona handed both Madeleine and Elisabeta an article of clothing to wash, and she followed the others' examples by carefully dipping it into the hot water and scrubbing it clean.

"What is your name?" Madeleine asked, and she found herself unable to stop staring at her pointed ears. She was a vampire? But also an elf? Was it even possible?

She forced herself to tear her gaze away and focus on washing the clothing. After all, her main objective here was to gather information and learn more about the culture. "Elisabeta."

Madeleine stopped her task, her mouth twitching as if fighting off a smile. "Ah, my mate, Nicolae, told me about you. It's not easy to impress Dracula, but you somehow managed to do it."

Her heart gave a start at the mention of Dracula, her eyes widening involuntarily. They knew him? Could being stationed at their bin be a stroke of luck? This was her chance to learn more.

"You know Dracula?"

"He's our dear friend," Ilona answered, a faraway—dreamy?—look in her eyes. The look alone instantly made her wary. Could Ilona be competition? Or worse, was she his mate?

Carefully treading the waters, she tried hard to sound disinterested in the turn of topic and continued to wash the blue dress. She found it difficult to hide her interest without tipping her hand. "I've heard Dracula is a brute. Is it true?"

Both Madeleine and Ilona snickered, and suddenly she felt foolish for asking such a question. Had she said something wrong?

With a playful swat to her shoulder, Madeleine answered, "Have you been listening to tales from his soldiers? He's particularly harsh on them because he needs to be. To turn recruits into warriors is no easy feat."

"Not to mention his moods," Ilona giggled, looking from Madeleine to Elisabeta. "He nearly drowned five vampires just this week."

Alarm coursed through her. Her pulse raced. "Drown?" she squeaked.

"You make it sound worse than it is." Madeleine rolled her eyes before offering her a soft smile. "He threw them over the bridge into the river. Vampires don't drown, otherwise he never would have done it. Despite the front he puts up, he's actually one of the most caring vampires I know. Once you have his loyalty, he would die for you. He's intense, but passionate about everything he does." She leaned closer as if sharing a secret. "Besides, he's a gull for female tears. I can practically make him do anything with a watery gaze."

Her heart surged with hope. She planned to use tears to her advantage if the opportunity arose.

Ilona and Madeleine shared a look, and Madeleine raised an eyebrow as if they were having a silent conversation. Could vampires speak telepathically? Or were the two of them such good friends as to read each other's facial expressions? And what were they talking about? Were they talking about her?

Finally, Madeleine turned and gave her a bright smile. "As you probably already know, tomorrow night is the blood moon. Our group of friends has a tradition to hike up the peak and watch the raining stars where the clouds don't obscure the view. As it is...Lucian Dragomir doesn't have a female companion for the excursion, and if you joined us, you would make the numbers even between males and females. Would you like to come?"

Triumph flowed through her and she worked hard to hide a smirk. She had an in. True, she wouldn't be paired with Dracula, but at least she would be close enough. Besides, she wasn't yet sure if Dracula had a mate, and this would give her the perfect opportunity to find out.

She smiled. "I'll be there."

Chapter 6

Dracula huffed for the dozenth time in the past thirty minutes, glancing up at the position of the blood moon above them in the dark sky. If Madeleine and Ilona kept them waiting any longer, they would all miss the raining stars. He didn't care if Madeleine was with child. If she didn't hurry and meet them, he just might march up the trail without everyone else.

He propped his foot behind him on the rock face and fingered the black handkerchief in his pocket. Tonight, he would give it to Ilona. No more excuses. Especially not Elisabeta. She was too young and ignorant for his taste.

"Will you stop sighing?" Lucian chuckled. "They will arrive when they arrive."

Nicolae narrowed his eyes suspiciously. "Or are you impatient because of Ilona? You're actually going to court her, aren't you?"

"That's none of your bloody business," he snapped. "I think you should be more concerned about Madeleine. Can she even climb the trail?"

"She can climb it just fine," Nicolae said with a wave of his hand. "In fact, she's been itching to get some exercise between being cooped up with the children and working as a laundress. Between her and Ilona, they've been talking my ear off over seeing the stars tonight."

Their conversation ceased at the shuffling noise on the path below, and moments later, Ilona appeared by herself. She looked nice tonight, wearing a nice dress and her curly hair tied back with a ribbon. Disappointment filled him when no spark accompanied her touch as she threaded her arm through his. Why didn't he feel it? He knew it existed, just not with Ilona. Still, he held onto the hope that feelings might develop over time.

"Good evening, Vlad," she said quietly, and it surprised him when she kissed him on the cheek. He wasn't sure what to do. He hadn't given her his handkerchief yet to officially begin the courtship. But if they were to start courting after tonight, he should welcome kisses on his cheek.

Yet, a pit of disappointment formed in his stomach. There were no pleasant emotions present in her company.

Turning to Lucian, she said, "You will no longer be the odd male out. Madeleine and I have procured a female companion for you tonight."

Lucian raised his eyebrows. "You have?"

"Indeed. Here they come now."

In the darkness, he made out two shapes coming their way, though he couldn't recognize them in the darkness. As they came closer, one of them appeared to be Madeleine by the large belly and waddling footsteps, and the other...

Heat spread through him as his eyes raked over red hair, a feminine face, and lips that smirked at him without seeming to be aware of it.

Elisabeta.

A dozen emotions coursed through him. Panic

because he didn't want her to see Ilona draped on his arm. Embarrassment because he didn't know how to act around her outside his usual captain persona. He was giddy at the thought of being around her but annoyed no one had warned him ahead of time.

A fire grew inside of him he quickly tried to put out.

Jealousy fueled the fire burning in his veins. She was Lucian's female companion tonight and not his.

He frowned as the two females stopped before them, he and Elisabeta staring each other down. "Ugh. You again."

Madeleine gasped. "That's no way to speak to Elisabeta."

But her words went unheeded.

"Hello to you too, Drac," Elisabeta said, her smirk growing wider.

"Never call me that." He looked her up and down, his frown deepening at each passing moment. "And why in Ylios' name are you wearing men's trousers? Your lack of femininity is atrocious."

She placed her hands on her hips. "Your lack of manners is atrocious."

"Vlad," Ilona said, tugging on his arm and snapping him away from his churning emotions. "Let's not miss the stars. I'm sure you can argue some other time."

His eye twitched. He hated when people called him Drac. He hated when people called him Vlad. How difficult was it to call him what he liked to be called?

"Send her away," he said to Madeleine. "She's unrefined. She's naive. And she gets on my nerves. I will not have her with us tonight."

"That's a shame," Madeleine said with a shrug. "Because she is Lucian's companion and not yours. I believe you have no jurisdiction here."

"Hello, my dear," Lucian said, bowing low and kissing Elisabeta's hand. "I am honored to meet you."

Why did everyone ignore his request? How infuriating!

"I'm not as naive as you think," Elisabeta said to him. "Forgive me for my lack of knowledge. My mother was a human. I don't know who my father was."

His lips pursed in surprise, especially because the story sounded all too familiar. His own disgusting father was a human and his mother a vampire. That would explain quite a bit. Her father must be the vampire then, but if she was raised by her mother... Then her naivety made sense.

Suddenly, his shoulders hunched with guilt for his comment and he turned away to hide it. He always judged people too quickly. But he almost willed his judgement to return because his desire to flirt with danger came raging back at full force. Why did she have to come? She ruined everything.

"Shall we?" Lucian asked, and a moment later, Elisabeta latched onto his arm.

Jealousy once again pricked at his twitching eye. He wanted to trade partners.

Nicolae and Madeleine led in front, he and Ilona in the middle, and Lucian and Elisabeta in the back. It took all his self-control not to scowl at Lucian over his shoulder every ten seconds.

"It's a lovely night," Ilona said, holding his arm in a way that allowed her to rest her head on his bicep—

like everyone else, she was short compared to his towering height. He scratched his head with the discomfort of Ilona acting familiar with him within Elisabeta's view.

"It is," he replied, taking a deep breath, and trying to pretend Elisabeta wasn't behind him.

"How many raining stars do you think we'll see?"

He shrugged. "Is it something you count?"

She nodded. "Last year, fifty-four stars rained from the sky. I believe Ylios sends them to warn us. An even number means good luck for the year. An odd number means bad luck. Let's cross our fingers he will send an even number."

Like usual, he wasn't sure how to reply. She was far too optimistic for his realistic views on life. With how things have been going lately in Ichor Knell, he expected an odd number of stars.

He snuck a glance behind him, and his heart skipped when he found Elisabeta returning his gaze. He quickly stared forward again and chided himself for the giddiness churning in his stomach. He hardly knew her, and he needed to put her in the back of his mind.

Which meant he needed to go forward with presenting his handkerchief.

He took a deep breath. It was something he needed to at least try.

Clearing his throat, he reached into his pocket and—

Elisabeta shrieked behind him, and he spun around to find her on the ground, clutching her ankle.

"I'm sorry!" Lucian cried as Dracula rushed forward without thinking. "I turned to admire the view and she must have rolled her ankle. I am such a horrible companion. I should have been watching."

He crouched down beside her and gently placed his hands on either side of her foot. "Can you move it?"

She shook her head, her eyes watering. "It hurts quite a bit."

"But she'll heal quickly, won't she?" Lucian asked, apparent worry in his eyes. "Every vampire does."

Again, she shook her head. "I'm half-vampire. It takes longer for my injuries to heal."

He narrowed his eyes at her. That wasn't true. He was half-vampire himself and he healed just as quickly as any regular vampire. But he didn't think more on it because his worry for her took over.

"Dracula," Nicolae said calmly. "You are familiar with battle wounds. You should take a look. It could be broken, and if that's the case, she might not make it to the top."

"Go on without me," she insisted, though she grimaced as she tried to move her foot. "I never meant to ruin your fun. Please. I would feel better knowing you enjoyed your night rather than fussed over me. I'll survive."

"Oh, cry me a river," he growled, rolling his eyes. "In battle, we leave no male—or female so to speak— behind. Let me take a look. And stop being a martyr. It's getting on my nerves."

Lucian's forehead creased with worry. "Allow me to help. What can I do?"

"You can escort Ilona to the top of the peak while I tend to Elisabeta. We needn't all stay behind. Besides, Ilona wants to count the raining stars."

For a moment, he looked like he might argue—or Ilona who appeared completely put out—but finally he nodded and offered Ilona her arm. The rest of the group continued up the trail.

Dracula was very aware of her proximity, and he tried his hardest to ignore the excitement coursing through his blood.

He guided her to a tree stump and helped her sit. When she put weight on her foot, she grimaced and clutched onto him tighter. Now how was he supposed to give Ilona his handkerchief when Elisabeta tied his stomach in knots?

Her scent hit him as a powerful surge, and he involuntarily trembled as he breathed it in. Daggers, her scent! It drove him wild.

"You rolled it?" he asked as he unlaced her boot. Boots and trousers? She dressed with such a lack of femininity. Yet, she still exuded grace and poise.

"Yes," she replied, her eyes starting to water. Protectiveness surged through him at seeing her tears, and he cursed his weakness. He could face dozens of vampires in combat and not even blink an eye. But a female's tears? It undid him.

Very carefully, he peeled off her stocking to reveal her bare foot. Much to his surprise, he liked the shape of her foot. Dainty but elegant. And skilled. Her footwork in their skirmish had been practiced and perfected.

He puzzled over the seemingly unafflicted foot. He found no bruising, no inflamed skin, and nothing to indicate an injury. If anything, it was just a miniscule fracture.

"Forgive me," he said, surprised at his own words. He rarely apologized. "I misjudged you. You may be naive, but you have a good reason to be. Where is your mother now?"

She frowned and looked away from him. "Like my father, I never knew her. She died giving birth to my triplet. It's just been me and my brother for nineteen years."

He raised his eyebrows. Triplet? So she had a twin? Did he look like her? How had they gotten by all these years? Especially as vampires outside of Ichor Knell?

But he kept his mouth shut and allowed her to continue her tale.

"I wanted to find a better life for me and my brother, which is why I am here."

He snorted, continuing to feel along her foot to make sure nothing was out of place. "I'm sorry to say Ichor Knell isn't the place you want to build a better life right now. You've made a poor choice."

"Have I?" Heat sizzled in his blood at the way she looked at him. He thought he heard the innuendo in her voice, but perhaps he just imagined it.

His hands paused on her ankles, and he studied her face for a moment. The mystery that shrouded her intrigued him. Both parents unknown? An elusive twin? Appearing out of the blue during a dangerous time to be in Ichor Knell? Not to mention her beauty. Her alluring eyes ensnared him. The slight curve of her lips tempted him. And although other ladies in Ichor Knell might disagree, he found her freckles wholly endearing.

Another puzzle stared back at him as his gaze roamed over her freckles. Freckles formed from exposing the skin to sunlight. If she was born a vampire, how did she get them?

"Your father must be the vampire," he commented

finally as he carefully pulled her stocking back on and started to lace up her boot.

"It seems that way."

He frowned. "How odd. Once a vampire mates, they are fiercely loyal. Even to their children if what you say about your mother's death is true. I find it strange you don't know your father."

"And who are you fiercely loyal to?" she asked as if attempting to avoid the subject of her family.

He gave her a playful grin after he finished tying her boot. "To be determined."

This game they played was fun. And it had only just begun.

"Can you walk?" he asked. "In truth, the raining stars isn't something you want to miss if you've never been to Ichor Knell before."

She attempted to stand, but her foot collapsed from under her, and he only just barely caught her before she fell. His heart pounded at her nearness, fire crawling through his blood where she touched him.

"Well, I'm not about to miss the stars because of you," he grumbled as he averted his gaze and rubbed the fluster from his neck. "Climb on and hold on tight."

"Climb onto your back?" she asked with wide eyes. "That's a breach of propriety if I ever heard of one."

"Yes, and so is a female wearing men's trousers. I am half-tempted to leave you here."

"Fine. But don't you dare drop me."

He helped her onto a rock, and from there, she climbed onto his back and held on tight. His pulse raced when she wrapped her arms around his neck and pressed her cheek against his. Every coherent thought fled from his mind, quickly replaced by her maddening wildflower scent.

But he forced himself to take a deep breath before he started jogging up the path. The raining stars was about to start at any moment and although he wanted to watch, a part of him wanted to share it with Elisabeta too.

Too soon, the others came into view at the top of the peak. Lucian appeared concerned, and Ilona annoyed. A guilty pit formed in his stomach. He was here with Ilona and *not* Elisabeta.

"Here's your companion back, Lucian," he grumbled as he deposited Elisabeta next to his friend. "She's more trouble than she's worth."

"Is her foot broken?"

"I can't tell just by looking at it." He took a seat in between Ilona and Elisabeta. "A fracture is my guess. But it already seems to be getting better. She'll probably be able to walk back down."

Lucian turned to Elisabeta and smiled. "Weak ankles?"

She returned his smile, which irked Dracula even more than the idea of them sitting close to one another. "Not usually. I must have stepped on a rock the wrong way. I'll be fine before you know it."

He tried to ignore them. After all, Elisabeta wasn't his companion for the night, but Ilona.

"It didn't start yet, did it?" he asked as he turned his attention to the dark sky above them. They were far enough from the castle to give them a clear view of the blood moon and the stars in the night sky.

"Not yet," Ilona replied, the previous annoyance he spotted in her expression now wiped clean. "Oh, wait!" She eagerly pointed to a red star that shot across the sky. Another one followed after, and then another one. He watched in awe.

In fact, he was in so much awe he nearly missed the breathless way Elisabeta watched the raining stars, as if she had never seen anything more beautiful in her life. He only wished to watch her reaction longer, but Ilona would likely notice.

"Do you know what makes them red?" Elisabeta asked.

Nicolae answered, "The blood moon happens once a year, and in turn, the stars become red and fall from the sky. As vampires, we believe our god, Ylios, weeps for the loss of devout vampires. If you are lucky when you die, you will become one of those fallen stars to give hope to the family you left behind."

"That's very poetic."

With a frown, Dracula said, "If that's the case, there will likely be a lot this year with how many deaths have occurred."

"Dracula," Madeleine warned. "Don't ruin tonight with your pessimism."

"It's not pessimism," he muttered under his breath. "It's reality."

Their group quieted as they observed the red stars fall from the sky. A deep ache settled in his bones. A part of him didn't want to believe it was true. Yes, it was poetic. But it was also sad.

Wanting to share this moment with Elisabeta, he inched his fingers toward her while continuing to gaze up at the sky. He rested his fingertips on top of hers. Her breath hitched, but he still didn't meet her gaze. Especially because he didn't want to draw attention to his actions.

To his delightful surprise, she returned the gesture by intertwining the tips of their fingers together, making his stomach become a jumble of nerves. He found the jumble of nerves to be pleasant. Exciting. A little bit dangerous.

Also to his surprise, her hand was warm. Vampires had colder skin than humans, elves, or dwarves. Why was her hand warmer than his?

He didn't get the chance to think on it more when she caressed the top of his finger so lightly, he could easily mistake it for a gentle breeze.

He craved more.

His fingers traveled up hers, across the top of her hand, and then he stroked her wrist, now hardly able to pay attention to the raining stars. There was someone much more exciting sitting beside him.

"Vlad," Ilona said quietly. He jerked away from Elisabeta, but Ilona didn't seem to notice. "Look at Madeleine and Nicolae."

He turned his attention to his friends and snickered when he found them nuzzling each other's noses and giving each other kisses. He couldn't help but whisper, "It's no wonder they have five children and one on the way. I've never seen two vampires more in love."

"Have you ever been in love?" she asked with wide, innocent eyes. He recognized the question to be a trap. To say no would be to hurt her feelings. To say yes would be to lie. He wasn't sure which direction was the safest route.

"I thought you were supposed to be counting the stars," he said instead.

"Oh, I am." One last star shot across the sky, but to his dismay, Ilona only frowned. "That makes one hundred and three. Maybe you were right. It's a bad omen. Not only is it nearly twice as many as last year, but it's also an odd number. Something terrible is going to happen."

"Don't say that," Lucian said, giving everyone an optimistic smile. "There is no bad omen. You're looking too much into it."

Dracula frowned. His friends were too optimistic. He didn't need omens or signs when he could feel imminent danger in his gut.

"Are you two done lip clapping over there?" he grumbled. Madeleine and Nicolae broke apart, both of them flushed from head to toe. "Some of us have to wake up early tomorrow for training."

"How long have you two been together?" Elisabeta asked. Her voice alone brought a wave of nerves to his stomach. Those waves increased in strength when he met her gaze, reminding him of her friendly touch only a few minutes earlier.

"Fifteen years," he answered for them. "But no one knew they were mates until Madeline started showing."

Nicolae huffed. "In my defense, we had eloped beforehand."

"Back when union licenses were actually affordable," he joked as he picked himself off the ground and helped Ilona to her feet. "It looks like there's no hope for the rest of us."

"Don't start on this topic again," Madeleine laughed, her eyes sparkling. "We all know how you think you could do better as Shah."

He glared. "I *could* do better as Shah. The first thing I would do is abolish that wretched, wicked church. And then I would next abolish the fee on union licenses, so any vampire who wants the ceremony can have it. And don't get me started on rising feeding costs."

"Feeding costs?" Elisabeta asked. "Not everyone hunts for their food here?"

Madeline shook her head. "Don't encourage him, dear. He has strong opinions on the way Jorin rules Ichor Knell."

"Jorin doesn't rule," he said with a roll of his eyes. "The church does. And what do you think would happen if the church decides to take matters completely into their own hands? Vampires would be oppressed. I believe Ichor Knell should be a safe haven for vampires and other beings alike. We have jewel trees, and *that* would be our staple to help spur the economy. No one else in the entire kingdom has what we have."

Lucian sighed. "And yet, you are not Shah, and in no life would you become Shah."

"I don't want to *become* the shah. But I think change needs to happen."

"Nicolae," Madeline said. "We need to get back to the children and make sure they're in bed. You know how lax Miss Sammy can be about watching them."

He took a deep breath and let it out slowly. He always got in a fit when they spoke of Shah Jorin. If only he had the power to create change, then he would do it in a heartbeat. Unfortunately, he had no power, and he was poorer than a dead man.

Thankfully, enough time had passed that Elisabeta was able to walk on her foot again as if it hadn't been hurt in the first place. However, he wouldn't have minded carrying her back down the trail...

"I'm glad we got to go together," Ilona said,

pulling his attention away as she took his arm.

Thinking of Elisabeta, he grinned. "I'm glad I was able to come."

Chapter 7

Elisabeta was not yet ready to face Dracula again the next day, early in the morning before the recruits even started to show up. But she forced herself to walk across the foggy field to where he readied weapons and armor, his back to her.

She took a moment to admire his profile from this distance. He was extremely tall and exuded confidence in every movement he made. He wore an intense look of concentration, and she might have been able to scare him out of his wits if she snuck up on him.

She smiled, brazened by their interaction last night. She had him within her grasp again, and this time, she planned to keep him there. At least until she found the treasury key.

"Dracula," she said, and he did indeed jump before he spun to face her. She gave him a coy smile despite the way he glared right through her. "You aren't one for sleeping in, are you?"

"What are you doing here, Red Cat?" he asked. Although he continued to glare with his arms over his chest, she couldn't help but smile at his nickname for her. No one had ever given her a nickname before.

"I'm here to see you, of course. Before your soldiers get here. I wanted to see what the training field looked like before getting littered with weapons and blood."

He swept a hand across the field, still not dropping his rough demeanor. "You've seen. Now get out of here."

With a start, she took a step backward. This wasn't the same Dracula she had interacted with the night before. That Dracula had been kind. Caring. Passionate about change. And he had held her hand. What happened to him?

Trying a different approach, she tried to ward off the morning chill by rubbing her hands up and down her arms. "Is it always this foggy in the mornings? I've never seen anything quite like this."

Except for the foggy nights out on the ocean water.

But she couldn't tell him as much because the ocean contained salt. Salt was a vampire weakness. He couldn't know she wasn't a vampire.

"Yes. Spring and winter have foggy mornings. Summer is too hot for fog, and autumn has few foggy mornings because of the rainy season. Any more questions? Or do you plan to waste more of my time?"

She frowned, shuffling her feet uncomfortably. She didn't understand. What had she done wrong this time? Last time, she had messed up because of her ignorance. This time... Had she not acted in a way that befitted his advances? Were they advances at all? Or did vampires hold each other's hands on a casual basis?

"You held my hand last night," she said, deciding to be upfront.

Dracula arched a dark eyebrow, giving her a stare cold enough to make her blood freeze. "I'm not sure what you're talking about. Now if you'll excuse me... I actually have work to do."

He walked toward the armory, leaving her staring

after him with a disbelieving slack jaw. Did he not remember? Surely, she couldn't have imagined it. But why would he pretend it hadn't happened? Perhaps for Ilona's sake? Could what the two of them have actually be deeper than she'd previously thought?

Nothing made sense anymore.

She wandered away, trying to figure out what she'd done wrong. As it was, today was the day she was to meet Miles. He would probably know. He knew everything.

Slipping into the cover of the trees, she wandered off the beaten path, continuously looking over her shoulder to make sure no one followed. As far as she could tell, she was completely alone.

She crossed the river and waded downstream for a few minutes to throw off her scent in the case of a pursuer, and only when she thought it safe to resume her trek, she sloshed out of the water and looked for each landmark to help her locate her brother. A triangular notch in the bark of a tree. Two fallen logs in the shape of an "X". A heap of pine needles at the base of another tree. And finally, dried leaves forming a circle on the ground. This was it.

Moments later, a figure dropped down from a tree, and she immediately lowered her gaze to the ground. Something about Miles made her submissive. She would do anything he asked of her, and despite the confidence she felt in Ichor Knell, she didn't have the same confidence in front of her own brother.

"Well?" he asked, his green gaze boring into hers. "Please tell me you have good news."

"I-I-I don't know," she said, suddenly afraid he might strike her for her lack of success. "I've made friends with his friends. They invited me on an outing last night, and Dracula was there too. But…"

He raised an eyebrow in a similar fashion to how Dracula had done it. "But?"

She took a deep breath. "He acted friendly one minute and the next completely cold."

"All right. So what is he doing?"

"He held my hand last night when no one was watching and today he pretended it didn't happen."

Her brother began pacing back and forth, and she watched him warily. He wasn't angry, which she took as a good sign. But he wasn't happy either. She was trying her best, but she just didn't understand Dracula. He was…complicated. And she couldn't figure him out.

She knew better than to interrupt her brother. As he paced, she took out her notebook and crossed off "fake an injury" on the art of seduction list. To Miles's credit, it had worked far better than she had hoped, especially because it had separated Dracula from Ilona and gave her the perfect opportunity to be alone with him.

"I see what he's doing," he said suddenly as he stopped his pacing and tapped a finger against his chin. "Dracula is playing a game with you. He wants the chase. So you give him the chase."

"The chase?" She didn't even know what it meant.

He nodded. "Like cat and mouse. As soon as the mouse plays dead, the cat loses interest. But as long as the mouse keeps running, keeps playing the game, the cat will pounce. In other words, if you give Dracula what he wants, he will lose interest."

Her head spun as she tried to follow. "I don't understand. Aren't I supposed to give him what he wants?"

"Not in this case. What you need to do is play his game and keep him interested long enough before giving him what he wants."

She pinched the bridge of her nose. She thought females were supposed to be the complicated ones. "All right, so what am I not doing that I need to be doing?"

He began pacing again, his eyes sparking as he worked it out in his mind. Guilt consumed her once more. The longer she spent in Ichor Knell, the more she came to like the people around her. Tricking them wasn't right. But though Dracula still had to determine who he was fiercely loyal to, she had known for a long time already. She was fiercely loyal to her brother. After all, he was all she had left of her family.

"Be aloof, but not detached," Miles said, ceasing his pacing once more, and she hurriedly jotted down each suggestion. "Make him jealous but do it in a way that lets him know you're playing his game. Let him come to *you*. Let him seek you out, not the other way around. And make sure to touch him, but only occasionally to make him crave more. Got it?"

Her hand paused her writing and she started to panic. "I am not skilled enough for this. What if I mess up? What if I accidentally play dead?"

Miles's expression darkened and she immediately regretted expressing her self-doubt. "Don't make me strike you," he said coldly, clenching and unclenching his fist. She forced herself to swallow her fear. Fear only encouraged his behavior. "But if you didn't heal quickly, they will know you are a human."

He handed her a pouch full of elixirs to help mask her human scent, and she immediately unstopped one and downed its contents, grimacing at its too-sweet taste. She needed to consume two a day. It seemed to be working—everyone in Ichor Knell thought she was a vampire.

"I can do this," she whispered, relaxing when her brother grinned. Though, she didn't know *how* to do it. Especially because she still didn't know nearly enough about vampire culture. In addition, something was brewing in the city she didn't quite understand.

Dracula and his friends talked about it enough, but they were vague, and she only picked up bits and pieces.

"Good," he said, patting her cheek. "I expect you to have more to report next time we meet."

She nodded and after she pocketed the newest vials of elixir, she turned back the way she came, leaving her brother far behind. Each step she took away from him felt like a breath of fresh air, but the feeling only lasted for so long. Anxiety followed behind her and trepidation waited in front of her.

She glanced up at the sky, frowning when she couldn't locate the sun behind the thick, dark clouds. She found it difficult to tell time in Ichor Knell, but she felt certain a couple hours remained before her shift as a laundress.

"Excuse me," she said, stopping a female vampire selling white flowers she must have picked outside of Ichor Knell. "Is there a library in this city?"

The vampire nodded. "Several. One in the palace, but peasants aren't allowed inside. Many others have personal libraries. And there is another library townsfolk can access just down the street. It isn't very large, and most of us can't read anyway. But it's there."

Nodding her thanks, she set off in the direction

indicated, but stopped short when she spotted a plume of smoke drifting upward into the sky. An acrid odor entered her nose. Could it be…?

Her feet moved on their own accord as she ran toward the smoke, but when she rounded the corner, her eyes widened in shock. The townsfolk library was a pile of rubble, only embers keeping it glowing like a flicker in a hearth. Small flakes of ash floated in the air around her, but when she reached out to touch one, it disintegrated immediately.

Her heart gave a start when she spotted a male vampire standing in front of the rubble, a tearful crowd around him. He was bald with tattooed designs around his eyes. He wore long, silky red and gold robes with long sleeves that flared outward when he lifted his hands to the sky. This must have been someone from the church Dracula had spoken about.

"Hear me!" the vampire shouted, his voice rising to the clouds. "Peasants are now prohibited from reading, and anyone in possession of books or other reading materials will be executed. Forfeit your books, or we will seize them from you."

Her heart pounded as she quickly turned in the other direction, thinking of the notebook she hid underneath her cloak. Would the vampire church execute her for it? Would they search her?

Dread filled her to the point of suffocation.

If they searched her, they would discover the vials on her person, and if they discovered those, she had no doubt she would be killed. Either way, she was in a lot of trouble.

She breathed fast and heavy as she darted down the cobblestone street, but to her horror, more vampires with tattoos and robes appeared and she diverted her path to avoid getting caught. Terror unfolded around her as they stopped others on the street and searched them, some getting executed right before her eyes with an iron dagger to the heart.

Her eyes widened as she watched homes go up in flames, females and children dragged into the streets, and tortured screams lifting into the sky. She was terrified, and suddenly, she found herself lost in the winding streets.

She was going to die.

She was going to die.

She was going to die.

An arm wrapped around her waist and pulled her into an alley, concealing her from view. She hadn't realized she was crying until a thumb wiped a tear away from her cheek.

"You are not a vampire," the voice said, and horror seized her heart for another reason. Her gaze darted to the speaker and her eyes widened when she found piercing blue eyes staring down at her, long blond hair pale against the dark alley walls.

"Nicolae," she breathed, flinching away from him, but she dared not leave the temporary safety of the alleyway. "I don't know what you mean."

He frowned as if trying to work it out in his mind. "Were you aware vampires have red tears and not clear?"

Ice crawled into her heart and made a nest for itself. No, she was not aware.

She clasped onto his arm, her eyes pleading. "Don't tell anyone. I beg you. They will kill me if they find out."

For a moment, he looked uncertain, as if he had more questions than answers, but then his eyebrows knitted together as he looked over her shoulder at the terror beyond. "We have more pressing things to worry about. Madeleine is currently emptying my entire library onto the streets to keep the family safe. But these…"

He gestured to the stack of books in his arms. "These are the books they want. The history of Ichor Knell and the intricacies of vampire culture and religion. They must be preserved. But…" He took a deep breath and finally lowered his gaze to her. "There is nowhere I can hide them. However… If you truly are not a vampire, then you are not bound by our restrictions. You can enter a building without permission. You can hide them."

"Me?" she squeaked. She was terrified as it was just to be a human walking around with elixirs that made her smell like a vampire. But if she carried banned books as well?

"This is my price for keeping your secret," he said urgently, his expression serious. "What will it be?"

She clenched her jaw, warring with herself. Her ultimate goal was to obtain the dragon egg. If she didn't help Nicolae, he would reveal her, and she would never get what she came here for if she didn't get killed first. But if she helped him, she risked her own life by doing so.

Finally, she nodded and took the stack of books from him. "Just tell me where."

With a protective hand on her back, he led her out of the alley and guided her through the city, careful to keep them out of notice of the monks. Fear closed around her throat with its icy claws, hindering her ability to draw breath. She wished it was Dracula leading her through the city and protecting her instead. Yes, he was dangerous. Yes, he sometimes frightened her. But she felt safe by his side.

"In there," Nicolae said quietly as he gestured to the open window of what looked to be an abandoned theater. "Shah Jorin retracted permission for all vampires to enter, as the theater was banned from Ichor Knell several years ago. Can you get in?"

She nodded and tried to still her pounding heart without success. "What if I die? How will you enter to retrieve them later?"

"That is an obstacle better worried about another day. Right now, time is of the essence."

After she set the books aside, he heaved her up to the window and with a small amount of difficulty, she shimmied herself through. A male would never have been able to fit.

She dropped to the floor, coughing when she breathed in a plume of dust. It was obvious no one had entered the theater in a long while, as she could hardly see through the thick dust coating the very air itself. A pang of sadness hit her as her eyes swept over the velvety seats, the shredded red curtains, and the worn and broken furniture that looked as if they had seen better days. She could imagine this building once looked magnificent in its red and golden splendor. Now it lay in shambles from neglect.

This was the perfect place to hide books.

She pushed a table beneath the window and stood on it to look down to where Nicolae stared up at her with a concerned expression. "I'm in," she whispered.

"Where should I hide them?"

"I don't know," he answered as he handed the books to her one by one, constantly looking over his shoulder. "Where no one will find them but you."

"All right," she nodded, taking the last book from him before disappearing inside. She studied the room with a careful, trained eye. She had done this plenty of times before when she wanted to hide something from Miles, such as their mother's old necklace she currently wore beneath her tunic or coins she wanted to save for herself.

A floorboard creaked underneath her foot, and she stopped in her tracks. She knelt down and hooked her fingers beneath the loose board, and although it took several good heaves, it finally gave way, revealing an empty space large enough to conceal the books. As an extra precaution, she placed her elixirs and notebook inside as well in case someone should stop her on the streets. She would have to return for them later.

She covered the items with the board once more. Not wanting to linger longer than necessary, she quickly climbed back out the window, allowing Nicolae to help her down. Together, they hurried off in the other direction.

"You two, stop!" a voice called behind them, and her heart thrummed rapidly in her throat. She turned around slowly, her eyes wide as she found herself face to face with a male vampire wearing lavish robes and tattoos around his eyes. How many monks existed?

Her heart raced as the male patted down Nicolae and then her only moments later. Relief over leaving her vials and notebook behind cooled her rising temperature.

The vampire grunted in satisfaction before moving onto the next terrified vampire.

Nicolae grabbed her hand, pulling her forward and not stopping until they were well away from the danger beneath a sapphire jewel tree beside the river. She clasped her hands over her mouth and couldn't stop tears from escaping her eyes. It could have been *her* with an iron dagger through her heart. Vampire or not, iron would have killed her either way.

"Please forgive me!" she wept, wiping away tear after tear. "That was terrifying."

He sighed and opened his arms to her, and she gladly entered them, grateful when he allowed her to weep into his chest. She hardly knew him, yet he treated her kindly, even knowing she was a human and not a vampire. Would the others accept her as she was too? Would Dracula?

When her weeping died down, he held her at arm's length. "What is a human doing in Ichor Knell? It's dangerous enough for vampires right now, and even worse for a human. Why do you smell like a vampire?"

She didn't know how to answer his questions without revealing her plans. Surely, he would try to stop her, especially because her plans involved Dracula.

"There is something I need to do here. I am not obliged to tell you more. Please keep my secret."

"I promised, didn't I? At least consider telling the others. They would not treat you unkindly. Well, everyone except Dracula. He despises humans. But his opinion doesn't matter."

Yes, it does. His opinion matters the most.

"Why does he hate humans?" she sniffed.

He sighed again. "His father was a human who

hunted vampires for sport. That's all I will say on the matter."

Guilt settled as a brick in her stomach. If she seduced Dracula and left him for the dragon egg, she would be no better than his father. He would never forgive her. How could she do this to him?

Thoughts of Miles entered her mind and she shuddered as she thought of how he would beat her if she didn't do as he asked. Miles scared her. Dracula scared her. Which was the lesser evil?

"I don't want Dracula to hate me," she admitted. "His good opinion matters to me."

"Does it?" He raised his eyebrows, clearly surprised by her confession. "That puts everyone in a bit of a pickle. Ilona loves him. Did you know?"

She swallowed hard and stared at the ground. That much was clear from the way she had treated him last night. "And does he love her?"

"…In a way."

His words sounded hesitant, unsure. Did it mean she might have a chance?

Before she inquired further into the situation between Dracula and Ilona, a tall, brooding figure rounded the corner, a look of relief on his face. She hastily wiped her tears away so Dracula wouldn't see what Nicolae had seen—her tears were not red. She was only glad it had been dark the night before when she cried preventing him from seeing the color of her tears.

"Thank the stars," Dracula said, his knuckles white as he clenched the pommel of his sword. "You two were the only ones I couldn't locate."

Her heart skipped as she turned his words around in her mind. He had been looking for her?

"My family?" Nicolae inquired. Although he maintained a relaxed facade, she noticed the distress etched on his face.

"Everyone is safe. Lucian didn't have many books to burn. I only had letters from my late mother. The monks rummaged through your entire house, Nicolae. Although your family is safe, a lot of your belongings were burned."

Nicolae released a breath like a waterfall of relief. "Elisabeta and I saved what was important. That's what matters."

Dracula turned his attention to her, his expression becoming darker. "By Ylios, Elisabeta. Have you been crying?"

His voice carried a touch of concern, but still she panicked and wiped at her face again despite not finding any remaining tears. Were her eyes puffy and red-rimmed then? As long as he didn't see the color of her tears, it didn't bother her.

"It was a terrifying ordeal," Nicolae answered for her, much to her gratitude. "As a vampire who has never been to Ichor Knell before, she was in for quite a surprise."

She silently thanked Nicolae for keeping her secret. But even amidst the terrifying ordeal, she still remembered her list, physical touch being one of the items. She gently touched Dracula's elbow and offered him a pained smile. "Thank you for your concern, but it's not necessary. I'm fine."

She dropped her hand just as quickly, watching the confusion on his face. Confusion was better than rejection, right?

"I should go," she said and started to walk away,

but he called after her.

"As you are new to Ichor Knell, you probably don't know about the mandatory services tomorrow. You are required to be there."

Church was the last place she wanted to be as a human. But as long as she didn't carry her notebook or elixirs on her, she hoped she would be fine.

With a terse nod, she continued on her way, a sense of urgency guiding each step. The faster she left Ichor Knell, the better. She needed to make haste with Dracula.

Chapter 8

The mourning bell chimed one hundred times directly in the middle of the services, which meant twenty deaths, and each vampire was forced to listen with heavy hearts. Some of those lost had been family. Some friends. It reminded them of how little power they held, and how much control the church had over them. What would they do next? Ban dancing? Singing? At what point would the chaos end?

"You need to control yourself," Nicolae whispered.

Dracula hadn't realized he stood on the balls of his feet, his hands clenched tightly into fists as he glared at the monk giving the sermon at the front of the square.

"I *am* controlling myself!" he snapped. "What does it look like I'm doing?"

Silence wedged itself between them. He only half-listened to the sermon as he glared and seethed and glared some more. So many deaths… This wasn't right.

"—and the peasants shall be thrown into the pits of hell," the monk continued. "The unbelievers will be cleansed of the earth."

"That's false doctrine," a voice beside him quietly said, and he turned to find a scrawny fellow, not yet come of age. His brown hair looked like it was plastered to his head, his round face making him look younger than he was. "I've studied every book on vampire religion, every manuscript, every stone tablet.

71

The church is changing their doctrine, and no one will be the wiser because there will be no documentation on the truth. They burned everything."

Not everything.

But he planned on keeping that to himself.

He raised an eyebrow at the scrawny boy. "How old are you?"

"Thirteen," he answered, taking him by surprise. Young for someone who knew so much. Young and annoying. Something about his face annoyed him. "Frederick Arter, Captain."

He only grunted in response. The boy had an annoying voice too.

Frederick continued despite Dracula trying to ignore him. "There is no hell for vampires. Rather, if someone lives a wicked life, Ylios will give them an unending and insatiable thirst for the rest of eternity. Hell is not a place, but a state of being. And it doesn't only apply to peasants, but to nobles, shahs, kumaris. Every vampire of every station, regardless of wealth or status."

"Again, how old are you?"

"Stop pestering him," Nicolae chuckled.

"I'm not pestering him. He's pestering me."

He snuck a glance to his right and held back a growl when he found Elisabeta speaking in hushed whispers with another male. And then the two of them laughed quietly, spurring fiery hot jealousy. What were they talking about? Why was she giggling? And why was she paying attention to the other male? Was it because of what he said yesterday? About pretending they hadn't held hands? It was all a part of the game, but he was beginning to get the distinct impression she was ignorant of the game.

The loss of her attention smashed his heart like a regretful blow. He should have been straightforward. He should have left the games behind. Now he may have lost his chance. What had he done?

His eyes narrowed, glaring a hole straight through the male. He knew him. He was one of his soldiers—Hammond. When did the two of them meet?

A sick feeling grew in his stomach as he envisioned Elisabeta visiting the training grounds to see Hammond. The feeling festered inside of him like strangling vines when he imagined them courting.

Under his breath, he muttered, "I'm going to impale that bastard."

At long last, the service ended, and he tromped across the square toward Hammond and Elisabeta. To his sheer annoyance, she didn't notice him approach until he cleared his throat.

"Captain!" Hammond said, standing straight and striking a fist to his heart in a salute. "We aren't training today, are we? I wasn't aware."

"No," he growled, not sure what to say. He hadn't thought it through other than keeping Hammond and Elisabeta from spending time alone together. "Don't tell me you have plans."

"Actually, we do," she said, threading her arm through Hammond's. The heat of his envy burned hot in his enclosed fist. It took all his self-control to keep himself from knocking the other male senseless. "I'm glad he doesn't have training, or I wouldn't have the pleasure of his company. Ready, Hammond?"

Hammond nodded and they started off in the other direction. He glared after them, at least until Elisabeta turned her head and gave him a wicked grin that left his heart pounding and his head spinning.

He chuckled as soon as his initial surprise vanished, returning her wicked grin when she turned her back. She *was* playing the game. And he fully intended to continue it.

"Nicolae!" he called, his grin uncontained. "Let's make an addition to the team. It will be entertaining to see how our newcomer fares."

"Oh dear," Nicolae grimaced. "Are you sure it's wise?"

"Most definitely. Have Madeleine invite her. Don't tell her what it is."

The look of inevitable shock on her face was something he couldn't pass up.

Giving him a look of caution, Nicolae said, "I know how you are, Dracula. You act without thinking. I hope you know what you're doing."

He rolled his eyes and huffed. "Of course I do. If she doesn't want to play, she can sit on the sidelines with Madeleine."

"Fine. But do me a favor? Don't hurt anyone this time. This isn't one of your war tactics. This is just a game. Promise me?"

Dracula shrugged. "It's not fun unless *someone* gets hurt. I won't make that promise."

"At least promise to protect the females from harm. Especially Elisabeta."

That was odd. Why did Nicolae care to make sure Elisabeta didn't get hurt? After all, she would heal within seconds, or even minutes. Besides, he would never dare let Elisabeta get hurt like he would never dare allow Ilona or Madeleine to get hurt.

"I give my word. Now will you tell Madeleine to invite her?"

"Very well."

They walked together back toward Nicolae's house, and Dracula couldn't contain his excitement. He had been last year's champion, and this year, he hoped to follow in his own footsteps. But honestly, he was mostly excited for Elisabeta to come. He hoped to get to know her better.

The door burst open at their approach, and a gaggle of children laughed as they threw themselves on him. He suddenly found four children hanging on his arms and legs with one crawling after the others, fangs bared.

"Dracula! You came!" Violeta cried, tugging incessantly on his arm. "Do the fun thing you always do."

"This?" he growled playfully. He spun them around, two on each arm, while they screamed and laughed and clutched on tightly.

He laughed out loud with the others, grateful for the opportunity to release all his pent-up emotion. "Someday, all of you will be too big for me to spin you."

"I'm not too big yet," Zeidan, the oldest, said, puffing out his chest. "But I'm growing! I'm almost as big as Papa."

Dracula snorted and ruffed up Zeidan's hair. "Sure you are."

Madeleine waddled outside and smiled. "I keep telling Nicolae to hire you on as a nanny."

"No, thank you." He grimaced, fingering the sword on his belt, the metal hilt cool against his fingers. He wished to warm it up by practicing on the church's wicked monks. "I was born with a sword in my hand, and that's not going to change anytime soon."

Very suddenly, Madeleine's mouth turned downward, and she gave him a piercing glare with her bright silver eyes. He never enjoyed being on the receiving end of her glare. "I thought you were going to court Ilona. You haven't given her your handkerchief yet."

"I said I would *think* about it," he replied, craning his neck in search of an opportunity to make a timely exit. The housing district was crowded as vampires returned home from the service. Peasants, like himself, attended services in the square. Nobles attended services in the cathedral. Dracula had always wanted to see the inside of the cathedral, but as a peasant, he wasn't allowed. It was any wonder Shah Jorin entrusted him with the key to the Ichor Knell treasury in the first place.

"The time for thinking is over," she huffed, massaging her belly with her hand. Even from here, his ears picked up the child's heartbeat from within her. Alive and strong. "Ilona deserves to be properly courted. And as far as I can see, you are not courting anyone. Like I said before, it can't hurt."

He groaned, wishing to have any other conversation besides this one. He dug inside his pocket and waved his black handkerchief in her face. "What do you think I've been trying to do, Madeleine? I've strived to give it to her on multiple occasions, but I just can't. Do you know why? Because I don't feel good about it!"

"Stop," Nicolae said calmly, yet he gripped Dracula's shoulder hard. The strength of it nearly made his knees buckle. "My mate is with child. I will not have her laboring early. No more fighting."

"My apologies," he muttered. He breathed in a river of calm, covering him with its cool water.

Madeleine approached with both hands over her belly, looking up at him from where he towered over her. "But why not?" she asked, her voice now soothing as if she knew raising it would set him off. "You two are good together. You look good together. You fit well together. I don't understand why you won't court her."

"I think I know why," Nicolae said under his breath, and he turned to him with a snarl. He opened his mouth to reply, but his friend cut across him. "With you needing to sit on the sidelines for the Game, I thought it would be wise for us to take on another teammate. What do you think about Elisabeta joining the team?"

A smile blossomed across her face, the courting crisis completely forgotten. "What a splendid idea. I will see her at work. I will ask her then."

"Just...don't tell her what the Game is about," Nicolae said, giving Dracula a confused look. "It will be better for her to be surprised?"

"Great idea, Nicolae," he chuckled, though it had been his idea all along. "We can show her what being an Ichor Knell vampire is all about."

He grinned. This should be fun.

Chapter 9

Elisabeta had never been more confused in her life. Both Madeleine and Ilona invited her to a bonfire up at the lake, but they had been vague about what to expect. When she thought about bonfires, she envisioned roasted boar, singing, and dancing. But vampires didn't feast on boar. Thus far, she hadn't witnessed singing or dancing. So what was it?

She counted herself fortunate to have received an invitation at all. Although she didn't know if Dracula would be there, it still felt good to have friends, even if it was on false pretenses.

"Dracula won last year," Ilona sighed dreamily as they neared the lake, the bonfire burning as a beacon in the distance. Tall pine trees surrounded all sides of the water while several dozen vampires lingered on the rocky beach. "He impaled at least twelve vampires by the end, but that's what puts the thrill into the Game."

"I-i-impale?" Elisabeta stuttered. "What exactly are we doing?"

Ilona didn't get the chance to answer as they drew near the fire—and with it, dozens more vampires—because a deep voice spoke for her.

"We call it the Game," Dracula said in the darkness, his voice alone twisting her stomach into knots. The bonfire cast flickering shadows across his face, and for a moment, she couldn't hold his gaze, it was so intense.

He looked handsome tonight—more so than usual. He had shaved the scruff from his face, and he wore all black, which somehow made him appear taller. "Each person is a part of a team. The objective is to obtain the Golden Chalice hidden somewhere in the woods, and anything goes. Mostly. As long as it doesn't cause any permanent damage."

She nodded, her uncertainty fleeing. "That doesn't sound too hard."

Beside her, Lucian snorted. "Oh, it is. Last year, someone slit my throat and it took an hour to heal from the damage."

The blood drained from her face. She wasn't a vampire. She could die.

"But don't you worry!" Lucian quickly said. "Because you are a female, males will often go easier on you." He mumbled his next words with furrowed brows. "But then again, you wear trousers and can easily be mistaken for a male."

Terror gripped her heart and squeezed. Why hadn't she thought to bring a dagger with her? Then at least she could protect herself. But as she eyed the other teams eyeing her, a queasiness churned her stomach. There were a lot of vampires here tonight. She wouldn't stand a chance.

Nicolae lightly touched her elbow, which helped ground her. "The Game is very dangerous. Especially if you are *new* to Ichor Knell. Perhaps it would be better for you to sit out this year and keep Madeleine company."

"Pathetic," Dracula muttered. "I should have expected cowardice. Well, at least that gives us four on the team, assuming you plan on playing, Ilona?"

"Yes," she nodded. "My transformation gives me good eyesight in the dark. That should help."

Elisabeta put her hands on her hips, staring Dracula down. "Now wait one bloody minute. I'm playing."

"But it's dangerous—" Nicolae started but she cut across him.

"I don't care." Besides, she wanted to impress Dracula and she knew sitting on the sidelines wouldn't help her accomplish her goal. She tried not to think about what would happen if she spilled even one drop of her own blood... "I'm playing and that's final."

Dracula grinned and untied a dagger from his belt, handing it to her. The sentiment filled her with warmth. This was Dracula's dagger. It was plain. It was simple. But it was his. "I hoped you would say that. Each of our transformations can aid us in the ultimate goal of obtaining the chalice. Well, all except Nicolae. His transformation is a harp seal. Ilona's transformation is a bobcat, Lucian's is a hawk, mine is a bat. What's yours?"

Her pulse thrummed loudly in her ears. She didn't *have* a transformation! She was as human as a human could get. She glanced to Nicolae for help, but he only gave her a look of concern. He was truly concerned for her safety.

"My transformation is...an owl."

A big fat lie, but Dracula grinned from ear to ear at her answer.

"Perfect. Three flying transformations. Three nocturnal. This will give us a competitive advantage."

Ilona wrapped an arm around Dracula's waist and the most unexpected emotion surged through her.

Jealousy.

The blood drained from her face for an entirely different reason other than for her own safety. She was developing feelings for Dracula. Real feelings. And that was dangerous. He was a vampire, for heaven's sake! She was a thief! A swindler! A pickpocket! A fake... And he had no idea. She hated herself for what she planned to do to him. It wasn't right. It was cruel.

She couldn't do it.

"We will stick together, right, Vlad?" Ilona asked as she looked up into his eyes, and Elisabeta turned away, unable to handle the pang inside her heart. She wandered closer to the lake and busied herself with strapping Dracula's dagger to her belt. Playing the Game seemed important to him, which made it important to her too. However, she couldn't afford to get her throat slit. Neither could she afford to spill a single drop of blood.

Ice froze her blood over as she imagined vampires tackling her, their eyes flashing red as their sharp nails tore through her body. And the fangs...

A shudder crawled across her skin in the form of gooseflesh. She needed to stay clear of the chalice during the Game while making herself appear busy.

"Are you ready?" Lucian asked, coming to stand beside her next to the water.

"Truthfully?" she asked. "I'm terrified. My heart feels like it might collapse from fear."

"I know," he chuckled. "I can hear it. I'm sure everyone can hear it."

"That's disheartening." She placed a hand over her heart, her face heating with embarrassment. Could everyone also hear the way her heart tumbled and danced around Dracula?

He gave her a reassuring smile. "You aren't the only one with a fast heartbeat, as I'm sure you can hear yourself. This time of the year is exciting and terrifying, especially for newcomers. However... There are a few things you can do to protect yourself if you are afraid of getting hurt. First..."

He reached up and tugged the pins free from her hair. Her red tresses fell around her shoulders. She looked at him inquisitively.

"If you insist on wearing trousers," he said as he handed her the pins, "then wearing your hair down will show others you are female. Even Dracula won't attack a female unless she attacks him first."

She looked over her shoulder and found Dracula unashamedly watching them as he sharpened his sword, Ilona no longer draped over him. Could he hear their conversation?

His mouth twitched as if fighting off a coy smile.

She looked down at her feet. Simply holding his gaze proved to be too much for her. But she didn't want to be a coward. She wanted to be someone worthy of his attention.

So she forced herself to lift her gaze and bite her lip while she tucked a strand of hair behind her ear. Momentarily, his eyes widened before he dropped his sword, the metal clattering against the rocks. She refrained from snickering. If he wanted to play this game, she would play it to the best of her ability.

"Listen up!" a voice called, rising above everyone's conversations until the air fell into a hush. "You all know the rules. No iron weapons. No permanent damage. Otherwise, everything goes. The first to get the Golden Chalice wins bragging rights for the entire year and the pool of coin. Get in positions, and when you hear the pitch, prepare yourself for chaos."

Her throat constricted as everyone moved in a flurry of activity, taking positions on the outskirts of the forest. She wasn't ready. She was terrified.

She wasn't sure she could do this.

Dracula jumped right in as if he was born ready for a war to rage. He led their group toward the forest with long, purposeful strides, his eyes tense and focused. "Nicolae, you are useless with a weapon. But you are lithe. You are the most likely to move in without being seen. Ilona, I need your eyes. Keep low. You and Nicolae will be the only ones on the ground. Lucian, you are fast. I want you attacking from the skies. I will use my echolocation to find vampires in the area. And Elisabeta, you can be a good distraction from the skies for any vampires who get too close. Are we all clear?"

Nicolae glanced at her and the waves of panic began anew. How was she supposed to keep up this lie? She couldn't even turn into an owl!

"You insisted on playing," Nicolae said quietly in her ear. "You either tell them the truth, or you risk getting killed."

"I *can't* tell them the truth," she hissed. "You don't understand."

Their conversation was cut short as they stopped at the edge of the trees. Her heart pounded so hard she thought she might faint. There was no point in trying to hide her thrumming heart now that she knew everyone could hear it. She just hoped everyone else's heart thrummed wildly too.

Dracula passed behind her, touching the small of her back, and her heart hammered for an entirely different reason. The simple touch flustered her, preventing coherent thought. Even as her mind drew a blank, everyone around her hadn't noticed the exchange and readied themselves for the Game.

He turned the slightest bit and cast her a devilish grin.

"There's the signal!" Ilona cried, and everyone rushed forward, leaving Elisabeta scrambling after them. What signal? She hadn't heard *anything*!

She entered the woods in a wild fit of panic as she glanced every which way. People flew past her in a blur of shapes and images, both animals and vampires. A horrifying thought struck her—she had already lost sight of her group.

Fear consumed her, the pulse of her blood deafening in her ears as if it struggled to surge through the ice slowly eating her alive. Never in her life had she seen war other than the skirmishes between pirate ships, and this certainly felt like a battle as vampires stabbed other vampires, littering the forest floor with bodies not quite dead but healing from their wounds. Anxiety slammed into her as she watched a vampire slit another vampire's throat, blood spurting from the wound and soaking his shirt.

I should never have agreed to play.

A vampire screeched behind her, and she turned just in time to find a female rushing at her with a long, wavy dagger. She reacted on instinct as she pulled her dagger free of its scabbard and stabbed the vampire first, straight into the gut. She didn't have time to reflect on what she had just done as she scrambled away, dodging an attack from the skies as an eagle flew at her with long, vicious claws.

This was a war zone.

"Vampires are mad," she gasped. Forget the winning prize. She had to find somewhere to hide.

However, as she ducked beneath a bow of trees, she ran smack into a male vampire. He grinned maliciously and before she could dodge, he kicked her in the ribs. What she hadn't expected was the superhuman power behind the kick. She flew backward and slammed against a tree, choking against the pain inflicted upon her ribs. Something was broken. A rib or two. Maybe her whole body. She couldn't tell.

The vampire stepped toward her as if to finish the job, but he stopped short as a bat flew downward from the skies and turned into a vampire right before her eyes, standing protectively above her.

Dracula.

The vampire hesitated, his eyes flashing from Dracula to her and back to Dracula, and finally, he turned and fled in the other direction.

"How did you lose us so easily?" he growled, helping her to her feet with a steady hand. "Can you not hear us communicate?"

No, she couldn't. How *did* vampires communicate? She was starting to suspect human ears couldn't hear what vampires could hear.

She wanted to cry, and it took every ounce of her self-control to hold back her tears. She didn't want him to see her weakness.

"This is my first time," she said, taking a deep breath but instantly regretting it when a burst of fire surged through her chest. Bones may have been broken, but she counted herself lucky the attack hadn't drawn blood. "I got lost instantly."

"Understandable." He backed her out of the way of two vampires brawling in a fist fight. "You will be safer in the skies. Come on. Let's go find the others."

"I'm nervous," she said with wide, fearful eyes. "I can't transform when I'm nervous."

"Seriously, Red Cat?" He sighed but took her hand, the contact bringing comfort and reassurance in a forest full of bloodshed and chaos. "Then I suppose we will have to continue on foot. Stick close to me and don't sheath your dagger. You will be safe by my side."

Despite the situation, despite her fear, she smirked. "If you wanted me to stay by your side all night, you should have just asked."

He snorted, glancing at her while leading her through the twists and turns of the trees. "Now where's the fun in that? Besides, you were practically *begging* me to come to your aid."

"I can take care of myself."

"Of course you can. But do you want to?"

His question took her off guard. She had a feeling he was asking about more than just the Game. Was he implying that he could take care of her? Provide for her?

But she quickly shook the thought away. Of course he wasn't. They hardly knew each other. "My brother takes care of me just fine." That was a lie, but she found herself lying to him more than she wanted to.

"And where is your brother now? I've been keeping an eye out for a second Elisabeta in Ichor Knell, but so far I've only found you."

A pit formed in her stomach as she thought of

Miles and what he expected her to do here.

An unexpected rush of discomfort raced through her. She had only just met Dracula, yet she had never wanted someone's good opinion more in her life than she wanted his. But it was far too late for that.

"Miles is away on business."

To her relief, they reached a quiet part of the forest, finding themselves very much alone. She wished it could last.

She took a step forward, but he yanked her back to him. She gasped in surprise when she bumped against his chest. Heat flared alive in her cheeks as she tilted her face upward, looking into a pair of dark, serious eyes.

"Will Miles take you away?" he asked. "Will you leave Ichor Knell?"

She wasn't sure what to think about the intensity of his words. From how it sounded, he didn't *want* her to go. For a moment, hope surged within her as a very dangerous, very selfish idea entered her mind. Perhaps she didn't have to leave. She could steal the key to the treasury, get Miles the dragon egg, return the key before Dracula knew it was missing, and then she could stay and build a new life without her brother.

While she had previously feared the idea of being separated from Miles, being in Ichor Knell these past days had shown her a new way to live, with friends she could rely on, especially Dracula. She didn't need Miles anymore.

Her heart fell at the thought. It didn't change the fact that she was still human.

And Dracula despised humans.

Swallowing against the emotion building in her

throat, she asked, "What if I wasn't a vampire? What if I was an elf? Or a dwarf? Or a human? What then?"

"That's an odd question, Red Cat."

"Answer it anyway."

He shrugged, the Game completely forgotten as they stood so very close to one another, only inches apart. "You certainly aren't an elf, as your ears are normal length. I suppose you could be a dwarf because you are so much shorter than me."

She pinched his arm. "I'm being serious. If I wasn't a vampire, would you want me to stay?"

He lifted a tendril of her hair to his nose and breathed in deeply. "You smell like a vampire, so I don't know why we're having this conversation. Will my answer affect whether or not you will stay?"

"Perhaps."

For the first time since they'd met, a flicker of uncertainty flashed across his eyes—she had never seen anything but confidence instilled in him, so she didn't know how to proceed.

His fingers lightly trailed up her arm, raising gooseflesh on her skin in their wake. "Do you want to stay?"

Although he didn't answer her question, she decided not to press. Instead, she hoped he might accept her for what she was when the time came.

She looked at him coyly as she answered. "I've never had a place to call home before. For once in my life, I was hoping for something more...permanent." She let her innuendo hang in the air and found it to be the truth. She tried hard not to think about her problematic position as a human among vampires. Surely, she could work around it.

Somehow.

Dracula didn't get the chance to reply as a chorus of battle cries echoed nearby moments before a group of vampires burst into sight, all with their weapons raised. She couldn't even lift her dagger before he pushed her behind him.

With skillful movements, he stepped around them like a carefully choreographed dance, easily dodging their attacks and stabbing each one straight through their midsection. Only one remained and she moved forward, but once more, he pushed her behind his back and finished off the last one with a slice to the back of the leg.

He took her hand and dragged her away from the scene of groaning, healing vampires, all while she scowled. When they were far enough away, she snatched her hand back and glared.

"I told you. I can take care of myself."

"And I told you I know you can. But I like taking care of you for a change."

Now *his* innuendo hung in the air, and she couldn't stop her lips from twitching as she fought off a smile. Their flirty banter was fun. She enjoyed this little game of theirs.

"Can you transform now? The immediate danger is gone."

"Is it?" she whispered, trailing her finger across the defined muscles in his forearm while doing her best to ignore her pounding heart. "I still can't transform after all."

"Elisabeta," he growled. "You're crossing a dangerous line. Once you cross, you can never uncross."

She didn't want to uncross. She wanted Dracula for herself.

He gasped suddenly, and her eyes widened in horror at the knife protruding between his shoulder blades. She wrenched it free and ignored his hiss of pain. She spun around and threw the knife at the attacker. Only a moment later, a male vampire with short-cropped blond hair fell from a branch, holding his neck with a look of surprise still evident on his face before he hit the ground with a *thud*.

A fearful shudder ran through her. As sorry as she was to see Dracula hurt, it could have been her.

"Are you all right?" she asked, frowning as she watched the wound reknit itself in seconds.

"I'm fine," he grunted. "We need to keep moving—"

The ground crumbled beneath her feet and she shrieked as she lost her footing altogether. Strong arms reached out for her, but they weren't enough to stop her from tumbling down the steep slope. She rolled over branches, across rocks, over Dracula a couple of times, and her trajectory didn't stop until they reached the bottom and landed in a heap.

She groaned and released a shaky breath, assessing her damage. Her ribs flared like a billowing torch, but now she felt the aches and pains of newer bruises on her arms and legs. To her relief, she didn't notice any cuts or scrapes. Her secret was still safe.

"The Game is too dangerous to exist," she grunted and tried to sit up, but Dracula pushed her right back down, pinning her while an overly intense expression took residence on his face. For a moment, her heart stopped. He was inches away—closer than he had ever been before.

"Now look what you did," he said quietly. "You just broke the rules."

Panic clutched her from the inside out. "What? I thought the Game had no rules."

"Not that game," he said, rolling his eyes. Her breath hitched as he trailed his thumb across her bottom lip. "This one. Distracting me in battle."

She trembled beneath his touch. He had never looked at her that way before, with an intense passion seeping from his eyes. Warmth spread from her toes to her fingertips to her heart and to her lips that desperately wanted to be kissed. Right then, seducing him no longer mattered because she couldn't do it. She didn't want to use him for her own personal gains. But what did matter was how close he was, close enough to feel his breath on her skin.

"Kiss me," she breathed, not able to handle the tension anymore.

"Dear Elisabeta," he grinned wickedly, "that's not how this game works. There are rules."

He kissed her below her ear, and her heart nearly collapsed as the tension thickened. It was all she could do to force out her words. "I don't like rules."

"I've noticed," he whispered in her ear. He kissed the corner of her mouth and she sighed. It was too much for her to handle. She turned her head in an attempt to meet his lips, but he turned it right back to keep her out of reach, effectively teasing her.

Desperation clung to her like sunlight in a grassy meadow. She had never been more desperate for anything than she was for the taste of his lips.

He placed a kiss on her jaw, and she lost her breath

completely. Wrapping her arms around his neck, she attempted to pull him closer, but he hovered a tantalizing few inches away.

"Kiss me," she repeated, a hint of pleading in her voice.

"No," he murmured, his lips against her neck. "We still have a chalice to retrieve."

She groaned and dropped her hands, the loss of contact baking her heart dry like a parched, withered desert. "We'd be the last ones to find it at this rate. We should split up if we want to get anything done."

A grin pulled on the corners of his lips as he helped her to her feet, but the grin immediately dropped as he glanced toward the sky, as if listening. Again, she didn't hear anything.

She stood straighter, concentrating. She couldn't hear anything, but she could feel it. A faint vibration emanated from Dracula's throat. Vampires were fascinating, she decided. They communicated in ways the human ear didn't hear. They transformed into animals of all types and sizes. And they lived forever if an unfortunate fate didn't befall them first.

Dracula, especially, fascinated her. He consisted of many different layers from his rough, cruel demeanor to his sweet, compassionate heart. He was cautious but flirty. He was aloof but caring. Getting to know his many sides was only half the fun.

"The others have found the location of the chalice," he said, their intimate encounter forgotten. "It's a complete bloody brawl over there. Let's go."

"B-b-bloody?" she stammered. "Shouldn't we stay *away* from the bloodshed?"

He raised an eyebrow as she followed him. "If you

wanted to be alone with me, you should've just asked."

A nervous chuckle escaped her when she recognized her own words he threw right back at her. "You better make this bloodshed worth it."

"I plan to."

****

The Golden Chalice was as beautiful as Dracula remembered it—a wide, golden base, intricate designs in the collar, knop, and cup, and a rim any vampire would covet to place their lips to drink. Only the Game's champion got the privilege to drink from it, and last year, the privilege had been his. This year, he strived for the same privilege and nothing would deter him from his ultimate goal.

He jumped straight into the bloody chaos, his sword drawn as he fought his way closer to the prize. The first vampire to hold the chalice in their hands won the Game.

When it came to reserves of strength, he had a near-endless supply. He impaled vampires right and left, using caution to make it a clean wound for flawless healing. He dodged attacks from the skies. He sidestepped blows coming at him from all directions. And like the thrill of battle often did to him, he focused intently on his end goal, the others in his group completely forgotten.

He laughed as he struck down the next vampire, which put him directly in front of his goal. The chalice was his. It—

A shriek broke him out of his reverie and his eyes widened when he spun around to find Elisabeta on the ground, a heavyset male hovering over her with one hefty boot pinning her wrist. She desperately reached for the dagger he had given her with her other hand, but no matter how much she writhed in an attempt to escape, she couldn't free herself.

The heavy vampire raised his sword, a malicious smile on his face as he looked down at Elisabeta's helpless form.

He swallowed as he glanced from Elisabeta to the chalice and back. She stared fearfully at her attacker, and it seemed as if the entire world halted around him. Nicolae rushed toward her, but Dracula knew he wouldn't get there in time. It was then he had to make a decision. A quick decision. And his body acted on its own accord.

Leaving the chalice behind, he charged toward the heavyset male and tackled him to the ground, punching him in the face again and again until his knuckles bled. Fury enraged him. Wrath consumed him. He didn't care that Elisabeta could have recovered quickly from a stab wound, but he was furious over the idea of someone stabbing her at all.

Lucian and Nicolae dragged him off the vampire, for if they hadn't, he might have beaten the male to a senseless, bloody pulp in his fury.

"Scum of the earth," he spat, kicking the male in the side for good measure and taking satisfaction in his grunt of pain. "Attacking a defenseless female. I am ashamed of you."

"That's enough, Dracula," Nicolae cautioned, still holding him back by the elbow as if he might attack again. Which was possible. He couldn't decide yet. "The Game is over. Dimitrie Gabor won. No more fighting."

"Dimitrie," he scoffed, turning his attention briefly

to the brunette vampire celebrating with the chalice in his hands. "I bet you my entire fortune he let his team do all the fighting while he took the credit for it."

Nicolae raised an eyebrow. "Your entire fortune, you say? What is that, exactly? A few shillings? I'll take you up on that bet."

Despite having lost the Game, he chuckled past his aggravation. "If he did, indeed, lift a finger to obtain the goblet, I will give you my entire fortune. If I am right, I get to name your child."

With a grimace, Nicolae shook his hand. "Madeleine will be put off with the both of us if I lose. For your sake, I hope you lose."

A bobcat burst into the clearing and turned into Ilona in a split second. She threw her arms around his neck and held him so tight he couldn't breathe. "Vlad, I thought something awful happened to you! Where did you disappear to?"

He peeled Ilona's arms off him and glanced toward Elisabeta, who looked to be recovering from her terrifying experience as her trembling fingers sheathed his dagger. He admired her bravery. Not many vampires would throw themselves in the midst of the final battle, but she had. He deeply admired her courage. Even Ilona hadn't set foot near the battle.

"Leaving no female behind," he murmured partly to himself.

"Glad that's over with," Lucian said with a characteristic smile. "I've been looking forward to this banquet all year."

Each year after the Game, the vampires in attendance held a banquet around the fire. It was nothing fancy like the nobles experienced in their lavish houses with their lavish goblets wearing their lavish clothing. But it was a banquet among friends—and some enemies. Would Elisabeta sit by him if he asked?

"Let's go," Ilona laughed, pulling him by the hand back the way they had come. He couldn't help but compare the emptiness at her touch to the way Elisabeta's touch filled him to the brim with excitement. He needed to return Ilona's handkerchief before she started getting ideas that they were courting.

There was someone else he thought he might want to court instead.

Chapter 10

Dracula couldn't stop thinking about what Elisabeta had told him. About her never having had a permanent home. He wondered what it must be like. For most of his life, he had lived in Ichor Knell after his mother had sought refuge following the ordeal with his father—his eye twitched with anger just thinking about the vile man—and he had lived here ever since. His mother died of iron poisoning fifteen years ago after stepping on an iron nail. The seemingly insignificant wound hadn't been treated soon enough and it had killed her.

He missed her terribly.

The bonfire raged brightly, fiercely, with all vampires that had participated in the Game—and a few others who had sat out like Madeleine—surrounding it. To his dismay, he hadn't been able to ask Elisabeta to sit beside him when Ilona commandeered his attention. He didn't want to hurt her, but the truth was he couldn't court her. His attention lay…elsewhere.

His gaze drifted across the fire where Elisabeta sat in between Lucian and Dimitrie. A flash of jealousy caught onto his heart like a fishing hook stuck in a gnarled branch when Dimitrie told a joke and she laughed. He quickly reminded himself she had asked *him* to kiss her. Not Dimitrie. A part of him wished he had taken the chance when it arose.

Suddenly, he scoffed when he saw a familiar face across the fire. "Who invited Frederick?"

"For the last time, I'm not Frederick," the vampire replied, rolling his eyes. "I'm Julian."

"Could've fooled me."

Julian didn't get the chance to reply because a vampire humbly stepped forward, holding the Golden Chalice filled with human blood and presented it to Dimitrie with a flourish. Cheers and applause lifted into the sky and begrudgingly, Dracula clapped his hands to honor the new champion.

"Speech!" someone in the crowd shouted.

The vampires sitting around the fire chanted the word until Dimitrie silenced them with an obnoxiously arrogant hand. He appeared self-important as if he had single-handedly fought his way through every single vampire in the Game and earned the prize. Honestly, the chalice would have been Dracula's if he hadn't been worried for Elisabeta's safety. But alas, preventing her from getting stabbed had been more important than obtaining the glory of winning.

He didn't regret his decision.

"I am humbled to be holding this in my hands," Dimitrie said, reverently staring at the chalice he held. "I wouldn't be here without my team. And although I fought my way through two vampires to get it, I would be nothing without the trust and action of my teammates."

Dracula frowned as he glanced at Nicolae who gave him a pointed look. He had lost the bet that Dimitrie hadn't lifted a finger to get the chalice. Now he owed his friend his fortune—which, admittedly, wasn't much. He owned some farthings. Perhaps a few shillings too. But otherwise, he had hardly a penny to his name.

His frown deepened as he stared moodily at the fire. What did he have to offer *any* female? He lived in the soldier barracks in the small, barely livable captain's quarters. The quarters were truthfully just a single room large enough for a bed and a dresser. And he couldn't afford to buy a house, let alone rent an apartment. Not only was his wage too small, but the price of homes and goods were on the upward increase.

With a sigh, he ran a hand down his face. He felt like a failure. He realized he could never support a mate, let alone any future children.

Unless he moved away from Ichor Knell.

But his home was here. With Nicolae and Madeleine and Lucian and Ilona, and dare he say it, Elisabeta. He could never leave them, even if it meant a higher wage and a better life.

Besides, he enjoyed being captain of the army. It gave him a satisfying sense of purpose.

"Here's to vampires!" Dimitrie continued, and finally, he took a long swig of blood from the Golden Chalice. Subsequently, another goblet was passed around, each vampire taking a swallow of blood before handing it to the vampire next to them.

Dracula took the goblet, and when he swallowed a sip of human blood, his eyes flashed red, a scratchy burn rising in his throat. He needed to feed. And soon. Between training recruits, flirting with Elisabeta, helping provide for Nicolae's children, and worrying over the state of Ichor Knell, he had forgotten one very important detail—taking care of himself.

He passed the goblet and lifted his gaze, finding

Elisabeta watching him curiously. One would think she had never seen a vampire with red eyes before. Still, he didn't look away, but rather returned her curious stare with one of his own. Someone passed the goblet to her and she stared at it, her eyes staying the same shade of green. They didn't flash red. She raised the goblet to her lips and swallowed. Strangely enough, her eyes remained green. He had never seen anything more peculiar. No matter the age, every vampire's eyes turned red when consuming blood.

"Are you all right?" Ilona asked, touching his hand.

Her sudden intrusion startled him from his thoughts. As he looked into her also-red eyes, a feeling of guilt hit him like a relentless rainstorm.

He didn't answer. Instead, he stood and placed his hand on top of her dark, curly hair. It was a gesture of tenderness, but not in the courting sense. She looked up at him in confusion, but she must have seen the guilty look in his eyes because she took his offered hand and allowed him to pull her to her feet. Together, they walked along the graceful curve of the lake, silence stretching between them as if she were bracing herself for his words.

"You don't need to say it," she said first, hugging her arms to herself and looking to the ground. "I already know what you mean to say."

"I have to say it," he insisted as he fished into his pocket and pulled out her blue and yellow handkerchief, placing it gently into her hands. "I thought I could court you, but I cannot. I'm sorry."

She nodded and wiped her tears with her own handkerchief, setting the guilt in his heart on fire. He had never wanted to make her cry. "Is there someone else?"

"Yes."

Her tears flowed faster, and he forced himself to look away toward the glassy surface of the dark lake. Breaking a female's heart was not an easy thing to do. He wished he never had to do it, but for Elisabeta, he had to push through.

Ilona took his hand and squeezed, offering him the barest hint of a smile before turning around and starting back to the others. For a moment, his guilt nearly made him retire early from the festivities and return home, but he was no coward. He would face his guilt head on and try to not let it affect him.

He took a deep breath and walked back toward the raging bonfire, but he didn't return to his seat next to Ilona—who refused to look at him, with good reason. Instead, he leaned against a nearby tree and watched vampires continue their small banquet with laughter and games—albeit much safer ones.

"That's a nice sword on your belt!" Grigore shouted, and it wasn't until Dracula turned his head that he realized the vampire male was talking to him. "How many vampires did you impale this year, Dracula?"

"It would have been fourteen," he grunted as he glared at the heavyset male who had nearly stabbed Elisabeta, "but I found my fists did a much better job than my sword ever would."

To his annoyance, this earned a chuckle from anyone close enough to hear, and a slap on the back to the heavyset male who had earned the infamous Dracula the Impaler's wrath. It was a shame vampires healed fast because he would have liked to see him sport a broken nose for a few more weeks.

"I heard a female tried out for a position in the army," Grigore snickered. "I also heard she didn't make the cut."

Dracula noted the way Elisabeta shrank lower where she sat, her eyes downcast. He had to admit his surprise. She appeared confident and capable on the outside, but he noticed she occasionally hid her insecurity and uncertainty.

"Nonsense," he said with a wave of his hand, standing taller and glaring at Grigore. "I cast her away because she was a female. Had she been a male, I would have made her a squadron leader. She is more talented than ten of my new recruits combined."

A murmur of surprise shifted through the crowd, and across the fire, Elisabeta met his gaze with gratitude written on her face. He looked away and grumbled under his breath. He hadn't said it for the gratitude, but because it was the truth. Besides, he still wanted to ask her where she learned how to fight. Did Miles teach her? Or did she learn from someone else?

One thing he felt sure of—she was far too interesting to pass up.

In a lull in the conversation, someone struck a long note on the gamba, followed by a cornamuse, and a lute joined in. Vampires started clapping along to the music and formed in couples. He groaned. He hated dancing. He should have gone back home when he had the chance.

He glowered when Elisabeta approached him, but even his expression wasn't enough to ward her off.

"Will you ask me to dance?" she asked, her eyes beautiful and sparkling in the bonfire-lit night. Despite her atrocious trousers and tunic, she looked ravishing, and he desperately wanted to kiss her like no one was watching.

"No."

She frowned, perfectly mimicking his own expression. "Do you have something against dancing with me?"

He crossed his arms over his chest and shifted to avoid looking directly at her. "You and everyone else wanting to look like a prancing lunatic. Go dance with Dimitrie. He's been fawning over you all night."

The words escaped his mouth before he could stop them.

As always.

But he had been jealous of Dimitrie all night from being this year's Game champion to winning over Elisabeta's attention with his jests and his quips and his charms. And Dracula's loose lips couldn't be contained, no matter how hard he tried. Words often slipped from his mouth, and he felt powerless to stop them.

"I may not be from here," she said, anger flashing in her eyes as she poked his chest, "but I don't understand you, Dracula. You are maddening. You are rude. And I'm sure you meant nothing that happened in the forest tonight."

She spun on her heel, not giving him a chance to reply. Of course he had meant it. Blast it! But that didn't mean he wanted to prance around like a moose!

"Infuriating female," he muttered darkly as he watched her join a dance with Dimitrie. The bloody vampire smiled so wide that if he smiled any wider, Dracula would knock the smile right off his face with a well-aimed fist. He despised the way they laughed together and danced in a lively circle. He hated the way she touched him and allowed him to lead her in the dance. And he especially hated Dimitrie for dancing with her at all.

He changed his mind. He most certainly would punch the smile right off Dimitrie's face.

He pulled up his sleeves and tromped forward with a death glare in his eyes, but before he managed to get any closer, Madeleine stepped in his path, her sweet smile immediately dissolving his malice.

She placed her hands on her belly—a habit of hers—and said, "Dance with Ilona? She's aching for a partner."

"I have one already," Ilona said quickly as she pulled the surprised Lucian by the hand toward the dancing. Guilt pricked his conscience for the strain his lack of interest put on their friendship. More than anything, he hoped it didn't affect his friendship with Madeleine. But for the time being, it seemed as if she wasn't aware of what had happened between him and Ilona.

"Dance with me then?" Madeleine asked, holding out her hand to him. "Nicolae is currently engaged in a heated debate about why Manuel Busca is a better philosopher than Theodore Florea, and it's boring me to death."

Of course, she had never been the scholarly type like Nicolae, but she was still smart enough to keep up with him.

He rolled his eyes. "Dancing is for lovestruck kittens. Not battle warriors."

She craned her neck and looked every which way. "Battle? What battle? I only see a lovestruck kitten in front of me. Come on, Dracula. Don't leave me without a partner. I had to sit out of the Game after all."

To his dismay, she grabbed his hand and dragged him along. Her brute strength surprised him. Even when he dug his heels into the ground to try and impede her progress, she still managed to pull him toward the other dancers. To his annoyance, Elisabeta witnessed the whole spectacle beside Dimitrie.

She still glared at him, and he scowled right back. How could she possibly think him rude? He hadn't done anything to warrant such a description, had he?

They stopped in the middle of the dancing couples, and his scowl deepened as he stood straight with his arms crossed. He refused to dance.

"Getting you to dance is like pulling teeth." She tugged on his arm to try and pry his hands free, but his arms didn't budge.

"You would have more luck prying Nicolae away from his heated philosophical debate," he grumbled. "If you want to prance like a moose, you go ahead. I will not prance."

She sighed and rolled her eyes. "Dancing is not prancing, Dracula. It's celebrating. Tonight, we are celebrating those we have left behind. Think of your mother. Once, she had been a raining star to remind you she is still with you. You can dance to celebrate her memory."

"Don't bring my mother into this."

"Then dance with me. It may be the last dance I have for a while." She looked at him with a quivering lip, and he knew he had given in before she even started to tear up. He didn't want to make *two* females cry tonight with the possibility of a third. He had already seen enough tears to last him a lifetime.

"Females are impossible," he muttered under his breath. He still scowled, but he offered Madeleine his hands, which she gleefully accepted. He still refused to prance, but he danced through the steps with stiff movements, not even a flicker of a smile on his face.

Regardless of his attitude toward dancing, she still laughed joyously when he spun her through the movements. He nearly cracked a smile at her happy demeanor, but he pushed it back when he saw Dimitrie and Elisabeta dancing together, and the same jealousy from before sparked again.

Why, he oughta smash some sense into the bloke.

The song ended and Madeleine grinned from ear to ear. "See, dancing didn't kill you? Did it?"

"It just might have."

She rolled her eyes but continued to smile as she playfully smacked his arm and sought out a different partner. He watched as several males ventured Elisabeta's way, but he hurried forward and beat them to it, wrapping his hand around hers and pulling her to the other side of the makeshift dance floor. She tried to tug her hand free, but he held onto it tighter and pulled her close. She winced as if in pain, but her glare quickly eased his worries for her welfare.

"I meant it," he whispered, his lips grazing her ear. "I meant all of it. There is no one else quite like you, Elisabeta."

Her scowl melted away as she returned his gaze, and he found his desire to kiss her stronger than ever. But he played by his own rules. He wouldn't kiss her. At least not today. However, none of his rules said he couldn't kiss her tomorrow.

"You are still rude," she sniffed and turned her

head away while they rocked slowly back and forth to the music. Just holding her hand made him feel…complete. Whole. Like a breath of relief. "Just because you think something doesn't mean you have to say it."

"Are you talking about my loose lips? Well, you can't change that one. Believe me. I've tried multiple times."

Her mouth twitched as if fighting off a smile, but she finally gave in and snorted in laughter. "Fine," she chuckled. "I can look past it if you can look past my *atrocious clothing.*"

His attempt to hide his grimace was unsuccessful as he looked her up and down. Her tunic was tucked into her trousers, and her trousers into her boots. Her clothing was something he would find a boy wearing in Ichor Knell. It was plain. It was unfeminine. And he most certainly found it atrocious.

Despite the clothing, she still looked beautiful wearing it. He couldn't fault her for that.

With a shrug, he replied, "I might be able to look past it."

"That's good enough for me."

He sighed with contentment, his envy dissolving as he held her. This felt *right,* despite their short acquaintance. She fit well in his arms. Their fingers were made to intertwine. She made him feel more alive than ever since she had arrived in Ichor Knell. He believed her arrival was divine intervention. Ylios was good and kind. Dracula didn't plan on wasting this opportunity given.

He smiled a real, genuine smile as he danced— swayed—with her, his head resting on top of hers—

though he still hunched because he was so bloody tall. The ball already started rolling and he planned to ride it out, excited over the idea of getting to know her more. Tonight, everything was perfect, and it was only the beginning.

Chapter 11

Elisabeta hummed softly as she consecutively ate her breakfast and pinned her hair up while trying to avoid agitating her injured ribs, her thoughts revolving around Dracula. She may have swooned a few times as she remembered his gentle kisses beneath her ear and on the corner of her mouth. Dancing with him had been the highlight of the night. Calm. Safe. Sweet. Wonderful. For someone so dangerous and foreboding, he made her feel safe and protected in her arms.

"Drat!" she groaned as her hair fell out of its pins for the second time. "I can't do anything without a bloody mirror."

Vampires didn't have mirrors in Ichor Knell because they couldn't see their own reflections. As frustrating as she found the drawback, it was actually for the best because she *did* have a reflection. Anyone paying close enough attention would see she was a human and not a vampire.

Giving up completely, she kicked her feet up on the table and took a large bite of her porridge— something she had snuck into Ichor Knell earlier. She often found herself starving because long stretches of time passed before she could eat. But at least she was still alive. That counted for something.

She grimaced, remembering the blood she drank last night. Honestly, it hadn't tasted horrible—more metallic than anything. Knowing she had consumed human blood made her uneasy. But with so many watching her, she hadn't had a choice.

A knock sounded on her door and she spooned a large mouthful of porridge into her mouth, venturing across the room. She assumed it was the landlady's daughter leaving a plant at the foot of her door again.

However, when she opened the door, she didn't find a plant waiting for her but a large, hulking mass of vampire. Her eyes widened with panic. She slammed the door in Dracula's face, swallowing her porridge so quickly it hurt on its way down. And then she scrambled around her room, kicking anything under the bed that might reveal her deadly secret, including her vials, her remaining porridge, and the incriminating notebook she'd retrieved from the old theater.

She wasn't ready to face Dracula yet today. She had thought she had at least a few more hours.

"Heaven help me," she whispered.

Taking several deep breaths to steady herself, she tentatively placed her hand on the door handle and turned it. A small part of her hoped he'd left after she had rudely slammed the door, but he still stood in the same spot with his arms crossed, an eyebrow raised higher than the clouds hanging over Ichor Knell.

"Dracula," she breathed. She tucked a strand of hair behind her ear and grimaced when she realized half her hair had fallen out earlier. In her frazzled state, she tore out her remaining pins, but ended up dropping one. Both she and Dracula reached for it at the same time, their fingers brushing.

A rush of blood entered her cheeks, followed by a pounding hammer against her heart.

"Did I come at a bad time?" he asked.

"No," she nodded, but stopped halfway through to shake her head instead. "Not at all. What brings you this way?"

She closed the door behind her when he craned his curious neck to get a peek inside her apartment. He must never be allowed inside, which brought an alarming reminder that she still needed to find the treasury key. When he was away from his quarters, she would search his room.

Obtain the key. Give the egg to Miles. Sneak back before Dracula even finds the key missing.

Everyone could win in this scenario if she was careful, and she needn't use him for her own purposes.

He returned his gaze to her, now seemingly distracted himself. "I'm headed out to hunt. I might be gone several days depending on how long it takes. Would you like to accompany me?"

"Me?" Excited jitters fizzled through her at the idea of spending time alone with him.

He rolled his eyes. "Of course, you. Is there anyone else nearby?"

The smile on her face melted when she remembered what, exactly, he would be hunting. Not in any way, shape, or form was hunting with him a good idea. Not only would she be incapable of keeping up with him, but she had absolutely no desire to drink human blood again. Besides, as a human, her life would be in danger on a hunt.

"I already ate—err, fed—recently," she lied, avoiding eye contact with his intense, dark, swoon-worthy eyes. Where was a fan when she needed one?

"So? Come anyway."

111

"No."

A grin spread across her face as she found enough courage to lift her gaze. He had denied her request to kiss her last night, so she denied his request to accompany him this morning. "If you insist on making up rules for our little game, then so will I."

He groaned, obvious annoyance in his voice. "Why in Ylios' name would you make up a rule like that? You won't hunt with me? What harm could it do?"

"Plenty."

He released a long-suffering sigh, a grave look of disappointment in his eyes and a pout on his lips. Somehow, it made him look adorable and, dare she say it, more approachable.

"Fine. But at least accompany me to the border. I won't see you for a few days, after all."

His words incited giddiness in her stomach. Although she had come to Ichor Knell under false pretenses, with the intent to steal from him, she found herself drawn to him. Warmth spread through her whenever he touched her. Her heart misbehaved whenever he came near.

Feelings of guilt surfaced, though she tried to push them away. If he found out about her deceit, what would he do?

The thought of procuring the petrified dragon egg and leaving the vampire city with Miles created a deep ache within her heart. She didn't want to leave. She wanted to stay. To belong.

But…a little flirting couldn't hurt in the meantime, right?

"I have no rule against doing that much."

She smiled, biting back her excitement as she

slipped into her apartment to grab a cloak and returned a moment later. She threw her cloak over her shoulders and took a deep, steadying breath as she walked side by side with him. A gentle fog rolled into Ichor Knell, obscuring them from view. It felt like they were the only people within the entire city, especially with the quiet and serene atmosphere.

"Why a soldier?" she asked suddenly. "What made you choose that life?"

He reached for her hand and a flush crept into her cheeks as their fingers intertwined. Warmth trickled from the tips of her fingers, up her arm, and encouraged her pulse to thrum harder and faster. He was wonderful. Despite his brutish capabilities, he was sweet, and kind, and tall. So very tall.

"Not everyone gets to choose," he replied quietly, his dark eyebrows pulling together. "My mother had always been frail and weak, despite being a vampire. I made it my job to take care of her. Provide for her. I asked the shah's advisor for work and he pointed me in the direction of the soldier training grounds. I've been there for twenty years now, even though my mother is gone. It's where I belong. I wouldn't fit anywhere else."

She recognized the wistful reverence when speaking of his mother. He must miss her terribly. Memories of her own mother evaded her.

Subconsciously, she touched the necklace around her neck, turning the pendant around and around. Her fingers brushed the warm, silver metal. The simple pendant was invaluable to her. She wouldn't trade it for all the riches in the world.

"What about you?" he asked. "What did you do before you came to Ichor Knell? I'm sure you haven't always been a washerwoman."

She laughed and shook her head. "No, I certainly haven't."

A frown replaced her smile. She had no desire to tell him lies, but she also had no desire to tell him the truth either. But she found she *wanted* to tell him the truth. She *wanted* him to accept her as she was, and not because of a lie.

Pulling her hand out of his grasp, she concentrated on a small indent on her necklace, ready to face whatever scorn he might throw her way.

"You won't like me once I tell you," she whispered huskily. "I am afraid you will never speak to me again."

"Of course I will. Goodbye is a word, is it not?"

His jest lifted her from her sulky mood, and a burst of laughter escaped her mouth. She playfully smacked his arm, but when she attempted to fidget with her necklace again, he grabbed onto her hand and squeezed her fingers. She was no coward. At least she kept telling herself that as she tried to form the words on her tongue.

Their footsteps slowed on their way to the border, giving them more time to converse. She took a deep breath, and she told the truth.

"I mentioned before I came to Ichor Knell for a better future for myself and Miles." She didn't tell him the part about the dragon egg. Some secrets were better kept hidden. "Our mother died giving birth to our triplet and I never knew my father. Miles and I…we grew up on the streets. There is no honest work for children without a home. We learned to pickpocket. We lied. We cheated. We stole. I am not the person you seem to think I am. I am not honest, but I want to be. I had hoped Ichor Knell could change the hand fate dealt us."

With a swallow and a grimace, she finally looked up at Dracula, who watched her with an expressionless mask, and she braced herself for the goodbye.

"You are nineteen," he finally said, his lips twitching as if swishing his words around in his mouth. "That's still hardly old enough to provide for yourself under normal circumstances. It's commendable of you to attempt a fresh start."

She raised her eyebrows at him, noting how he still held tightly onto her hand. "Where is the goodbye? I am still waiting for it."

He smirked, surprising her when he pulled her closer to drape an arm across her shoulders. She sucked in a breath at the ache in her ribs, but the pain faded as the powerful, musky scent of male caressed her nostrils. A desire to turn more fully toward him to breathe him in surfaced, to run a hand down his chest, to kiss the soft skin beneath his jaw.

"If you think I would turn you away for petty thievery, you certainly don't know me very well, especially if you turned over a new leaf. As long as you don't steal from me, we won't have a problem."

Except she *was* planning to steal from him. She would give the key back once she finished the job, and she hoped more than anything he wouldn't find out. If she played her cards right, he would never learn of her act of betrayal.

Still, she could hardly believe he didn't turn her away. There was no scorn. No contempt. No judgement.

Perhaps he could accept her for being a human too.

"Have you thought about my question?" she asked

carefully. "If I was any other race other than a vampire, would you want me to stay?"

He groaned. "This question again? I thought we were past this. It doesn't even matter. You are a vampire. I am a vampire. Why entertain a pointless scenario?"

"It matters to me," she murmured, but today wasn't the time to press, just like last night wasn't the time to press. He opened his mouth to reply, but she cut across him, giving him a coy look from where she was tucked nicely under his arm. "How much jealousy do I have to inspire before you admit you kissed me in the forest?"

"Bah!" he grumbled, the previous question completely forgotten. "Those weren't real kisses. If I kissed you for real, you would know it. Believe me."

Heat flashed through her veins at the idea of him kissing her. It seemed like a very real possibility.

With one hand, he moved aside the boughs of a willow tree, and they entered within its private embrace. Her jaw dropped at the beauty of it. She touched the willow branches, watching as they sparkled beneath her fingers. This wasn't a jewel tree, but something else entirely. The boughs shimmered like sparkling diamonds when the wind weaved through the lazy, drooping foliage. It reminded her of how the sun reflected on the ocean water as the wind moved the surface in soft ripples.

Breathtaking.

She turned back to Dracula, and she suddenly didn't see the tree anymore but only him. The way he looked at her stole her breath away. His expression softened as he gently trailed a strand of her hair through his fingers. Her thoughts fled from her as she gazed into his eyes. It was then when she realized the truth.

She was in love with Dracula Ardelean.

This time, she didn't have to ask him to kiss her. His masculine scent wrapped around her as he leaned down and touched his lips to hers. A fire sparked to life in the shape of butterflies in her stomach. But as she returned his kiss, the fire turned into something softer. A warmth. A ray of sunshine. Clouds danced under her feet. Stars glimmered in the sky. All sense of time and space evaporated before her, and the only thing she was aware of was his kiss and the way he pressed her close to his body, safe within his muscular arms.

But it ended too soon, bringing her back down to earth in a gust of wind.

"Oh, heavens," she breathed, lightheaded as she placed a hand on his chest to steady herself. "That was worth waiting another day."

He chuckled and kissed her palm and then her wrist, sending a delightful shiver rushing up her arm. "Now you see why there are rules."

"It still doesn't change my view on rules."

He smiled at her. A true, genuine, beautiful smile. He rarely gave her those. "Are you sure you won't come hunting with me? I would enjoy your company at the very least."

She wanted to say yes. She wanted to go with him. But then she reminded herself *what* he was going to hunt. It would be dangerous for her to accompany him.

"I'm sure." She flirtatiously trailing her finger across his chest. "Perhaps it would give you time to miss me."

He didn't answer, but rather looked at her with an intense gaze, as if contemplating something. What could he possibly be thinking about?

Lightly gripping the dagger in his belt, she pulled it free, the metal singing on its way out. He watched her curiously, but he didn't stop her. She felt his gaze on her back as she took the dagger and scraped the tip against the rough bark of the willow tree. It wasn't until she finished half a heart when he sighed.

"Ugh. You are really going to do that?"

"I really am," she laughed, finishing the other half of the heart, and then scratching her initial into the bark. She held the dagger out to him handle first, but he didn't take it. Instead, he huffed and turned his head to the side, color climbing his neck.

"My initial is very lonely," she insisted. "It would be heartbroken to be left behind."

He rolled his eyes. "Your initial doesn't have feelings."

"Yes, but I do…"

Immediately, his rough demeanor melted like candle wax under the heat of fire. "Give me that." He snatched the dagger from her hand, and she watched as he carved his initial under hers. She tried to bite back a smile, but it broke through anyway.

"Happy?" he grumbled, sheathing his dagger.

"Are you?"

His mouth twitched, and despite trying to put up a grouchy facade, his dark brown eyes reflected the workings of her own heart. He was as happy as she was. Happy and in love.

"You dropped something," he said, his gaze flickering to the ground.

She frowned, puzzling over the black handkerchief lying at the base of the tree. She stooped to pick it up, running her thumb over the soft fabric. Her eyebrows furrowed even more. Never in her life had she owned a black handkerchief.

"This isn't mine."

"I know. It's mine."

Her eyebrows pulled together. Now she really didn't understand what was going on. "Then what…"

He sighed, an eye roll escaping in the form of his breath. "Are you too much of a foreigner to not understand the customs of vampire culture? Figure it out, Red Cat."

Panic lodged itself in her throat as she watched his retreating back. What had she done wrong this time?

Worry after worry ran through her, at least until he turned his head and offered a grin. He called out to her, "You have a few days to figure it out. Don't make me change my mind."

And then he was gone.

She lifted the handkerchief and inspected it closely as if she might find a hidden message within the fibers of the cloth. However, it was just an ordinary handkerchief. Nothing special about it. No magical qualities she could see. No special design or embroidery. But it had to mean something, otherwise he wouldn't have given it to her.

Elisabeta scratched her head over this new puzzle. Gifting a handkerchief? What odd vampire custom did she need to learn about now?

The mourning bell tolled, startling her out of her thoughts. Alarm raced through her as she burst out of the cover of the willow tree and ran quickly toward the city. She was late for work! Madame Glover wouldn't throw her out, would she?

She hastily tied her hair back as she burst through the building. Madame Glover gave her a disappointed frown, but otherwise said nothing as she located a garment waiting to be washed and knelt down at the tub beside Madeleine and Ilona. However, she paused after dunking the rich clothing into the water. Ilona sobbed, her red-tinted tears trailing down her cheeks and dripping into the laundry water. Crying and sniffling, not seeming to care who saw—or heard—her do it.

"Ilona!" she gasped. "Whatever is the matter?"

Ilona mumbled a few incoherent words, but she couldn't understand through her tears, so she looked to Madeleine for help.

"Someone returned her handkerchief," Madeleine explained with a sympathetic look. "I truly thought this would work out, but it didn't."

Despite Ilona's obvious distress, she perked up at the mention of handkerchiefs. She had to ask now while the iron was hot. "I'm new to Ichor Knell... What does giving or receiving a handkerchief mean?"

Madeleine dipped a coat into the water and scrubbed vigorously as if avenging Ilona. Poor, sweet girl. Elisabeta wished she wouldn't cry.

"Receiving a handkerchief means someone is interested in courting you. To give a handkerchief means you are also interested, and thus begins the courtship."

Excitement bubbled up inside of her. She accidentally dropped the garment into the basin of water and fished around to find it again. "I received a handkerchief only this morning!"

Both Madeleine and Ilona glanced up, interested in the promise of gossip. Madeleine leaned forward with animated eyes, touching her arm. "You must tell me who."

She dug inside her pocket and pulled out the black handkerchief. Madeleine's face became pasty white before Elisabeta even uttered his name. "Dracula."

Immediately, Ilona choked on a sob before covering her face with her hands and weeping on her way out of the building. Elisabeta trailed her with her eyes, guilt clouding her mind as she realized *who* returned Ilona's handkerchief.

What had she done?

"*Dracula* gave you his handkerchief?" Madeleine hissed, retracting her hand as if her arm had burned her. She shrunk away from her apparent anger. "How could you seduce his attention away with your unfeminine wiles? Dracula and Ilona were just about to strike up a courtship. Did you not know?"

She had never wanted to cry more in her life than she wanted to then. She had few friends in Ichor Knell, and she managed to tear everyone apart. If she courted Dracula, she would create a rift between not only herself and her new friends, but between him and his friends too.

She had known all along Ilona was competition, but she hadn't realized just how serious Dracula's and Ilona's relationship might have been if she hadn't shown up in Ichor Knell. It didn't matter that she was in love with Dracula. She had planned to hurt him in the end by either seducing him or leaving Ichor Knell with her brother and the dragon egg. She was a human in a vampire's world. She didn't belong here.

It would be better if she left.

"How could you?" Madeleine snapped with a hiss

of betrayal in her eyes. "I wish you had never shown your face in this city."

Her words hit Elisabeta like a horse's hoof to the chest, and this time, she *did* start to cry. She quickly hid her eyes so Madeleine wouldn't see her clear tears, but she knew she couldn't stay here any longer.

"I'm sorry," she whispered, standing up and fleeing out the same door Ilona had. But unlike Ilona, Elisabeta didn't plan on returning. She planned to make one last effort to find the treasury key, but afterward, she would leave Ichor Knell for good.

Chapter 12

Hunting had always been a relaxing activity for Dracula, but with Elisabeta on his mind, it was anything but. Instead, he found himself itching to return home if only to see her face again. Unfortunately, hunting was not easy. There were no laws regarding hunting. Any human was fair game. The hard part was finding a human *he* deemed acceptable for a meal. Despite his hatred of humans, he personally believed they were people too, with not many differences from vampires themselves. They were wives, mothers, husbands, fathers, children. Even his hatred of his own human father didn't change that.

Which was why he followed his own belief system closely. He refused to feed on mothers of young children, especially those still suckling their babies. He refused to feed on men providing for a family if he could help it. He also refused to attack a group of humans just to get his fill.

However, he found it acceptable to feed on humans by their lonesome, the elderly, and men who were criminals.

His morals made hunting difficult.

He gritted his teeth in frustration as he watched the small town before him in the gathering darkness. An entire day and a half had already passed, yet he had nothing to show for his efforts. Any other vampire would have found someone to feed on by now.

"Finally," he muttered, watching as two guards dragged a man through the village in the dead of night, the light from their torches glinting off their steel armor. The prisoner fought against the guards, but his weak, pathetic attempts did nothing but annoy them. The guards bound the prisoner to a wooden post, kicking him in the side as if he had personally offended them.

"Don't leave me here!" the man cried, struggling against his bonds as the guards turned away. "There are vampires out there!"

"Good riddance," one guard spat. "May God cast judgement upon your sins."

A criminal. Even better.

He watched the guards' retreating backs, waiting for the opportune moment to strike. The torchlight disappeared around the bend, and then all became quiet in the small town except for the man's whimpers of fear. Some vampires enjoyed torturing the humans they killed, but despite his formidable reputation, he liked to end their lives quickly. He preferred to not hear his meal's cries of pain.

He didn't even pull out his weapon as he rushed forward with a burst of speed. The man's eyes widened as he saw him coming, but he otherwise had no time to cry out before he snapped the criminal's neck. The body became limp.

A raging thirst clutched his throat, burning hot as the promise of blood consumed him. He nearly fed then and there, but he forced himself to remain in control.

Using his sharp fingernails, he sliced the ropes that bound the criminal to the wooden post and slung him over one shoulder. The man's limp body swayed with each step he took away from the town, but he didn't stop until he was far enough away to enjoy his meal in peace.

Settling down on a patch of dried pine needles, he eagerly sprouted his fangs and sank them into the man's wrist. Warm, delicious blood greeted his throat. All human blood more or less tasted the same, though the younger the human, the fresher the blood.

He had never finished feeding so quickly in his life, as he yearned to return to Elisabeta. He would return to Ichor Knell sooner than he had anticipated, and he hoped by then, she would have figured out what his handkerchief meant.

He had no doubt she would agree to court him.

He grinned as he wiped the blood from his mouth and left the human body behind. He looked forward to hearing a simple but delicious word come from Elisabeta's mouth. A fiery, satisfying courtship was about to begin.

Chapter 13

Nothing terrified Elisabeta more than breaking into Dracula's room.

She had known she would have to do it eventually, but somehow, it felt like betrayal. It had been easy to pretend she belonged here. That she had friends. That she was wanted. But it was all just a farce. She had no friends. Those who she had thought were her friends hated her. She got caught in her own lie, believing she belonged with Dracula.

Madeleine's painful spurn had put her focus on the right track.

The treasury key...

That's what she had come to Ichor Knell for. Nothing more.

She took a deep breath and pushed back her heartache, telling herself again and again she didn't belong here. Madeleine had said as much. Ilona didn't want her here either. And if Dracula learned she was a human, he would shun her too.

Her fingers trembled as she took a pin out of her hair and fit it into the keyhole, but to her surprise, the door wasn't locked. Did vampires not lock their doors? It made sense, as vampires couldn't enter a room without permission. Still, it was a strange habit. One she couldn't wrap her mind around.

Looking both ways to make sure no one saw her,

she slipped into his room and quietly closed the door behind her. Guilt at trespassing consumed her, not just because it was wrong, but because it was *Dracula*. She loved him. But she didn't deserve him.

"Forgive me," she whispered and turned around.

The state of Dracula's room sent her into a shock. To say he was a slob was an understatement. Weapons littered nearly every inch of the room, and it looked as if every article of clothing he owned lay in heaps on the floor rather than his closet. Not to mention his unmade bed or the candle wax that had dripped onto his bedside table and seeped into the wood.

How was she supposed to find a key in this mess?

She tiptoed carefully, making sure to return anything she touched to how she found it. She searched shirt pockets, pants pockets, and inside shoes. She hunted through drawers, rifled through weapons, and dropped to her hands and knees to scan beneath the bed. Unfortunately, the key was nowhere to be found.

"Do you even have it?" she whispered to herself, her hands on her hips as she surveyed the disastrous room, like a windstorm had taken all his belongings and scattered them about.

What if the captain of the ship had been wrong with his information? Did Dracula truly have the treasury key? Did the vampires have the petrified dragon egg? Since she had arrived in Ichor Knell, she hadn't gotten a single whiff of talk of the egg. Had she come all this way for nothing?

Both disappointment and relief filled her. Disappointment because the dragon egg had been a chance at a new life. Relief because the last thing she ever wanted to do was betray or hurt Dracula. Miles would be immensely upset at her failure, but there was no helping it.

Or perhaps she had befriended the wrong people. Should she instead have impersonated a noblewoman? That might have given her access to the castle, and perhaps even access to Shah Jorin. Still...she was done meddling in the lives of the vampires she cared about. She would lie to Miles if she had to, if it meant making Ilona, Madeleine, and Dracula happy.

The handle of the door turned, and she froze, staring at the door opening before her. Her heart pounded, her blood pulsed loudly in her ears, and every instinct inside her shouted at her to flee. But she remained rooted to the spot, her eyes wide.

Dracula stood on the other end of the door, but his back faced her. Instead, he appeared preoccupied with something else.

"Captain!" a soldier called out. "You have returned. A court messenger awaits. From the palace."

"From the bloody palace?" Dracula grumbled. "Can Jorin not send letters anymore?"

"Letters are outlawed to peasants," the other vampire reminded. "And books. And reading in general—"

"I get it. Where can I find the messenger?"

She glanced wildly around the room for an escape. She could hide underneath the bed, but she felt sure Dracula would notice her scent and find her. She could also escape out the window. But opening the window might make noise, alerting him to her presence. The only way out was through the door he currently held open, oblivious to her presence within. What would he do if he turned around and saw her there? He would immediately figure out she wasn't a vampire. Would he hurt her? Would he be upset?

A horrible feeling churned inside her. What would he be more upset with—the fact that she was a human or the fact that she had lied to him?

"I come home for two minutes and I don't even get a chance to sit down before someone needs something of me," he said, annoyance lacing his voice. "Fine. I'll get this over with. I'll grab my sword first. I may have to impale a vampire or two on my way. And don't look so terrified. I'm not going to impale you. Get back to training."

Again, she panicked. She warred between unsheathing her dagger to protect herself from his inevitable wrath and ducking underneath his arm, running as fast as she could away from him.

She hated getting caught red-handed.

In the end, she ducked underneath his arm at the exact same time he turned around. They smacked hard into each other, enough to knock the air right out of her lungs, send a flare of fire through her ribs, and trip her to the ground in the hallway. She didn't know what was more humiliating—crashing to the ground at Dracula's feet or getting caught doing something she wasn't supposed to be doing.

And why was he already back from his hunting trip? He said he would be gone for a few days!

"Elisabeta?" he asked, surprised. "Are you all right?"

He helped her to her feet, concern in his eyes, and for a moment, she couldn't breathe as she stared back at him. Now she finally understood how it felt to be a doe with an arrow trained right at its heart. As soon as

Dracula released the arrow, she felt sure she would die.

Chapter 14

Dracula couldn't fathom why Elisabeta had come to see him at his room. How had he missed her on his way there? Had he walked right past her? Had she slipped right past him? And why in Ylios' name was she here? She didn't want to...mate...did she? As tempting as it sounded, he was far from ready to form a bloodbond with anyone. Besides, he didn't even have the means to support a mate.

But he tried to play it off casually, as he didn't want to reveal his uncertainty.

He leaned against the doorframe, a smirk lifting his lips. "Couldn't get enough of me earlier?" he teased, enjoying watching the blush rise to her cheeks. But even more confusing than her sudden appearance was the way he heard her release a sigh of relief, her heartbeat slowing.

She still didn't say anything, and his uncertainty grew. His relaxed posture firmed into rigidness. Something didn't feel right here. And it made him immensely uncomfortable. Why did she look at him with such sadness in her eyes? After the kiss they had shared beneath the willow tree, shouldn't she be smiling radiantly instead of looking close to tears?

She answered his unspoken questions as she lethargically produced his black handkerchief and tucked it into his shirt pocket. "No, thank you," she whispered.

His mouth fell open in disbelief. That hadn't been the word he had expected to come from her mouth. "No, thank you? Elisabeta… This isn't a part of the game. I'm completely genuine. Absolutely serious."

"I know."

Truth shone in the dull, lifeless look in her usually fiery eyes. She had no desire to court him? None at all? Did she not feel what he felt? Did she not feel the fire? The spark? The happiness? Had he just imagined it all? She truly didn't want to court him?

"But…but you seemed interested before I left hunting. What changed?"

She turned her back to him, and the loss of eye contact snapped the thread that conjoined their two hearts. He felt the snap like a kick to the chest, and suddenly he understood what heartbreak felt like. It was agonizing. Torturous. His stomach churned and his heart twisted painfully.

Her words escaped as a whisper, "I should not have come to Ichor Knell. I offset the balance. I only got in the way and you deserve much better than me. Believe me. I'm sorry, Dracula. Someday, you will be able to see why this is for the best."

"No," he replied with a disbelieving shake of his head, feeling their near-courtship slip through his fingers. For days, he had been joyous beyond belief, and for a moment, he thought she felt the same. "Why would you say that? You gave me reason to believe you felt the same as I did. Do you not?"

She didn't answer, and the silence tortured him. He didn't dwell over the agony for long when he noticed the full bag she wore on her back.

Once again, heartbreak kicked him in the chest, but harder this time to the point of stealing every inch of his breath. "You are leaving?"

"I don't belong here," she said, her words pained. "Just ask Nicolae. Perhaps when I'm gone, he will tell you why. Goodbye, Dracula."

When she started to walk away, he reached out for her but dropped his hand, unsure of what he could do or say to bring her back. Therefore, he simply watched her go, each footstep she took away from him like a hammer smashing into his heart. He wanted to race after her, demand she stay. But he didn't know how.

He puzzled over why she had acted interested at first and now shied away from him. What had he done wrong? Did he say something rude? Did she find his poverty unattractive? Most of Ichor Knell lived in poverty. It couldn't be helped. Or was she simply not interested in courting him?

Her rejection stung like the bite of an iron sword.

Finally, he gathered his bearings enough to jog after her. "Elisabeta, wait!"

However, before he reached her, the court messenger his soldier mentioned earlier stepped in his path, preventing him from delivering his pleas. He nearly pushed the messenger aside, but he didn't dare, especially as the danger in Ichor Knell increased by the day. Trading the messenger's attention for Elisabeta's could put her in unnecessary danger.

"What?" Dracula snapped, balling his fists at his sides.

The messenger frowned, but he said nothing at his outburst as he straightened his court robes and stood taller—though he was still much shorter than Dracula's formidable height.

"Shah Jorin requests your immediate presence."

"Now?" he asked, craning his neck in the direction Elisabeta had disappeared in.

"Yes, now. Hurry along. He does not like to be kept waiting."

He internally groaned. Now was not a good time. He wanted answers! He wanted an explanation. Something must have happened to change Elisabeta's mind and he needed to know what.

Still, he reluctantly agreed and followed the messenger toward the looming black castle. Only a handful of times had he set foot in the castle, but he never stayed long enough to explore. Even if Shah Jorin invited him to wander the spacious building, he doubted he could traverse the large structure within a day. Not only did it contain numerous rooms and hallways, but ballrooms, a throne room, and courtyards. Peasants weren't allowed inside the castle—let alone the cathedral; however, he was an occasional exception.

With trepidation rising within him, he followed the messenger through the large double doors leading inside, immediately intimidated by the grandeur. The hallways stretched endlessly from one end of the castle to the other, the walls contained paintings centuries old or even older, and the ceilings stretched high with colorful portraits of vampires past. He felt small in the castle, not at all like he belonged.

"This way," the messenger said, tearing his attention away from the high-vaulted ceiling and leading him to what he recognized to be the throne room.

Nervousness formed a pit in his stomach as he

thought of every little thing he had done to warrant a personal visit with Shah Jorin. He hadn't done anything *too* horrible. Sure, he may have impaled a handful of vampires, thrown insults around like the dropping of leaves in autumn, and kissed the loveliest vampire he had ever met... But none of those things were against the law. Did the shah plan to strip him of his position as Captain?

A sick feeling churned in his stomach at the thought. He refused to lose Elisabeta and his job on the same day.

He stepped into the dimly lit throne room to find Shah Jorin sitting slouched in his throne, a crown placed upon his chin-length golden hair. Jorin looked like a young adolescent with insolent brown eyes and a sharp, angular jaw, though he was approximately four hundred years old. Dracula hated him. He was selfish, arrogant, and easily swayed. If he could knock the vampire right onto his tail end, he would.

"You are late," Jorin said, staring a hole straight through him. He struggled to keep his hands at his sides to keep from throttling the male around the neck.

The shah looked expectantly from Dracula, to the ground, and back to him, his mouth forming an irksome pout. "Bow."

Forget throttling him, he wanted to run him through with his sword and throw him over the side of the deep ravine bordering Ironfell. He bowed to no one, but he had little choice in the matter.

He held his anger in check as he knelt to one knee and inclined his head, beating down his rising fury. This conceited male before him was responsible for many vampire deaths. With the church using him for their own means, Jorin was not fit to wear the crown. As Dracula thought time and again, he believed he could do a better job as Shah. However, there were two things wrong with that sentiment—he didn't want the position, and in no way, shape, or form would he ever have the opportunity to become the shah, especially because of his position as a peasant.

"You summoned me?" he asked, but instantly regretted it when Jorin frowned and pushed himself off his throne. Although he knew what was coming long before it happened, he forced himself to stay still as Jorin struck him across the face.

His cheek burned, but the pain didn't hold a flame to the rage festering inside him. If it hadn't been for the dozens of royal guards lining the room, he just might have snapped every bone in Jorin's body.

"Never speak unless requested," Jorin spat, righting his crown as if slapping him across the face had been a great undertaking. "Do you still have the key?"

He nodded, not trusting his own voice to refrain from speaking a string of curses. As he dug into his pocket and handed it over, the anger in his eyes nearly boiled over. He didn't want this bloody key. If he didn't have morals to ground him, he just might have stolen every bit of coin from the treasury and dispersed the wealth among the peasants.

"Good," Jorin said, slumping into his throne once again. He handed the key to one of his advisors, who disappeared with it as if on their way to the treasury. "I like to know exactly where it is. As for the other reason I summoned you..." He casually inspected his nails, as if he found even the slightest trace of dirt deplorable.

"I am officially disbanding the army. No more training. No more soldiers. I will allow them to remain living in the barracks, but I will not give them a wage. As for you... Your only wage will come from keeping the treasury key safe. You will receive half a wage of what you used to make. And you better think twice before making a fuss. I have plenty of ways of keeping vampires in line. Do you understand?"

For a moment, he couldn't think, let alone speak, so great was his rage. *Someone* needed to keep the citizens of Ichor Knell safe, and with the army disbanded, he had a horrible feeling something awful was about to happen. With no soldiers to protect Ichor Knell, what would become of the city?

He knew one thing for sure...

Lucian, Ilona, Madeleine, Nicolae, and the children needed to leave Ichor Knell immediately. The time for safety was over. He would do his best to care for all of them outside the city. They were his family. And he swore to keep his family safe.

Taking a steadying breath, he forced himself to nod.

"Speak the words," Jorin said impatiently, and he found himself clenching his fists so tightly his knuckles turned white.

"I understand."

"Good. If I see any soldier activity, there will be consequences." The advisor returned with the key and gave it back to him. "You are dismissed."

He held in his rage as he rose to his feet and saw himself out of the castle. He held in his blistering anger as he calmly walked across the square, past dozens of royal guards watching him warily. He held in his fury as he headed away from the castle as the day turned into dusk. And finally, when he could no longer contain his seething rage, he turned to the nearest tree and punched the bark as hard as he could.

Bones crackled and snapped in his hand, but the pain didn't deter him. He struck the tree once, twice, three times, until he successfully channeled all of his anger into the object. His fingers bled like a river of blood. His entire hand throbbed with scorching pain. He breathed heavily as if his remaining rage could exit through each breath he released.

"Damn Jorin," he muttered, resting his forehead against the cool bark as he waited for his body to heal the broken bones in his hand. A cool relief entered the base of his wrist, traveled upward into his palm, and coursed through each of his fingers. Slowly, the pain disappeared, and he gained the ability to move his hand once more. He wasn't sure how much time had passed. Perhaps seconds. Maybe minutes. But he knew he could no longer stay here and deliver his anger to an undeserving tree. He had much to do.

Unsheathing his sword, he heaved it onto his shoulder and marched toward the training grounds where his soldiers continued their exercises. Each eye trailed him, and everyone ceased fighting as if they knew something awful had just transpired. He stopped in the middle of the training grounds, looking each vampire directly in the eye. These soldiers had potential. Now all that potential was lost.

Raising his voice, he called out, "Each and every one of you has made exceptional progress since day one of training, and I encourage you to remember the skills you have learned. Shah Jorin has disbanded the army and decreed army activity is now illegal."

A murmur ran through the crowd as he let the new information sink in. "I also encourage you to find a new profession, because although you are still welcome to live in the barracks, you will not receive a wage."

The murmuring turned into full-blown complaints, and he didn't bother easing their outrage at learning they no longer had a means of supporting themselves or their families.

"Is this true?" Lionel asked, and all voices quieted to hear his answer.

"Yes. Keep your weapons at your side. Always be on your guard. Keep your families safe."

"Why is our shah doing this? Having an army is essential to any city."

He frowned, unease settling in his heart. "I don't know. Which is why I caution you to be ready for anything."

His own unease transferred to the ex-soldiers, as they conversed with one another, voicing their fears and doubts he wished to block from his mind. But those fears and doubts were very real, and they were terrifying.

As if on cue, the mourning bell tolled thirty-five times, meaning seven deaths, and each toll hit him hard. Those tolls meant someone's loss. Mothers, fathers, sisters, brothers... And they could very well be *his* family. He refused to stay in the city any longer. The only problem he knew he would encounter was Madeleine. She was due very soon, and in her state, it would be difficult for her to flee. For her safety—and her child's safety—she needed to leave. Even if he had to carry her the entire way.

And Elisabeta…

He swallowed hard at the thought of her leaving Ichor Knell. She would be safer away from the city, but on her own, she would be in danger. He had to go after her, if only to convince her to travel with them.

Leaving his soldiers behind, he sheathed his sword and flared his nostrils as he attempted to pick up Elisabeta's scent. It wasn't easy amid the dozens of sweaty scents from male vampires, but finally he caught a trace of wildflowers and started following.

The faint scent led him away from the training grounds, over a hill, and it became stronger as he followed it toward the forest. His frown deepened the further he traveled. How had she managed to get so far in such a short time? Not being able to keep an eye on her concerned him. Of course, she was certainly capable of taking care of herself, but he *needed* to be able to protect her.

Suddenly, her scent disappeared when he reached the river, as if she had taken to the skies rather than continued on foot. Had she turned into an owl?

An urgency set in, and he transformed into a bat. His eyesight became sharper, almost too sharp. He relied on his echolocation to guide him through the forest. He flapped his wings quickly, flying erratically as he dipped under a branch, turned sharply on one wing to dodge a cluster of trees, and flew higher until he skimmed the top of the forest. However, a ray of sunset nearly burned him, forcing him to fly lower beneath the safety of the boughs.

Elisabeta, where are you?

Worry pushed him faster. Mice and moths scurried away from his high-pitched screeches. He listened for any signs of flapping owl wings, but he heard nothing. He searched the ground, but he didn't spot any red-headed females wandering about. His echolocation didn't sense any movement besides normal woodland animals. Had something happened to her? Did someone from the church get to her first?

Lifting his gaze to the skies once more, he narrowed his eyes when he caught sight of a plume of smoke rising above the trees. A surge of hope burst through him and he flew faster in the direction of the smoke.

He tilted his wings and cut through the air, flying lower and weaving between trees. The smoke came closer with each second until he landed on a branch, shifting upside down with his sharp claws digging into the tree. He sighed in relief as he finally found Elisabeta. She sat with her back to him, her chin resting on her knees while she stared somberly into the fire. Why did she look so sad? It broke his heart. Perhaps even more than her rejection had.

He shifted on the branch, which seemed to get her attention. She turned her head to look, but then she shrieked, leaping to her feet, and pressing a hand to her racing heart.

"Don't do that!" she gasped. "It's terrifying."

On another day, he might have laughed for scaring her, but tonight, he didn't have it in him. He held onto the branch with one hand and slowly untransformed until he reached his full height, letting go of the branch and dropping deftly to his feet.

"I didn't mean to frighten you," he said, approaching cautiously as if she was an animal that spooked easily. He slowly sat beside the fire, making it clear he didn't plan on leaving anytime soon. "I was worried. I couldn't find you for a good while."

"That was the point."

She released a long sigh but joined him beside the fire, poking at it with a stick. Red embers floated upward, curling, and twisting, and dancing until they turned ashen and disintegrated in the gentle breeze.

Silence filled the space between them, and he sought to cut through it. "You built this fire on your own? I don't know a single female who knows how."

"None?" she asked, surprised. "It's one of the most fundamental skills I believe everyone should know."

A grin spread across his face. "Finally! Someone who gets it. Basic survival skills are a must. Tell that to Nicolae. He hardly knows how to handle a simple knife."

"You're jesting."

He shook his head. "I'm not. That's what happens when you spend too much time with your nose in a book and not enough time in the great outdoors." Of course, he had begged Nicolae time and again to pick up a sword and learn a thing or two, but he always refused.

"Why do you hate humans?" she asked suddenly, taking him by surprise. "Nicolae told me your father was a vampire hunter."

At the mention of his father, his nostrils flared with anger.

"That bastard," he said in a low growl. "I hate that man. My mother was a mated vampire. My human father killed her mate and took advantage of her. He kept her around. Beat her. Even with me in the womb. Not even I could protect her as I got older. The only

142

thing I could do for her was help her escape to Ichor Knell where he could not follow. I hate humans because they are selfish. They are greedy. They take what they want, not giving a care in the world for the destruction they leave behind."

"I see…" she whispered, her voice hardly audible even to his vampire ears.

He sighed into his hand, thinking his outburst had frightened her. Of course, he had only known one human, but his father had tainted his view on their race. "Forgive me. I can hardly contain my rage when I think of my father. I would rather not speak of him."

"I understand all too well," she replied quietly. "Greed breeds hurt."

Another awkward silence created tension between them. Her shoulders tensed as if bracing herself for his next question. He needed to ask it. He needed to know.

"Why?" he said quietly. She curled herself into a ball, seeming to make herself as small as possible. "Did I do something wrong? I must have if you are willing to leave the city just to get away from me."

"You've done nothing wrong," she said, lifting her head to return his gaze. Her normal happy, fiery spark in her eyes was gone. What had he done to take it away?

"No?" he asked, raising an eyebrow. "You are not offering any other explanation. Therefore, I must have done something wrong. Perhaps I am not wealthy enough for your tastes? If that's the case, I will never earn your favor. I got sacked."

Her jaw dropped. "You lost your job?"

"Me and every one of my soldiers. Jorin disbanded the army." He flexed his fingers, now completely healed.

"I'm sorry," she said regretfully, placing a hand on his arm. His heart stopped for a moment as he stared down at her hand. His entire being burst to life when she touched him. "I don't care that you don't have a lot of money. I am sad you lost your job, however. You loved it."

He shrugged, though he tried to hide how much losing his position as Captain hurt. "There are other worthy professions." Unfortunately, he didn't know what those were. "But you still haven't answered my question, and I refuse to leave this spot until you do."

She retracted her hand, and immediately, the warmth she offered left his body, leaving behind a trail of ice. "I have already told you," she said, staring once again into the fire. "I don't belong here. I never will. And I am certainly not welcome."

"Not welcome?" He recoiled as if struck. "We have all been welcoming toward you. Why would you say that?"

To his dismay, she didn't answer, but rather shrank smaller into a ball. He couldn't even understand her reasoning. Lucian treated her kindly. Nicolae was getting more and more chummy with her by the day. Madeleine and Ilona were her friends. And he... Well, he was *very* welcoming.

He heaved a great sigh and fidgeted with the treasury key in his pocket. As soon as he was able, he would get rid of this bloody key once and for all.

He pulled it out of his pocket and inspected it, watching as the firelight glinted off its shiny, silver metal. It was a large key, and he found it burdensome. He didn't want it. He had never wanted it. Not for the first time, he wondered why Jorin had thrust this burden upon his shoulders. Why not keep the key on his own person? Or entrust it to one of his advisors?

"What is that?" Elisabeta whispered, making him jump. Her voice startled him out of his thoughts.

"Nothing important," he replied, shrugging his shoulders. "Just a key I've been carrying around for years. I don't understand why Jorin entrusted it to me. Most likely to watch me squirm."

She leaned closer, her eyes wide with fear. "What door does it unlock?"

"The royal treasury," he replied with confusion. What about this key frightened her?

"Oh, Dracula," she said, swallowing as she returned to her ball and stared back into the fire. "Why did you show it to me? I cannot lie to him."

"Lie to who?" What on earth was she going on about?

She took a deep breath and looked at him. The deep fear settled in her eyes made him uneasy. "I need to tell you the truth."

Now he was beside himself with uneasiness. A dam broke loose inside of him and created a path for a flood of disappointment. He finally understood her hesitancy of courting him. She was seeing someone else. That was the last thing he wanted to hear.

"You already have a mate."

Her eyebrows furrowed. "What? No, I don't. Miles would skin me alive for courting anyone."

"So this is about your brother then? He would not allow you to court me."

She shook her head. "I have reason to believe he *wants* me to court you."

Infuriating female! Why didn't she give him answers? He came here for answers, but all he had gained was confusion. She didn't have a mate. Her brother would want her to court Dracula, yet he would skin her alive for it? Was she simply afraid of the idea of courtship? What could he do to change her mind?

He reached out a gentle hand and caressed her cheek with the back of his fingers. "Kiss me."

"Dracula," she whispered, gazing back at him with sorrowful eyes as she placed her hand over his. Her touch brought warmth, but there was something missing still. It was a despondent touch. A goodbye. "I cannot kiss you. I am sure everyone will be much happier if I am gone. Even you."

"Daggers, Elisabeta, kiss me!"

"No!"

He dropped his hand and angrily jumped to his feet, tromping to the nearest tree, and leaning his hand against it with his back to her. How infuriating! He could see the desire in her eyes. Why wouldn't she kiss him? She still hadn't given him a straight answer about why she wouldn't court him.

Running a hand down his face, he forced himself to take a deep breath and let it out slowly. Nothing was going as planned. He lost his job. The female he cared for didn't want to court him. And Ichor Knell became more chaotic by the day. If Elisabeta wouldn't court him, then he could at least keep her safe. Her safety was what was important right now.

"It's too dangerous for you to be out in the woods alone," he said, turning around as if the incident moments earlier had been forgotten. "Come back to Ichor Knell, at least for tonight. I will try to convince the others to flee the city tomorrow night. Shah Jorin disbanded the army for a reason, I just know it. I'm afraid the city will collapse under theocracy. At that point, it will be too dangerous to live in Ichor Knell."

Elisabeta opened her mouth as if to protest, but he cut across her. "We will locate Miles along the way. He will come with us. You don't need to worry about your brother."

She shook her head, glaring defiantly from where she sat on the ground. "No."

He groaned. "I hate that word. Honestly, this is for your own safety."

"I said no. You don't understand."

"I'm *trying* to understand! You are being elusive with your answers to my questions."

They glared at one another, each unbending in their decision. Why couldn't she see the voice of reason? Whether or not she liked it, she had become a part of his family, and he took care of his family. He would find a way to make her see reason. But he had to do it soon, otherwise he might not get another chance.

Without another word, he transformed into a bat and flew away from her and her infuriating stubbornness. She would accompany them if he had to stuff her into a bag and drag her along.

He made circles in the skies overhead, intent on watching over her through the night when the realization hit him. He had been gone for a couple of days on his hunt, and in that time, Elisabeta had seemingly lost interest in courting him, yet the desire in her eyes remained. Only one person would dare meddle in his courting life.

Madeleine.

He frowned as annoyance overcame him. What had Madeleine said to Elisabeta to make her feel unwelcome? What had she said to drive her away?

He didn't know, but tomorrow, he planned to find out.

Chapter 15

Elisabeta watched Dracula fly away in his bat form, a heaviness in her heart. She was in love with him, but she had to let him go. And she had to do her best to forget he ever showed her the key. She had no desire to hurt him, and if she led Miles to believe she didn't know its location, perhaps she could avoid causing him grief.

She sighed, recalling each time Miles saw through her lies. The task would be impossible.

She absently braided her hair as she pondered alternate solutions. Her attempt to tell Dracula the truth about her race had been interrupted by heated arguments. Leaving Ichor Knell was in everybody's best interests.

Madeleine wanted her gone. Ilona wanted to court Dracula—after all, Ilona had been in love with him first. And Dracula would soon realize he never wanted to court Elisabeta in the first place when he found out her secret. He hated humans because of their greed. Unfortunately, she had come to Ichor Knell because of greed. She only managed to prove him right.

"Where are you, Miles?" she nervously asked the darkening skies. They weren't supposed to meet for a couple more days, but she had hoped she might find him out here anyway. Especially now that she had nowhere to go. She was at the mercy of the woods. And the darkness.

Kicking dirt over her fire, she shouldered her pack and ventured further into the woods with the hopes that Dracula wouldn't find her again. This time, she didn't build a fire, but sat in the darkness with her back against a tree, her hand never leaving the pommel of her sword. Her lungs tightened with fear, making breathing difficult. She was a human in vampire-infested waters.

"Dracula," she whispered, though she knew he couldn't hear. "Come back. I'm sorry. Don't leave me by myself."

But of course, he didn't return.

She huddled beneath her cloak, jumping at every rustling bush and every hooting owl. But the terror of the darkness had only just begun. Her eyes played tricks on her. Dark shadows slithered across the ground and eyes blinked in bushes. Her heart raced with fear, and she pulled her hood over her eyes to block out the nightmares surrounding her.

The boughs rustled above her. She threw her hood off, leaped to her feet, and unsheathed her sword. Her fingers trembled as she spun in a circle. Nothing jumped out at her, but just because she couldn't see something didn't mean it wasn't there. Vampires had the ability to transform into animals. As long as she stayed outside in the open, she was in danger.

Tears streamed down her face as fear overcame her. Terror gripped her heart. She couldn't last the night like this. What had she done?

Sobs wracked through her body as she watched the breeze lift dark shadows through the trees. She swore something large skulked in the boughs above her. She swore several pairs of fangs sprouted from eager vampire mouths.

A screech echoed in the night, making her trembling fingers drop her sword. She wanted to scramble away from the dark shape darting downward, but her feet remained rooted to the spot. However, the dark shape turned into a large figure, and her entire body sighed with relief.

"Infuriating female," Dracula said, closing the distance between them and wrapping her in an embrace. She welcomed the embrace, sobbing into his chest. Her fear took precedence over keeping her tears hidden, but in the darkness, she hoped he wouldn't see their lack of pigment.

"You've given me no choice," he sighed. "I planned to keep watch from the trees, but it's not good enough. Come here."

He pulled her down with him, his back against the nearby tree while he held her closer. Her hands wouldn't stop trembling. Her tears wouldn't cease escaping. If there was one thing that frightened her more than being alone, it was the unseen terrors lurking within the darkness.

He soothingly rubbed his thumb over her shoulder, and even though his presence calmed her, it took several good minutes for her tears to subside and for her hands to stop shaking. Safely tucked into his side, a sudden weariness washed over her. She hadn't realized how tired she was until she felt safe.

"Afraid of the dark?" he murmured into her hair. She didn't answer, but it seemed she didn't need to because he kept speaking anyway. "Strange quality for a nocturnal animal like yourself. Aren't you supposed to be an owl?"

She still didn't speak, afraid her quavering voice might betray her.

"No matter…" he continued quietly as he began to stroke her hair. The action soothed all of her fears away. Here in his arms, she felt safe. "Plenty of people are afraid of the dark. And now that I know one of your fears… I suppose it's only a fair trade for you to know one of mine. I am afraid to lose the people I love. My family, as I call them."

Finally, she lifted her gaze to find him already looking down at her. Even in the darkness, she noticed the faint traces of his scruff growing back in on his face. "You are Dracula. You aren't supposed to fear anything."

He chuckled. "Is that what they say about me? I fear plenty."

"You have already lost your mother."

Dracula nodded, a wistful look in his eyes. "I still don't think I have recovered from the loss. Ever since, I swore I would protect my family with everything I have. Nicolae, Madeleine, the children, Ilona, Lucian, and now you… I protect my family, so I don't have to lose anyone again."

Her cheeks warmed despite herself. "You hardly know me. Why would you group me into your family?"

"I know enough. Besides, it's more of a feeling I have than anything else. Reject me all you want. It won't change that fact, draga mea."

"What does that mean?"

He smiled softly, churning happy feelings inside of her. "It means 'my darling'."

Guilt spread through her, but she did her best to

push it away. If he only knew the truth... He might not be so kind toward her.

She released her anxiety in the form of a sigh and allowed her eyelids to droop. With Dracula holding her close, she felt happy, safe, and warm. The last thing she was aware of was his soft kiss to the top of her head before she fell into a dreamless sleep.

Chapter 16

Elisabeta was one of the most stubborn vampires Dracula had ever met. She never followed the most logical route, even if it was common sense. For example, she had wanted to join the army as a female. She didn't wear clothing befitting a female. She refused to travel with him and the group for nonsensical reasons, and she preferred sobbing onto his shoulder over telling him what inspired those tears.

Infuriating.

Still, he smiled softly as the night turned into early morning, watching her sleeping face resting on his lap. She looked beautiful in her sleep. Peaceful. Calm. Innocent. His desire to kiss her increased with every passing moment, to feel her soft lips on his own once more. But he would never kiss her unless she wanted it, and to his dismay, she did *not* want it—a fact he needed to remedy before the day's end.

"I will see you again soon," he whispered, shifting to move himself from under her. She didn't stir as he took off his coat and placed it beneath her head, protecting her soft red hair from the ground. He was reluctant to leave her, but now that night had passed, she would be marginally safer from threats. If she stayed beneath the shady trees, she would also be safe from sunlight.

Gazing at Elisabeta one last time, he transformed

into a bat and took to the skies, careful to keep to the shadows. He allowed his rage and annoyance to build with every second he flew closer to Ichor Knell. He had no doubt Madeleine had meddled in affairs that were no business of hers. As soon as he located her, she would get more than just an earful from him.

Flying close to the ground, he transformed back into a vampire the moment his feet touched the earth. The early risers were up and about, which also included Madeleine. He easily caught onto her faint forest-like scent and followed. It didn't take long before the smell became stronger, and he found the vampire in question, her blonde hair and long ears standing out in the distance.

However, panic raced through him at the sight of her sitting on the ground with her back against a jewel tree, sweating and breathing heavily. "Madeleine!" he cried and rushed to her side. He felt her sweaty forehead. He grasped her clammy hands. Something certainly was not right.

"I'm just winded is all," she said, but he wasn't convinced.

"I'm taking you home." He picked her up into his arms, worry creasing his brow as he took long strides in the direction of the Covaci home. He had witnessed all five of her labors, and this exactly resembled them.

She wrapped her arms around his neck and didn't protest over him carrying her. When he reached the Covaci residence, he hurried through the door and helped himself inside. Nicolae stood in the main room, helping one of his children dress, but he immediately abandoned his task at the sight of Dracula and Madeleine.

"What happened?" Nicolae demanded, instantly at his side.

He laid her on a cot, standing back as Nicolae assessed her condition. "I found her like this. Could she be in labor?"

"I'm fine," she breathed heavily, but neither of them were convinced.

"What will we do?" Dracula asked, frowning as he took in Madeleine's feeble state. "I don't think either of us can hire a physician. How adept are you at delivering babies?"

"I have already thought this through," Nicolae replied. "Our nursemaid is also a midwife." He disappeared and returned a minute later with Miss Samantha, who hurried to Madeleine's side. She held a hand to Madeleine's head, felt her belly, and when she started to lift her skirts, Dracula averted his gaze. The entire room held their breath, waiting for the verdict, and he prayed for good news.

Finally, Miss Samantha spoke. "She's dilated at one centimeter, and she is contracting, but they are only practice contractions." Both Dracula and Nicolae released a sigh of relief. "However, I recommend bed rest, otherwise she could have the baby early."

"But I have to go to work," Madeleine started to protest as she tried to sit up, but Nicolae shook his head and pushed her back down into the pillows.

"We will survive without your income, Madeleine. I am more concerned about your health at the moment." Nicolae touched her cheek tenderly, and Dracula felt a pang in his chest at the intimacy of their bond. He wanted that too. He wanted it with Elisabeta, and he suddenly felt real fear that he might never get the chance to experience what the bond felt like.

He needed to get to the bottom of this. Before Elisabeta woke and decided to leave for good. Last time, he had a difficult time finding her. He feared the next time, she might disappear altogether, and he would never locate her.

He cleared his throat, interrupting their moment. "I am glad you are all right, Madeleine. Now I don't feel as guilty being upset with you."

Nicolae frowned. "This is not the time, Dracula."

"It's the *only* time!" He closed his eyes and took a deep breath, letting it out slowly. Despite his rage, he knew he shouldn't upset Madeleine and cause her to labor early. When he opened his eyes again, he found her staring back at him, biting her lip in a guilty manner. It was as he suspected... "What did you say to Elisabeta to drive her away? She returned my handkerchief and will hardly speak to me."

Madeleine's eyebrows shot up in surprise. "She returned it?"

"Yes," he growled, touching the black square of fabric within his pocket. "I feel like a horse kicked me in the chest. I don't like this feeling."

Tears began welling in her eyes, and although Nicolae shot him a glare, he said nothing, but rather soothed her by stroking her hair. But he quickly turned his attention to the sleepy child tugging on his clothing for his attention.

"I didn't know she would return it," she sniffed. "I admit I was angry. I told her about you and Ilona, and I said I wished she had never shown her face in Ichor Knell. I didn't mean to make her cry."

"You made her cry?" he thundered, but then he

took another deep breath and ventured to the window, looking out to help keep himself centered. It was no wonder Elisabeta left the way she had, despite being scared of the dark. Now everything made perfect sense. She refused to kiss him because she wanted to get out of Ilona's way. Her selflessness was admirable, but completely irksome.

"Forgive me," Madeleine said, wiping her red-tinted tears away from her eyes. "I wanted you to court Ilona. I know you had wanted to."

He shrugged, running a hand down his face. "Not really, no. I said I would think about it, remember? I thought it was safe to try, at least until I met Elisabeta. But now she has left Ichor Knell. She stopped for the night in the woods on the southeast border, but nothing I said convinced her to return. I don't know what to do."

Madeleine held out her hand to him, and he took it, kneeling by her bedside. "How do you feel about Elisabeta? Tell me."

He rested his chin on the bed, thoughts of Elisabeta swimming in his mind. "She's the most beautiful vampire I have ever met. When she's near, I feel giddy. When she looks at me, I feel like everything is going to be all right. When I touch her, I feel like my body bursts into flame. And when I kissed her…"

He tilted his head back and released a breath as he remembered those precious moments beneath the willow tree. "I never knew someone could make me feel the way she does." He frowned, his heart panging as he realized what he might have lost. "And now everything aches. She is leaving."

Madeleine sighed and remained silent for a long

moment. But finally, she said, "What you have with Elisabeta is what I have with Nicolae. It sounds like you're in love."

Dracula scoffed. "I am not in love. Love is for—"

"—lovestruck kittens?" she finished for him with a laugh. "You *are* in love and I am a fool for not seeing it earlier. I apologize for trying to force you to court Ilona. That wasn't fair of me. I am afraid I may have damaged our friendship because of it."

"Of course not," he replied hurriedly, patting her hand. Thankfully, it wasn't as clammy. Resting seemed to do her some good. "There is little you could do to drive me away." He frowned as he thought of the danger lurking just around the corner, and he turned to Nicolae. "I have been sacked from my job, the army disbanded. I feel something foul coming our way. I want all of us to pack up and leave Ichor Knell as soon as possible."

"The entire army?" Nicolae asked, a serious look in his eyes. "What about protecting the citizens?"

He clenched his jaw as he fought off his own fear. "I think that's the point, Nicolae. Peasants will have no way to protect themselves. I fear we will face a mass homicide."

"But why?" Madeleine breathed, shock in her voice. "How would it serve Ichor Knell?"

"I still don't know. But I want everyone to leave immediately. Tonight, even."

Nicolae shook his head, gazing back at his mate with immense worry in his eyes. "Madeleine is in no shape to travel. If we leave now, she will certainly start laboring for real before we even get far enough away from the city to safety."

"We will pull her along in a wagon."

"And pull her with what animals? If we get caught stealing either a wagon or horses, we will be killed."

"Then I will carry her."

Although Nicolae wasn't usually a pessimist, he was being one now. "And how far would you be able to get? Even vampires have their limits. What about the sun? It will be difficult to avoid."

Dracula stood at his full height, glaring down at Nicolae. "And would you stay here? Would you risk the lives of your family because you are afraid to even try?"

Nicolae didn't say anything for a moment, but finally he nodded. "I believe you are right. We are all in danger. Just hold on for a couple more days at least. Allow Madeleine to rest, and then we will set out."

"I can live with that. I will talk to Lucian and Ilona. And Madeleine, will you speak to Elisabeta for me? Perhaps you can convince her to return to Ichor Knell until we are ready to leave, because I already know I can't."

"Has she left the woods yet?"

He shook his head. "I don't believe so. Otherwise, I would track her down and drag her back by force."

She rolled her eyes and looked to Nicolae, who stood on the other side of the room rocking the littlest one to sleep. "Will you bring Elisabeta here? I'm sure she would listen to you."

Dracula frowned at her words. "Why is that, exactly? You two have been getting extra chummy lately."

Like Madeleine, Nicolae rolled his eyes. "Are you jealous? True, she confides in me, and I certainly know more about her than you do. But Madeleine is my mate. I'm not sure what there is to be jealous of."

Narrowing his eyes, he stared straight through his friend. "What, exactly, has she been telling you?"

"Now, I wouldn't be a good friend to her if I told you. I promised I wouldn't say. If you court her, I'm sure you will find out eventually."

He wanted to throttle Nicolae, but for the child's sake, he refrained. "Get Elisabeta *now*."

"Fine," Nicolae grumbled, gently handing him his near-sleeping child. "But you better not be here when I return. I have a feeling it will be difficult to convince her to stay, and it seems you will only make it worse."

"Get!" he hissed, shooing him out the door. Nicolae glared momentarily before disappearing.

He immediately turned on Madeleine. "What is this secret about Elisabeta?"

"I don't know. I wasn't aware he was keeping a secret about her. But if he hasn't told me, I'm sure there is a good reason for it." She released a long breath and closed her eyes, settling further into the pillows. "Sing me that song, Dracula. The one they sing in the human world."

He huffed. "I am not singing."

"Sing it *now*!"

He jumped at the tone of her voice, and even he didn't dare defy her when she was in a high-strung mood. Besides, the goal was to ward off labor, as it was too early to birth the child she carried. If singing helped keep her calm, then sing he must.

Gently rubbing the child's back as he slept on his shoulder, he started the song in a low note, his deep voice carrying throughout the room.

"Give us a place where the blue waters run
Find us a home where green fields stretch amber
We follow the starlight to escape these wintry holds
Down the steep slopes through an endless white
storm
*

Bring us the hope to dispel our loved losses
Show us the light that rains from above
Forward and onward from the northern dark caves
We follow the sunlight as east shows our way
*

Give us a home, a family to love
Give us the light that rains from above"

He finished his song on a quiet note, smiling softly as he noticed not only was the child sleeping in his arms, but Madeleine had fallen asleep as well. Her skin no longer appeared sweaty, and her breathing evened out. His goal to keep her from laboring early had worked.

Fondly resting his hand on top of her sleeping head, he smiled before carefully climbing the stairs so as to not wake the sleeping boy in his arms. He tucked him into his cradle, watching for a moment as he slept. Despite not being related by blood, Nicolae's children were a part of his family, and they always would be. And as soon as Madeleine gave birth to their sixth child, he would adopt him or her into the family as well.

"I'm not supposed to be here anymore," he whispered, though the child didn't stir. "If you are awake when Elisabeta arrives, make sure to put in a good word for me."

He chuckled at the thought. The child could only

say a few simple words, but he could use all the help he could get. Otherwise, he feared Elisabeta would leave all the same.

Please, he prayed to Ylios. *Please let her stay. I love her.*

And as he spoke the words in his mind, he realized they were true. He was, indeed, a lovestruck kitten, and he would do anything for the chance to be with Elisabeta. Anything. If she would have him. Although he didn't own much, and he didn't have much by way of coin—not counting he had bet his miniscule fortune away to Nicolae—he hoped Elisabeta might look past his shortcomings and see the things he *did* have to offer.

With a prayer in his heart, he transformed into a bat and flew out the window. He hoped Nicolae and Madeleine would be able to change Elisabeta's mind, because he didn't think he could bear the idea of leaving her.

Chapter 17

Elisabeta startled herself awake, bursting into an upright position. For a moment, she panicked when she didn't know where she was. Her fingers scrambled for a weapon, and she found one several feet away, unsheathed as if thrown aside. She picked up the weapon and glanced wildly around her, finding herself in the middle of the woods. It wasn't until she noticed a wadded-up coat on the ground when she remembered where she was and why she had come here.

"Dracula," she sighed—albeit dreamily—as she picked up his coat and brought it to her nose, inhaling the smell of him. But then her eyes widened as she scanned the boughs above her, searching for any sign of a black bat. She would be mortified if he found her smelling his coat.

No sign of him. Where did he go?

She tried to ignore her heartache at the thought of leaving Ichor Knell for good as she slipped her arms into Dracula's coat. A relieving safety enveloped her as if he held her in his arms.

"I think I'll keep this," she said, smirking. She didn't even have to steal it.

As a precaution, she checked the pockets to make sure the treasury key wasn't in any of them and felt both disappointed and relieved it wasn't there. What would Miles say when he learned of her failure?

A shudder wracked through her body at the thought of him beating her. She hoped an attempt at lying would pay off.

Picking up her things, she began walking in the opposite direction of Ichor Knell, scanning the woods as she traveled. Her stomach growled in protest—she hadn't eaten since yesterday morning. It didn't take long before she spotted a cluster of mushrooms. In any normal circumstance, mushrooms would be the last food item she would pick, but she was ravenous. Anything looked good at this point.

She cut the mushrooms free with her knife and took a big bite, grimacing at the bitter dirt taste. They would taste better cooked.

"You have caused quite a stir of drama lately," a voice said behind her. She spun around with wide, terrified eyes. However, she immediately relaxed when she found Nicolae and *not* Dracula. He stood straight with his hands clasped behind his back, his blue eyes piercing a hole straight through her.

"How are you vampires finding me?" she glared, taking another bite of the mushroom. "I made sure to cover my tracks!"

"You underestimate the capability of a vampire's sense of smell." He chuckled, watching with fascination as she ate. "Now if it had been Ilona, she would have been able to find you an hour earlier. She has the keenest nose of any vampire I've ever met."

She frowned at the mention of Ilona, her hands on her hips. "Why did you come, Nicolae? Did Dracula send you?"

His guilty grimace said it all. "Yes and no. Madeleine wants to apologize to you." He waved away his comment with his hand as if something more important weighed on his mind. "I don't know what you're trying to do here, Elisabeta. You are a human! What will Dracula do when he finds out?"

"He won't find out. I'm leaving."

Nicolae shook his head. "Not if he has anything to do about it. Dracula is dead set on courting you. I don't know what you did to make him so smitten, but he is in love with you."

The breath squeezed from her lungs as she stared back at Nicolae, her mouth falling open in disbelief. A smile began to surface, giddiness finding a home in her heart.

"He is…in love with me?"

She could have fainted from happiness.

"Yes. Now you better think very hard about what I'm about to tell you. Ichor Knell has become too dangerous of a place to live. We are all fleeing, and Dracula wants you to flee with us. But that would mean telling everyone your secret. That you are a human. Dracula, at least, deserves to know."

"I am afraid," she whispered, clutching her stomach with one arm as if to hold her nervousness inside. "He will be so angry with me."

"Probably. But it's best he finds out sooner rather than later."

Once again, she couldn't breathe. But this time, it stemmed from fear rather than twitterpation. "I cannot. I am *not* a vampire and I don't belong with him. Besides, I am loyal to my brother. He would be most upset with me if I abandoned him for Dracula."

Nicolae's expression softened, and he put his hand on her shoulder—a comforting gesture. "We all must move on eventually. One day, your brother will only be a small part of your life. It's up to you to decide who will end up being the bigger part."

"And you think it will be Dracula?"

"I am quite certain Dracula is already hoping you will be the bigger part for him. Think on it for a while."

"But…" She swallowed hard, torn between taking a chance and playing it safe. She knew what waited behind her. It wasn't a happy life, but it was familiar. She could only hope for happiness on the path in front of her. Still, it was completely unknown. "But I'm just a human. Dracula will change his mind about me."

"Maybe. But there is only one way to find out." He held out his hand to her, and she had never felt more uncertain in her life. To take his hand meant to betray Miles. To shy away meant to hurt Dracula. Wasn't there a way she could have both? Wasn't there a way she could make everyone happy?

Finally, she released a long breath and took his hand, nodding her head. She didn't know what awaited down this road, only that she needed to know if she could find happiness of her own.

"I honestly thought convincing you would be more difficult," he chuckled. "I took most of the work off Madeleine's shoulders. Come on. She would like to speak to you."

He led her back toward Ichor Knell, and with each step she took, the burden of nervous anticipation pressed on her shoulders. The last time she saw Madeleine, she had run from the room in tears. What could Madeleine possibly say that would erase the pain her words had caused?

They reached Nicolae's home, and she slowed her

steps as she stared at the building. The barely two-story house was by no means lavish, made of wooden logs and a straw roof. The wooden shutters that protected the windows from drafts were crooked and ill-kempt, and the wooden door contained large cracks between each plank that she was sure would invite pests inside. The only redeeming features were the vines climbing up the trellis on the side of the house and the window boxes full of green plants.

She put her hands on her hips as an idea surfaced in her mind. Ichor Knell needed flowers. Some kind of flowers that lived even without sunlight.

"You have a beautiful home," she said finally, nodding in satisfaction.

Nicolae chuckled. "I am glad you think so. Madeleine despises it. She would prefer living beside the river with an emerald jewel tree providing cover from the elements. I keep telling her we will find another home someday, but fifteen years have passed, and we still live here. I suppose we should be grateful we have a home at all. After all, Dracula lives in the soldier barracks."

I know.

But she didn't say it out loud.

They entered the small cottage and she glanced around in wonder. The cottage certainly appeared cramped, with two of five children playing with dolls in the corner, not even noticing their entrance. Her eyebrows rose in surprise when she noticed the children's ears were pointed, but not quite to the degree of Madeleine's. She didn't know much about elves, only that they were capable of feats of magic.

As if noticing her stare, Nicolae said, "Madeleine

is from a well-off family. Her elven parents are healers, but unfortunately, I never did get their blessing to take Madeleine as my mate because I am a vampire. Relations are getting better, at least. I only hope with time, we will be on speaking terms."

"Madeleine doesn't speak to her parents?" she asked. "They were *that* against the marriage?"

"Marriage is a human term," he replied. "We call it a union here in Ichor Knell. And yes, they were very against it, which is why we eloped."

"You turned Madeleine then?" she asked, shuddering at the thought of vampire fangs in her neck. She never wanted to become a vampire. It sounded awful. "How did she react to the venom?"

He tidied up the room, almost absently. "Better than most. She cast a healing spell on herself right before the transformation. Although she felt the pain, the spell protected our future progeny."

She opened her mouth to ask what he meant, but he quickly changed the subject.

"Would you like some tea?"

"Oh, yes. I would love some—" She cut off, narrowing her eyes at him before a grin pulled on the corners of her lips when he laughed. "I see what you did there. You are jesting. Vampires don't drink tea. Well, I wish they did. What I wouldn't give for some normalcy right now."

"You can make your own tea on the road as soon as we leave this city. Just don't offer to share. It would probably irk Dracula even more."

At the mention of Dracula, her heart sped up with nervousness. "He will be that upset?"

He turned to her with contemplation in his eyes,

and she found she didn't like to be the object of intrigue. "I don't know, but I am curious to find out."

"Nicolae, is that you?" Madeleine's voice called from the other room, snapping her away from her uncertainty. "Have you brought Elisabeta?"

"Yes, dear," he replied, giving her a reassuring smile. Though, he lowered his voice to a whisper, and she leaned closer to hear his words. "Madeleine is on bed rest to ward off labor. I've said this to Dracula, and I will say it to you. Don't you dare upset her. I will personally see to your end if you cause her to labor early."

She wasn't sure what to make of his threat. He said it with a smile, but his words were anything but friendly. Unfortunately, it only increased her nervousness as he led her into the other room where Madeleine lay on a cot, a guilty look in her eyes as she rested her hands on her belly. To her surprise, Madeleine cut right to the chase.

"I am so sorry," she said. "I didn't mean what I said to you. Ilona is my dearest friend, and for months, I have been hounding Dracula to court her. He has always been reluctant about the idea, and I should never have pressed so hard. I have a bad habit of meddling where I shouldn't. It is clear as day that you and Dracula belong together. I have never seen him happier than he has been since your arrival. All I want is for him to be happy."

For a moment, she stood speechless. She didn't know how to reply.

Madeleine beckoned her closer, and she obliged. "Just tell me one thing. Do you love him?" Her cheeks inflamed at the forward question, and her heart picked up against her will. Annoyingly so, Madeleine seemed to be able to hear it. She chuckled, lying back against the pillows as if finally at peace. "That is all I need to know. I hope you will forgive me."

"Of course I do," she said quietly, willing her heart to slow, but it didn't. Not when thoughts of Dracula filled her mind.

She took her bag off her back and rummaged through it until she found what she was looking for— the light blue silk slippers she had worn aboard Miles's ship. Sheepishly, she held them out to Madeleine. "I cannot sew, and I need to give Dracula a handkerchief. Will you help me?"

"Are you sure you want to use this fabric?" Madeleine asked as she caressed the slippers in awe as if remembering a time when she had worn such finery. "You can sell these for a pretty penny in Ichor Knell."

"I have nothing else to give. I want to give him something special, and not just any drab fabric I have in my belongings."

"I don't think it matters to Dracula."

"But it matters to me."

She studied her for a moment before nodding. "Very well. Helping you sew these pieces together is the least I can do."

"Thank you," she breathed. Honestly, she both feared and looked forward to this huge leap of faith, but she thought the risk was well worth it if it meant finding out what happiness she might find with Dracula.

Forgive me, Miles, she silently pleaded. *I may not see you again.*

As Nicolae had said, someday, she would need to

move on and find the person who would play the bigger part in her life. Although she felt terrified and horribly nervous, she hoped Dracula might be that person.

Chapter 18

In his bat form, Dracula crouched in the shadows of the mourning bell tower that overlooked the castle, scowling as he watched Shah Jorin converse with the Diviner himself. After the book burning, he had been watching the two as closely as he dared without being detected. Something was afoul in Ichor Knell, but he still didn't know what. And as he no longer had a job, he spent every moment he could trying to uncover the wicked atrocities happening in the city.

He frowned as he cocked his ears, but he was too far away to hear their hushed conversation below, even as a vampire.

If there was anyone he hated more than Shah Jorin, it was the Diviner. It wasn't his long chin and small eyes that set him off. It wasn't his bald head or cringeworthy coldness. It was his wickedness and greed.

He watched as Jorin handed a sack of coins to the Diviner, who took it with a triumphant smirk on his face. Now, what was this exchange all about?

The Diviner motioned with his fingers and two monks appeared, dragging a female between them. She kicked and struggled, but with her hands bound behind her back and a gag tied around her mouth, she couldn't escape.

Dracula's frown deepened as he watched the

display with his black bat eyes. He edged toward the corner of the tower, ready to take flight in a moment's notice. Who was this female? A criminal? She wore scroungy clothing, her hair matted, and her eyes a deep red. Even more, she bared her fangs and writhed with ravenous hunger.

Finally, they spoke loud enough for him to overhear.

"We have found an impure soul," the Diviner said calmly as if there wasn't a thrashing vampire beside him. "Uncontrollable thirst is a punishment from Ylios for those unworthy to bask in His glory."

Although Dracula certainly was no expert in vampire doctrine, something about this didn't sound right. Didn't vampires believe Ylios cast punishment only in the afterlife by cursing the wicked with an uncontrollable thirst? Not in this life?

"And there are more of these creatures?" Jorin asked, disgust in his eyes as if he faced a swamp grundling rather than a vampire.

"Plenty more," the Diviner confirmed. "The city is full of them."

Jorin plugged his nose and turned his head away. "I refuse to reign over such horrid monsters. I will not have it. Guards!"

The monks holding the female threw her to the ground as a couple guards approached. Dracula didn't have time to react, everything happened so fast. One guard drew his sword—an *iron* sword—and beheaded the female right then and there. His eyes widened, his heart beating so loudly he feared the others might hear it. The female received no trial. No hearing. She didn't even have the chance to defend herself. And now she was dead.

"Good riddance," Jorin said, unplugging his nose as if whatever stench he had smelled disappeared. "We need to have a conversation about these impure vampires. Come. Walk with me."

The Diviner followed Jorin away, and Dracula didn't wait any longer before he leaped off the bell tower, flying as fast as his wings could carry him to Lucian's home, where he lived with his three brothers. He didn't understand what was happening, but he feared for his friend's safety.

He found Lucian and his brothers outside, standing around a basin full of human blood. Each bared their fangs, their eyes closed as they raised their arms and muttered words in the Old Language.

Lucian was the strangest vampire he had ever known.

He would have stopped to grimace at the display, but he didn't come to mock Lucian's strange religious habits. At least not today.

Before his feet hit the ground, he transformed into a vampire and pulled Lucian aside, his gaze unfocused as if he had no idea where he was. His brothers continued on, not even noticing Lucian's sudden absence.

"Retract your fangs," Dracula growled. "Now is not the time for you to stand out."

"What are you talking about?"

With a roll of his eyes, he motioned with his head in the direction of the castle. "I have reason to believe the church will be hunting for vampires who are different. If you and your brothers want to survive, put your fangs away." He lowered his voice, doing his best to ignore the strange chanting in the background better suited to a witch's ritual than a vampire's. "The rest of us are leaving Ichor Knell not tomorrow night, but the night after. Pack only the essentials. None of this...eccentricity."

Lucian retracted his fangs, and somehow, the lack of made him look like a completely different person. "Is this one of your extreme moods, Dracula? I don't feel like playing one of your games today."

"I don't have moods!"

"You do. And they are tiresome." He glanced toward his brothers as if yearning to join them again. "What is this about leaving? Has Nicolae agreed?"

He nodded, focusing on the task at hand rather than the irksome chanting. "All of the Covaci coven and Ilona will accompany me. We need to leave while we still can. Madeleine is on the edge of labor, so she is resting, otherwise we would leave tonight. Nicolae is trying to convince Elisabeta to join us. I thought we could flee to Varmeth. I know it's a journey, but I believe putting distance between us and Ichor Knell would be wise."

Lucian studied him curiously, watching him as if he stared straight through his soul. Some days, he was convinced he actually could. "You have thought this through."

"Thoroughly, yes. Will you come? Perhaps you can convince your...strange...brothers." He looked over Lucian's shoulder to find his brothers still raising their arms with their eyes closed chanting words that hardly existed anymore.

"I will come," Lucian nodded. "I don't doubt my brothers will too."

"Good."

Without another word, he transformed into a bat and started to fly back to the Covaci residence to check to see if Nicolae ended up being able to convince Elisabeta to return. However, he only made it halfway when he caught a familiar scent on the wind—the scent of wildflowers.

His heart raced with anticipation as he dipped lower, weaving in between trees before he spotted her. Elisabeta *had* returned! And she paced back and forth below, an intense look of concentration on her adorable face. She wore his coat, which brought a smile to his face. He landed on a thick branch and transformed back into a vampire, his legs dangling over the side as he watched her curiously while she talked to herself. She didn't notice him yet.

"Yes, I am aware," she said, her eyebrows furrowing. She stopped suddenly, facing an unseen person. "No, it's not necessary, I don't think. It can work either way, right?" A frown pulled on her lips. "Right?"

"Who on earth are you talking to?" he asked. She jumped at his voice and spun around. Her hand flew to her heart, and even from where he sat in the tree, he heard the way her heart accelerated.

"Dracula," she breathed, tucking a strand of hair behind her ear. A blush crept into her cheeks and her gaze drifted to the ground. "How long have you been watching me?"

He hopped from the tree, landing lightly on his feet. He didn't know how to approach her yet. She had returned, and that's what mattered. But would she leave again? "Long enough to learn that you talk to yourself.

Do you do it often?"

"I have no one else to talk to," she admitted sheepishly, not lifting her gaze, but he wished she would. He wanted to gaze into her deep green eyes. "I have never liked talking to Miles, and friends are scarce where I come from. That only leaves myself…"

"How lonely."

"Indeed."

He took another step closer, a branch crunching beneath his foot. She still didn't look at him, but rather continued to stare with furrowed brows at a spot on the ground. Something about his presence unnerved her, otherwise her heart wouldn't thrum quite so fast. But why?

Finally, she lifted her gaze, the connection making his stomach churn in a bundle of nerves. Never had he felt like this for anyone before. He never knew he could feel breathless, weak, and vulnerable like she made him feel. Those feelings were very uncharacteristic of him. On the battlefield, he was strong. Capable. Skilled. Focused. But it all disappeared, completely unraveled in her presence.

She reached into his coat she still wore, and for a moment, he thought she was about to extract a weapon. He raised his guard. However, his defenses fell in an instant at what she produced—a light blue handkerchief made completely of fine silk.

"Elisabeta…" he whispered.

"I am not very familiar with the vampire customs in Ichor Knell," she said, her voice quavering. "Madeleine explained them to me as much as she could, at least where courting was concerned." The color in her cheeks darkened, but she didn't avert her gaze this time. He found her courage an attractive quality. "I admit I cannot sew. Madeleine helped me piece it together. But I hope it conveys the right meaning."

She handed the handkerchief to him, and he held it reverently in his hands. He'd never felt silk before, and it was softer than he'd imagined it would be. He ran his fingers along the fabric, happiness bursting to life inside of him.

"I didn't know you owned silk."

Surprisingly, she grimaced. "I have to be completely honest. I stole them off the human my brother killed. I am a thief, remember?"

He shrugged, still in complete awe over the fact that she had gifted *her* handkerchief to *him*. "Every vampire has to feed. I'm more disappointed that your handkerchief doesn't smell like you. You're supposed to sleep with it before you gift it."

Elisabeta snorted, but her smile faltered when she realized he was completely serious. "What?"

Just to make sure, he pressed the handkerchief to his nose and inhaled deeply. A frown formed on his face when he smelled something that more closely resembled ocean air than wildflowers.

How disappointing.

"Do you know nothing?" he asked, rolling his eyes, though his veins pulsed with so much excitement to not be *too* disappointed. "How else am I supposed to enjoy your scent when you are not around?"

He grinned wickedly at her fluster.

Before she could reply, he took her handkerchief and rubbed it against her hair, and as an added measure, he rubbed it into her neck, making sure to caress it against the spot just beneath her jawbone where her scent was strongest—and where it was, admittedly, driving him mad.

He brought the handkerchief to his nose once more and inhaled the sweet scent of wildflowers, a satisfied smile spreading across his lips.

"Is that truly a vampire custom?" she asked, her freckles hiding in the red fluster of her blush.

"Maybe not where you are from. But here? It's an age-old tradition we believe was started by Ylios himself when he presented a handkerchief to Iqris to petition her to become his mate. Since then, it evolved into presenting it for courtship."

"And to a potential mate too?" she breathed, and his wicked grin returned. He trailed his finger down her cheek, across her jaw, and caressed the soft skin covering her collarbone, enjoying the way her heart picked up at his touch.

"Eager already?"

She shook her head, but the emotion in her eyes betrayed her. "I'm only trying to understand Ichor Knell customs."

He chuckled darkly, wrapping an arm around her waist, and drawing her closer. A wave of her wildflower scent filled his nostrils, drowning out everything but the intense desire to claim her as his own. "I believe you are thinking of an engagement gift, though the tradition has been falling away in recent years. A male presents a gift of his choosing to a female, and if she returns it before mating, then that is most unfortunate for the male."

He reached inside his pocket and produced his black handkerchief with a flourish, tucking it into her belt. That was it. They were officially courting. A spark of pure joy stretched across his arms, up to his shoulders, and entered his heart as a billowing, eternal fire.

Dipping his head, he moved in to kiss her, but she placed a hand on his chest and pushed him away, her wide eyes carrying a trace of nervousness.

"There is something I need to tell you," she whispered, but he couldn't stop the flow of desire when it had already begun. He kissed her jaw and then worked his lips toward her ear.

"Can it not wait?" he asked, his breath caressing her skin. She stood tantalizingly close, which only managed to increase his desire.

"But it's important," she insisted. However, he quickly hushed her words with a kiss to the lips. "You might want to know—" He kissed her again, tangling his fingers in her hair. "I think you—" He kissed her once more, which seemed to do the trick. She wrapped her arms around his neck, pulling him closer to her, and he willingly obliged.

An "Mmm" escaped her, encouraging him to take the kiss deeper. A fire lit inside of him that started out as a small flame, but quickly turned into a raging forest blaze. Hot, delicious warmth spread from his toes to his fingers, and he breathed out the stream of fire through his nostrils. He loved this female. He only met her recently, and he already loved her. He would do anything for her. Anything at all.

Elisabeta broke the kiss and gasped. "What was that? I've never felt anything like it."

He smirked, lifting her chin with the tip of his finger. "Passion, draga mea."

She stared back at him, and his smirk grew wider at

her flustered expression. "Then we're in trouble."

"I certainly hope so."

"Dracula," she said, her nervous expression replaced by a characteristic grin. "You're not making it easy to stay away from danger."

He leaned closer, and she shuddered as his lips brushed her ear. "I like flirting with danger."

She stepped away, breathing in the fresh woodsy air. He watched as she ran her fingers through her hair, fluster claiming her long lashes as her eyes widened. He imagined she was coming to the same conclusion as he was—mating would be inevitable. He wanted her as his mate. Did she want the same? At this rate, it wouldn't take long at all.

"Nicolae said we needed to leave Ichor Knell," she said, and at the mention, his flirty mood instantly died.

He crossed his arms over his chest, images of the earlier beheading filling his mind. "It's too dangerous to stay. Just keep your hunger in check, don't show your fangs, and don't allow anyone to see you with red eyes. Not even me. Are you hungry? I can take you hunting right now."

She shook her head, and he noticed her swallow as she averted her gaze. "I'm just fine. I think you should be more worried about Madeleine. She wasn't looking too good when I visited."

"I know," he sighed, running a hand down his face. "Waiting until she is ready to leave is the only chance we have. But perhaps I can send you away with Lucian and his brothers. I would feel better knowing you were out of harm's way."

"And leave you behind? Not a chance."

Her words should have started an argument, but he

was too surprised to counter. No one had ever been worried about him before. All his life, he had been the one to worry about those he cared for. He had been the one to protect them, to see them to safety.

The fact that she cared about him sparked warmth inside him. At least until that warmth all too easily blazed hotter into desire. Her concern for him was a little too attractive for him to handle.

Clearing his throat, he replied, "Very well. Though, there is someone I must speak to about a pressing matter. Will you be fine without me?"

"I can take care of myself, Dracula," she said with a roll of her eyes. "Not everyone's lives need to be a burden on your shoulders all the time."

"My family, remember? I protect them with all I have."

He escorted her safely to town and forced himself to keep from kissing her again. He had a feeling he wouldn't be able to stop himself next time.

It took the better part of an hour to locate Frederick Arter after knocking on his door only to be met with no response. Eventually, he found the irritating lad in the market square, haggling for wool. He whistled as quietly as he could, getting his attention. Frederick furrowed his eyebrows in confusion for a moment, at least until Dracula motioned with his head for him to follow. He quickly obliged, leaving his haggling behind, and followed him into the shadows behind a building.

"Yes, Captain?" Frederick said in his annoying, nasally voice. Just the sound of it grated on his nerves.

"I'm not the captain anymore," he muttered, but he quickly lowered his voice, checking to make sure no one was near enough to overhear. "I haven't much money, and certainly not enough for what I seek. You seem to know a lot about the vampire religion... Could you bond me with another vampire?"

The boy appeared momentarily surprised before he shook his head. "I cannot because I don't hold the same power as the Diviner, no matter how corrupt he is." He grimaced, and it was his turn to glance around them to make sure no one heard his incriminating words.

He sighed disappointedly and leaned with his back against the building, trying to think of another solution. Not having much money had never bothered him before, but now there was something he truly wanted, and he couldn't have it because he was poor.

"I don't want to sin and become unfavorable in Ylios' eyes," he admitted finally.

The young vampire smiled knowingly, and a sliver of wisdom flashed across his eyes despite his youth. "If chastity is the sin in which you refer to, you should not be afraid. Unlike humans who must marry first before mating to preserve fidelity, vampires often love first and have a union later, because fidelity is a given between mates. When there will only be one female you will be mated to for the rest of your life, there is no room for sin."

He pushed himself away from the wall, his eyebrows knitting together as he tried to make sense of Frederick's words. "My friend, Nicolae, underwent the ceremony before mating."

"Ah, yes. But he also mated with an elf, those of which don't mate for life. To prevent her from living in sin, the ceremony was necessary first."

"And it's not necessary for a vampire?"

"If mating is between two vampires, then no. It is not necessary to undergo the ceremony first. That can come later. Two mated vampires will be true to each other for the remainder of their years. Infidelity is not possible. However, if you want her to assume your name, and for your future posterity to also take your name, a ceremony will need to happen eventually."

He released a sigh of relief. The last thing he wanted to do was offend Ylios.

And that was when he realized he was talking to a thirteen-year-old boy. It was easy to forget when Frederick spoke such wise words for his age.

Scoffing to nurse his wounded pride, he turned away from the young vampire. "What am I doing with the likes of you? There are prettier faces I can look at right now."

Instead of showing offense, Frederick simply smiled as Dracula walked away, pondering his wise words. He had a feeling if he sought Elisabeta out again, he'd be far too tempted to mate with her. Besides, he needed to watch over his flock. If what he suspected about Shah Jorin giving the order to purge "unclean" vampires from Ichor Knell was true, then he needed to be as alert as possible.

Ichor Knell had suddenly become an extremely dangerous place for even a vampire.

Chapter 19

Something sharp hit her window, followed by excitement churning in Elisabeta's stomach. Only one person could be throwing rocks at her window this late at night.

She jumped out of bed and stole across the room, her shoes softly tapping the floor with each step. As a human in a dangerous place like Ichor Knell, she didn't dare take off her shoes, even when sleeping.

Unable to contain her smile, she pulled the window open and—

And her smile dropped to her stomach, all traces of excitement gone in a flash. The figure wearing a cloak below wasn't nearly as tall as Dracula, nor did he have dark hair and eyes. Instead, she found herself staring back at her own reflection, except the man had shorter red hair and he was slightly taller than her, not yet having grown into his masculinity.

Miles.

She quickly closed the window and tried to push her panic back. Her breathing quickened and her pulse thrummed. She shuddered at the thought of her brother coming personally to fetch her.

If he had only waited two more days, she would have been free of him. Forever. For a moment, she had allowed herself to believe she had found a new family here in Ichor Knell. New friends. Someone to love. But it all came crashing down on her in an instant when she saw Miles standing below her window, reminding her she was bound to her brother.

She was loyal to him. She feared him. But she had conveniently forgotten.

Knowing better than to keep him waiting, she grabbed her cloak and threw it over her shoulders, making sure to conceal her hair beneath the hood. She took a moment to mask the trepidation in her expression, knowing Miles would punish her for showing what he considered weakness.

Confident her emotions were hiding beneath a rock in her heart, she exited the apartment and stepped into the darkness of the night, making her way toward the forest. She felt, rather than saw, a presence fall into step beside her, but he didn't speak. Not yet.

Through her anxious thoughts, she wondered if Miles had taken the elixir to make him smell like a vampire.

Of course he had. He wasn't stupid enough to enter vampire lands smelling like a human.

When they were out of view and earshot, Miles turned to her, his expression stern. She braced herself for his reprimand.

"You were supposed to meet with me this afternoon," he growled, and she instinctively lowered her gaze to the forest floor. "Or did you forget?"

"I…I couldn't get away," she lied. Although she was an exceptional liar, she could never get away with it with Miles. He always saw straight through her deceit.

"You didn't want to come," he accused, crossing his arms over his chest, and standing taller. His stance only made her feel smaller. "You are growing attached to these vampires."

There was no point in trying to lie again, so she nodded. "They are my friends."

He began chuckling, which turned into a full-blown laugh. But in only seconds, his laugh cut off abruptly as he grabbed a thick branch off the ground, and she didn't have time to react before he used it to strike her on the side of her head and sweep her feet right from under her. She landed on her back, the air whooshing from her lungs. Pain pulsed through her ear, one side of her hearing detecting nothing more than a deafening ring.

Releasing a pained breath, she touched her ear, grateful to hear the motion. For a moment, she thought her brother might have deafened her.

"You are fooling yourself if you think these *vampires* are your friends!" he shouted, holding the end of the stick menacingly over her heart as if it were a blade. She dared not move. "If they learned you were a human, you would instantly become breakfast. Or have you forgotten?"

She certainly had not forgotten. Although she had tried to tell Dracula she was a human, her words had been lost in his passionate kiss. She feared he would reject her if he found out. Now she didn't know what to do.

Without waiting for her to answer, he said, "Have you done what I asked you to do?"

She shook her head. "It's not right, Miles. I...I can't. Dracula deserves better than tricks."

He dug the stick into her ribs, and she whimpered at the flare of pain from the wounds she'd received during the Game.

"Dracula. Is. Not. Your. Friend. You will do what I say. And you will steal the treasury key—" Her brother stopped abruptly, slackening the pressure of the stick against her chest as he stared down at her. Her eyes widened as he grinned triumphantly. Oh no. "You know where the key is, don't you? You have seen it."

She didn't say anything, but she didn't have to. He laughed again and threw the stick aside. She pressed a hand to her ringing ear as she cautiously stumbled to her feet. Hatred for her brother rose within her. Her fingers itched to move toward the two knives in her belt. But he'd been the one to teach her how to fight. He moved quicker than her. He was more skilled.

And she both loved him and feared him.

Miles's tether wound around her soul, and she didn't know how to escape. Perhaps he was right. Dracula would never accept her for her humanity.

All her life, she had practiced hiding her feelings in front of Miles, but this time, she was unable to stop her tears from escaping, silently trailing down her cheeks. No matter what she did, she would hurt Dracula. How had it come to this?

"You know how to get the key?" Miles asked.

She nodded.

"Good girl. The next time I see you, you better have it in hand. From there, we can devise a plan to get the egg."

She nodded again, her entire body numb starting from her heart and stretching like smothering vines to her very fingertips. There had to be a way around this, but she feared Miles would come after her if she even tried to escape Ichor Knell with Dracula. No matter which way she turned, she found a wall of stone facing her. She was trapped, and her chains weren't quite long enough to escape.

He handed her more vials, which she struggled to conceal in her pockets when her fingers felt so numb. She nearly dropped one, and he glared at her, though he made no move to strike her again.

She started toward the vampire city, Miles's words trailing behind her. "Remember, the next time I see you, you better have the key."

A shudder ran through her at the thought of failing to bring back the key. Her chains were far too short to figure out a way around this.

The city came into view, and she clenched her fists as she realized what she needed to do. She would get her brother the key, Dracula would never find out, and then she would escape with him and her friends. On the road, only then would she tell Dracula of her humanity, hoping for Nicolae's aid. His friendship with Dracula might help soften the blow. There was no reason everyone couldn't have what they wanted, including her. If she played her cards right, she could possibly earn Dracula's forgiveness, and never have to be separated from him again.

Instead of turning toward the apartment to finish the night off with getting little to no rest, she veered in the direction of the palace.

Guards patrolled the area, putting her on high alert. Never in her life had she been more aware of her pounding heart than she was in that moment, fearing one of the vampires would hear it and locate her from the sound alone.

She shouldn't be doing this, but she felt like she

had no choice. If she gave Miles not only the key but a plan to retrieve the petrified dragon egg, he would more likely leave her be, free to pursue a future she desired.

Even as the thought crossed her mind, she knew it was a shallow hope. But she had to try. Dracula was her something bigger.

Her breath hitched when two guards walked her way, and she quickly ducked behind the corner. Despite her heart pounding ferociously, neither looked in her direction as they passed, iron swords clinking against their armor as they walked. She didn't move a single muscle until they were well out of sight, and even then, she made sure to walk on her toes to make the least amount of noise possible. A lifetime on the streets couldn't prepare her for this. Infiltrating the vampires' palace...

She was going to get killed.

She willed her fingers to cease their trembling as she touched her two knives hidden in her belt for reassurance. Knives made of steel could never kill a vampire, but perhaps they could deal enough damage to allow her a quick escape.

"I'm going to die," she whispered to herself, unsuccessfully trying to calm her heart. This was idiotic. What was she doing—

"Did you hear something?" a voice said from the window directly above her, and she stiffened against the palace wall.

"No," another voice answered.

"Strange... It must have been the wind."

She pressed herself closer to the wall, noting not a single wisp of her hair moved. There was no wind tonight. She needed to move before they figured that out.

She crept deeper into the shadows and acted like the street urchin she had grown up to be, always keeping a hand on one of her knives in case she needed to use it. She climbed over a stone wall and found herself inside the palace. Flickering torches lined the airy hallway, the open windows without glass or shutters to shelter the structure from the elements. Her shadow danced across the wall, at least until she turned a corner and crept along the darkness once more.

Her eyebrows furrowed as she took in every detail from the paintings on the wall to the number of guards that prowled about. She needed to remember these things because Miles would likely demand more information after giving him the key. But the only problem...

Where was the treasury?

"Your Highness," someone said just around the corner, and she slipped behind a stone pillar in time for two men to come into view. One of them wore a gaudy crown while the other trailed behind him, his bald head standing out amidst his robes. Elisabeta focused on breathing evenly. She knew who these two were even without an introduction—Shah Jorin and the Diviner.

"You may address me," Jorin said with an air of laziness, but she had seen enough dangerous people in her life to know he was anything but lazy. The muscles in his arms flexed as if ready to draw a weapon at any moment. And he looked...young. Nicolae had mentioned Jorin was four hundred years old. She had expected white hair, maybe a few wrinkles. But no. He looked to be in the prime of his youth. Not a day over thirty.

The Diviner easily caught up, and as they walked down the hallway in her direction, she pressed herself closer to the pillar, praying to whatever god might be out there she wouldn't be found. She knew praying was hopeless. No god would ever come to her aid with her sinful past and her sinful future. She was on her own.

"The nobles each have a bodyguard, as you have asked."

Jorin's mouth lifted into a grin, one with malicious intent. "Good. We will keep it that way for a while. To get them comfortable."

"Perhaps a little too comfortable—"

The shah held up a hand, and the Diviner immediately quieted.

"My apologies," the Diviner said as he humbly bowed his head.

They continued down the hallway in silence, walking right past the pillar she hid behind. When they reached the end of the corridor, she exhaled a breath of relief. She had very nearly been discovered.

Jorin stopped in his tracks, and she froze with fear. Her heart beat erratically, her fingers inching toward her knives, convinced even the sharp weapons couldn't cut through the thick tension in the air, let alone vampire skin. But he didn't turn around. He simply stood still.

She gripped the handle of the knife, ready to throw it straight into Jorin's eye socket should he turn around. But he didn't turn. He didn't give any indication he knew she was there.

"Tell me about the peasants," Jorin said suddenly, resuming his same leisurely pace from before. They turned the corner, and she could no longer make out their words aside from the faint echo of their voices.

She swallowed her uneasiness and cursed her idiocy as she followed after them on silent feet. If anyone knew where the treasury was located, Jorin would. He might possibly lead her straight to it.

The corridor became dimmer with fewer torches to light up the darkness, and although it made it more difficult for her to see, it also made it easier to hide. She followed after the faint echo, which became fainter and fainter with every second. She was going to lose them.

She picked up her pace, desperate to keep up. She needed to figure out where the treasury was. If she failed this simple task, how would she ever find the petrified dragon egg? She began to think she chose wrong by coming to Ichor Knell to worm her way into Dracula's circle. What she needed to have done was get closer to the shah.

However, she knew she wouldn't have traded anything in the world for Dracula. She was desperate to keep him. But she would worry about it later.

The voices ceased, and she slowed to a cautious walk. Where did they go?

She didn't get the chance to ponder the question when something grabbed her from behind, holding a fistful of her hair and dragging her into the next room. With a jerk, she twisted out of her attacker's grip and delivered a kick to the shin. Her hands flew to her knives, but they were no longer there, and she didn't have time to lash out again before her attacker held tighter onto her hair and threw her to the ground. The attacker was strong. Too strong.

"Ah, so we do have an intruder," a voice said, and her skin crawled at the sound. She lifted her head to find Jorin staring back at her, inspecting her curiously. "Who is she?"

"I don't know, Your Majesty," another voice said, and her gaze darted toward the sound to find another male wearing a high servant's clothing. "A peasant, I presume. She must be new to Ichor Knell."

Despite her attempt to jump to her feet, Jorin reacted swiftly and forced her once again to her knees with a too-strong hand. Fear coursed through her, and she wished Miles was here to save her. He always knew how to get them out of a tight spot. This time, she didn't know if she could save even herself.

"Only steel," Jorin commented, throwing her two knives to the ground in front of her, which she quickly snatched up. Why would he return them to her?

She swallowed the lump in her throat at the realization. Jorin was convinced he could overpower her, even when she was armed. After experiencing his strength firsthand, she was convinced as well. What had she done? Her haste had been necessary, but also foolish.

Jorin produced a dagger from his belt and used it to lift her chin. She didn't dare move a muscle lest the tip prick her skin and draw blood. He would immediately know she was not a vampire.

Her face paled as she remembered the vials on her person. But Jorin didn't search her person. He didn't find the vials.

"Why are you in the palace, especially this late at night?" Jorin asked, looking directly into her eyes. "Peasants are not allowed within these walls unless otherwise specified."

She fabricated a quick lie. "I was curious, Your

Majesty. I wanted to see what the palace looked like, and I hoped I wouldn't get caught if I came at night."

He studied her for several long moments before he finally sheathed his dagger. "Your name?"

"Marianne," she lied, and quickly added, "Your Majesty."

"Well, Marianne. We shall see if you are one of Ylios' elect. He shall be your judge tonight. Not I." He motioned to a servant, and only moments later, the servant brought in a wriggling, screaming man. She didn't need to be a vampire to know he was a human, and likely an innocent one.

The servant used his fingernail to slice the man's throat, and Elisabeta watched blood spill onto the floor all while Jorin watched her. Carefully, it seemed. She had seen spilled blood plenty in her life. Far too many times. She felt no prick of guilt. No sadness. She didn't even cringe. She often wished she wasn't numb to killing, but death followed her no matter where she managed to find herself. Even in Ichor Knell.

Jorin grabbed her chin and forcefully turned it every which way as he looked into her eyes. He said nothing as he dipped his finger into the spilled blood and forced Elisabeta's mouth open to drip the blood onto her tongue. Like the time she sipped blood during the Game, she forced herself not to react. Something gave her the impression that Jorin was watching for a reaction.

Finally, he released her chin and wiped his bloodied finger with a cloth a servant handed to him. "At least there is one pure vampire in this city," Jorin scoffed. "Ylios has made his judgement. You are free to go, Marianne. But if I ever find you near the palace again, that will be the end for you. Do you understand?"

"Yes," she nodded while she backed away from him, and she never took her eyes off him until she made it out into the fresh air. She turned on her heel, walking away as quickly as she dared, both her knives still in her hands.

She turned the corner and jumped when someone wrapped a strong arm around her shoulders. Panic raced through her and she slashed at her attacker with one of her knives, but her attacker easily swiped her hand aside and pressed her closer to him. The panic fled immediately when she saw it wasn't an attacker at all, but Dracula.

He held her close, guiding her away from the palace at a brisk pace without sparing a glance for her. He appeared even taller and more formidable than ever, a dark, frightening look in his eyes. It wasn't until they reached her apartment building that he stopped and rounded on her, the same darkness from earlier searing into her.

"What were you doing in the castle, Elisabeta? Were you trying to assassinate the shah? With these?" Dracula reached for her and wrenched the knives from her hands. "They aren't even iron."

"You saw me?" she gasped, wrenching her knives right back and tucking them into her belt. The entire purpose of doing this was to do it without his knowledge.

"Yes, I saw you," he spat. "I've been watching the palace for days. *Spying*. If they plan on going after my family, I want to know about it first." He ran a hand down his chin, facing away from her for a moment before turning right back. "How did you do it? You weren't baited."

"What are you talking about?"

He stepped closer and lowered his voice. "You are only nineteen, Elisabeta. A young vampire. You didn't even react when they killed the human. Not a twitch. Not a whine. Daggers, your eyes didn't even turn red when you tasted the blood."

Now it was her turn to glance away from him. She didn't want to deceive him anymore. But now wasn't the time to tell him the truth. First, she needed the key.

"I don't know," she replied, facing him, and looking him straight in the eye as she lied. "I fed recently. Perhaps that's why."

He sighed and rested his forehead on her shoulder. His own shoulders sagged as if a burden had just been lifted from him. "I thought Jorin was going to kill you. He would have if your eyes had turned red. And blast it, I would have killed every single vampire in the palace to save your life or died trying."

She couldn't answer. She didn't know how. No one would have ever done such a thing for her. Not even Miles. Dracula deserved better than this. And so he would have it. As soon as she procured the key for Miles.

"I feel like you've been avoiding me," she accused, and he lifted his head from her shoulder. "What on earth are you doing?"

Thankfully, the change of subject helped lighten the mood.

"Staying away from danger," he grinned mischievously.

"First, you insist to the ends of the earth that I court you. Next, you keep your distance because I'm too dangerous?"

"Precisely. But I'm beginning to rethink my strategy. There is far too less of you."

He trailed a lock of her hair through his fingers, and she shuddered delightfully at his touch.

Her heart started pounding harder, and as if he could hear it, he raised a questioning eyebrow. How embarrassing... Not even her heart was private. Thank goodness he couldn't hear her thoughts along with it.

"I love you, Dracula," she whispered, terrified of the rejection she might receive if what Nicolae had told her earlier about his feelings rang false.

"Oh, really?" he smirked, his mischievous smile growing wider. "That didn't take long at all. Coming from someone who refused to kiss me only two days ago."

"You talk as if I didn't want to."

"You could have fooled me." He trailed the back of his fingers across her cheek, and she sighed again at his touch—a fire that stirred the passion within her. "Do you love me because I am devilishly handsome?"

He said it with a twitch of his mouth, letting her know it was a jest. Well, she could jest right back. She placed a hand against his chest, feeling his strong heartbeat just beneath his shirt. "I think you have the devil part down."

"Then I have done my job right," he whispered in her ear. "I love you, Elisabeta."

In the next instant, his lips captured hers, igniting the flicker of passion into a raging wildfire. She returned his kiss, trembling both from excitement and from fear as she thought about what she was about to do. She wasn't going to do it for Miles. But rather, for herself, and she hoped Dracula would forgive her when he someday found out her secret.

He pinned her against the side of the building and trailed fiery kisses down her neck. She forced herself to take a deep breath and pushed him away. He obliged with a rather disappointed look in his eye, but she smirked as she took a hold of his hand, led him to her apartment, and unlocked the door.

She gave him a coy smile and pulled him into the room by hooking a finger around his belt. He returned her smile with a devilish grin of his own. And he shut the door behind them.

****

Elisabeta stayed awake long after Dracula fell asleep, even as dawn began to creep closer. Happiness warred with guilt as she waited for him to fall into a deeper sleep, clearly exhausted after nights of staying up late watching Jorin's every move.

She watched his chest rise and fall with each breath. His face looked relaxed and peaceful in his sleep, void of the burdens he chose to carry each and every day. Honestly, she had meant everything she said to him the other night when she told him her feelings. But she was supposed to have told him the truth about her before this happened. Miles had given her little choice, and now she hoped Dracula would forgive her for her deceit.

Careful as to not disturb his slumber, she quietly dressed and located his trousers in a heap on the floor. Sure enough, she found the treasury key in his pocket, shiny and silver without a speck of tarnish.

She gripped the key tighter as guilt overwhelmed her. She did not want to be a thief anymore, yet she was a thief through and through. It seemed she could not leave the life behind. Like death, it followed her wherever she went. She hoped to finally turn over a new leaf when she left Ichor Knell with Dracula. This plan would work. She was sure of it. All she needed to do was get Miles this key.

"Forgive me," she whispered as she shouldered her bag and stood at the door. Dracula did not stir. "I will return. I promise."

Without another word to the unconscious vampire, she left the apartment knowing this would be the last time she would stay in it. Dracula, Nicolae, and the rest of the group would escape Ichor Knell, and she planned to accompany them.

However, she took one step out of the building and froze.

More guards than she remembered littered the town in the early morning, similar to the ones she saw at the palace the night before. She ducked behind a tree and covered her red hair with her cloak to avoid bringing unwanted attention to herself. The guards hardly gave her a passing glance, but that didn't give her the relief she wished it did.

Panic rose within her when she thought they might have found Miles, but she took a deep breath and pushed the fear right back down. If Miles didn't want to be found, he wouldn't be. She needn't worry how her brother fared.

She pulled her cloak tighter around herself and slipped away from the building and toward the woods. But a guard quickly cut her off and stepped directly in front of her.

"Halt! No vampires are to leave the city."

She took a step back, eyeing the sword strapped to the guard's belt. She wore a sword of her own, but hers was only made of steel. The worst she could do was injure him enough to stall him. Nothing more.

"May I ask why?" she dared to say.

"We ask the questions around here. Go back home. Trust me. You don't want to push my patience."

She internally cursed her luck as she moved away from the guard and watched the woods from a safer distance. There had to be a way to get Miles the key. If Dracula found it on her, everything she was working toward would be ruined.

Chapter 20

She wasn't there.

Disappointment encompassed Dracula at Elisabeta's absence when he woke, but it didn't last long as warmth filled his soul. A desperate need to be near her drove him mad, an effect of the mating bond he had not anticipated. He needed to hold her. To kiss her. To laugh with her. To simply be near her. He needed her desperately. So much that his heart almost burst at the pressure his love for her put on him.

He pulled on his clothing and sat at the edge of the bed, forcing himself to take a deep breath. Elisabeta was now his mate, but he didn't need to be clingy about it. Daggers, if he had known the bond would be this intense, he would have prepared himself better.

He glanced around the room, only to find it bare of all her belongings. Panic raced through him as he thought she might have left Ichor Knell, but he braced himself against the wall, forcing himself to take several deep breaths.

"I will not be a clingy lovestruck kitten," he muttered to himself, running a hand over his scruffy face. "How do vampires survive this bond? I can hardly take it."

His mind fogged over with thoughts of Elisabeta despite knowing he needed to keep his family safe. He was losing focus. It was completely unacceptable.

Now where was she?

Her wildflower scent drove him off the walls, and as he followed it out the door. It weakened when mixed with the fresh outside air before it strengthened once more when he caught onto her trail. He followed the trail, though his jaw clenched when he noticed the increase of guards in town. They gave him no second glance, which worried him. What was Jorin up to now?

It was a good thing they wouldn't find out. They were leaving tonight.

Elisabeta's scent continued in the direction of the forest, and he forced his panic away once more when he noticed guards surrounding the outside perimeter of the city. Did she leave Ichor Knell? Did she get caught? Where was she now?

His worry fled when her scent became stronger than ever, somehow much more easily detectable with their new bloodbond. She stood with her back against a tree, her hood drawn over her head. If he hadn't been specifically looking for her, he might have missed her entirely upon passing by.

"Don't you have somewhere to be?" Elisabeta asked, and if it hadn't been for the twitch of her lips, he might have thought her comment cutting.

"At the moment, I am out a job. I have been waiting for a better opportunity to come along."

"And that opportunity includes stalking innocent young maidens into town?"

He grinned as he ran his fingers up her arm and leaned close to whisper in her ear. "Oh, you are anything but an innocent young maiden."

The intense bloodbond rushed over him, and he couldn't help himself as he leaned in to kiss her.

However, she turned her head, so he kissed her cheek instead of her lips. He pulled away in surprise, staring back at her in confusion. She didn't look him in the eye, and if she had, he was convinced he wouldn't like what he found there.

"You don't..." His eyebrows furrowed as he tried to make sense of it. Did she not feel the bond? Did she regret what happened? "You don't want to kiss me? Do you regret becoming my mate?" He didn't mean for the hurt to echo in his voice, but it did. Her aloofness made no sense.

She sighed and shook her head, finally lifting her gaze to give him a full view of her green eyes. "Of course I don't regret anything, Dracula. I just... I don't... I don't know how to do this. Where do I fit in now? What if your friends don't accept me? What if you don't accept me?"

He released a tense breath and smiled as he took her hands in his. "You had me worried for a moment, draga mea. You worry too much. We don't need to tell anyone just yet if it makes you more comfortable. As for me..." He tucked a strand of red hair behind her ear, glad he would get the opportunity to do this for the rest of his life.

"I know the female I am mated to. An orphan. A twin. Grew up on the streets. Stole and swindled to survive. Came to Ichor Knell for a better life but didn't find one. Beautiful. Kind. Brave. Good with the sword. Fun." He gave her a devilish grin for that one. "Our mating may have been hasty, but it was inevitable. I cannot possibly understand your worry that I won't accept you. I already have."

Although she still appeared troubled, she wrapped

her arms around his waist, and he held her close. His heart was so full to bursting that he had to restrain himself from squeezing the life out of her with his embrace. This bond was nearly too much to bear.

"Don't you dare tell Madeleine I said any of that," he murmured into her hair. "She would never let me hear the end of it."

She chuckled against his chest, and thankfully, she didn't let him go. Holding her brought warmth to his heart in ways he didn't know were possible. Ceremony or not, they were bonded together as mates, and he swore to himself he would protect her. Love her. Cherish her. Give her all the happiness he could offer a mate. Perhaps someday, they could afford a home and grow old together with a gaggle of children—why on earth was he thinking about children?

His body stiffened with tension as he thought of the one thing he overlooked.

Miles.

He held her at arm's length, searching her eyes. "Elisabeta... We are leaving tonight." He lowered his voice and glanced around, watching the increased number of guards in town with a wary eye. Escaping wouldn't be easy, but at night, it might be possible. "Where is Miles? If he arrives in Ichor Knell and we are not here... It could be dangerous for him."

"I don't think he will be coming," she replied and extracted herself from his arms.

"How do you know this? Have you been in contact with him?"

"No," she said hurriedly, but she quickly smiled at him. "He told me he might not make it for a while. I can write a letter to him at the first opportunity. You don't need to worry about Miles. I promise."

Her reassuring words hardly did anything to soothe his nerves, especially with the guards roaming about. But if she said everything would be just fine, he trusted her.

"If you're sure." He glanced hesitantly at the guards once more. He needed to come up with a new strategy.

Not wanting to dwell on worrisome thoughts right after their night together, his flirtatious smirk returned to his lips. He wrapped an arm around her waist and pulled her closer, so no space remained between them. She released a shaky breath as he backed her into the shadows and pinned her against the wall, the flames of desire eating him alive.

Making no attempt to douse the flames, he ran his hands down the length of her body, enjoying the way her breaths came in short gasps as if she struggled to breathe. He kissed the space below her ear and then trailed his lips down her jaw, to the base of her throat. Her scent tantalized him, called to him, lured him in. It became too much to withstand, and he needed more.

He sprouted his fangs—

She shrieked and pushed him away, her eyes wide with fear as she stared at the yellow liquid dripping from his fangs.

"What the blazes are you doing?" she cried.

He frowned and stared back at her, confusion taking a hold of him when he noticed her fingers inching toward the knife on her belt. She wouldn't use it on him, would she?

In a low voice, he said, "Elisabeta, I understand you weren't raised in vampire culture, but you have to know what a love bite is…"

Judging by the blank look in her eyes, she had no idea.

He sighed and retracted his fangs, desire nearly fleeing from him completely. Although her hand fell to her side, her air of caution remained.

"It's a bite a vampire gives to another vampire, to their mate or potential mate. It's supposed to…feel good…to have another vampire's venom in your blood." He scratched his head, wishing he'd known to tell her about it previously. But they still had time. Plenty of time.

"Promise me something," she said in a barely audible whisper as if she could hardly speak over the fear he had caused moments earlier. "Don't ever bite me, Dracula."

His eyebrows shot upward, and he nearly grinned and teased her back if not for the note of seriousness in her expression. He crossed his arms, his eyebrows now falling quickly into a furrow.

"Never?"

"Never. Promise me."

This promise was ludicrous, especially because he knew she'd like it. But he held onto the hope she'd change her mind with time. Their bloodbond was still so new after all.

Finally, he agreed with a nod of his head. "I promise. Now that we're past this ridiculous hiccup, do you want to accompany me to the barracks? There are a few things I need to put together."

She shook her head, and instant disappointment filled him, at least until he remembered they would have plenty of time together on the road.

"I would like to check on Madeleine and Nicolae," she answered. "See you tonight?"

He nodded, and this time, she *did* allow him to kiss her on the lips, sweet and gentle, but with a rush of intense emotion surging through him like a raging current. Desperation. Need. Worry. Anxiety. Love. He forced them all back. "See you tonight. Stay safe."

He swallowed his worry as he moved away from her and started toward the barracks. He was halfway there when he dug his hands into his pockets as a force of habit.

The blood drained from his face. The treasury key wasn't in his pocket.

After patting down his pockets and searching in his boots, he spun around to see if he had dropped it on the road, but he found nothing but dirt and grass. There was no trace of the treasury key anywhere.

Running his hand down his face, he cleared his mind to think for a moment. The last time he had seen it had been when he showed it to Elisabeta the other night in the woods. It could be anywhere by now. There were far too many places he might have dropped it.

He prayed Jorin wouldn't find out it was missing until he left Ichor Knell. Even then, they would be in danger. How could he have lost it? How could he have let this happen?

He continued toward the barracks as he tried to push away his growing anxiety. After tonight, the key wouldn't even matter. He would see his family out of Ichor Knell, and he would keep them safe, no matter what it took.

Chapter 21

Instead of visiting Madeleine and Nicolae like she told Dracula she would, Elisabeta spent the majority of the day watching for holes in the enemy's defenses. She found only one, and it was covered in what she assumed was dried human blood, though some parts were slick with a semi-fresh coat. A shudder raced through her as she stooped down and ran her finger through the thick, crimson slime, confirming what she already knew. This was where they slaughtered humans for their blood.

She pulled her cloak closer to her body as she followed the trail of blood, covering her nose with her arm in an attempt to keep the stench from permeating her brains. The trail ended at a crater in the woods, one filled with ash and scorched bone.

First, the vampires slaughtered the humans, and then they burned their bodies.

If she wasn't careful, she could end up in this pit too.

Trying to ignore the urge to flee from the horror of the city, she continued through the woods on deft feet until she reached the meeting spot. Miles was nowhere to be found.

She swore under her breath as she slipped her hand into her pocket and pulled out the treasury key. It gleamed with the light of day, the silver shiny enough to show her reflection on its surface. The face staring back at her screamed *traitor, liar, filthy thief.*

Dracula deserved so much better than someone like her.

Guilt left a crater in her heart the size of the one she'd seen earlier. She was his mate, yet he still had no idea of her deceit.

"I should have given you a choice," she whispered to the formidable breeze while she waited to see if Miles would show. "Now you don't have one."

Shame continued to prick her like a sharp needle. She deserved Dracula's wrath, and she felt certain she would receive it, sooner rather than later.

Hours passed and Miles still didn't show. She knew she couldn't wait around forever, nor did she want to leave the key in case someone other than her brother found it. With trepidation clinging to her heart like morning dewdrops, she pocketed the key and returned the way she had come, careful to remain out of sight until she entered town. Dusk fell, and she made her way to Nicolae's home. Thankfully, Dracula hadn't arrived yet.

Nicolae ushered her into the house and looked over her shoulder into the darkness before closing the door behind her. Everyone was already here—Nicolae, Madeleine, their children, Ilona, Lucian, and his brothers, and now her. Dracula entered the house minutes later, and all nervous chatter died down immediately. His mere presence brought her comfort.

He caught her eye across the room, and he crossed the small space to stand beside her. Although he said nothing to her, he gave her hand a brief squeeze before addressing everyone.

"I know of a path through the woods. It won't be easy to traverse, but it will keep us hidden until we are far enough away from the city. I have also taken weapons from the armory. Everyone will carry a dagger at the very least. Except the children, of course."

"I want a dagger," what looked to be the oldest of the children whined.

"I have an important task for you, Zeidan. You will help your mother climb over any obstacles on the path. That is far more important than wielding a dagger."

The child lifted his chin importantly. Her heart raced as Dracula studied their group for a few moments before saying, "We will stick together, Nicolae and Lucian at the lead, me at the rear. If we get split up for any reason, meet at the Black Dahlia Inn in Ravensford."

"What if we don't make it out of the city at all?" Ilona asked as she tightened her grip on her shawl.

"Let's hope it doesn't come to that."

After gearing up with weapons and other necessities, Nicolae extinguished the lanterns and they all filed out of the house one by one. She felt terribly conspicuous traveling in such a large group, and she was disadvantaged when all the other vampires could hear, smell, and see acutely while she walked blindly forward. Not to mention they could transform on a whim. This was not her idea of a good stealth strategy.

The darkness descended upon them, and she wished more than anything for a lantern to help her find her way through the darkened streets. All was quiet, which only caused her trepidation to grow. Silence was never a good sign.

She looked to the front of the group to find Nicolae

supporting Madeleine with an arm circling her waist. Her face was paler than usual, even in the darkness.

All at once, the vampires stopped in their tracks, and she nearly ran into Ilona in her disadvantaged state.

"Do you hear that?" Dracula asked Nicolae, who nodded with a grave expression. She glanced every which way, but she found nothing at all. However, only moments later, she heard something too.

Screaming.

"Run!" Dracula cried.

He took Elisabeta's hand and tugged her along on legs hardly able to keep up with his long, urgent strides. She stumbled in their haste to flee, and that's when she saw them. Perched in the trees. Waiting for them.

"Dracula!" she gasped as she produced a knife from her belt. She threw it at the same moment one of the enemy vampires loosed an arrow. Her dagger lodged itself in the vampire's neck, and he slumped forward and hit the ground with a loud *thud*. Beside her, Dracula hissed as he now began to usher everyone back the way they had come. An arrow protruded from his shoulder, the wound gushing blood.

"Dracula," she whispered in horror when she realized what metal it was—iron.

"No time," he growled, pushing her forward as more arrows flew in their direction. Having her secret revealed by an arrow spilling her blood was the last worry on her mind at the moment. She and Dracula could actually die.

As the lot of them ran back into the city, her eyes widened at the chaos surrounding them. Buildings burned with flames hot enough to sear her skin even from a distance. Vampires struck down other vampires right and left. The scene brought her back to the day vampires had burned down the library and killed anyone who refused to relinquish their books.

When she realized Dracula had disappeared from her side, she turned around only to find him ripping an enemy off an innocent vampire, stabbing him in the neck with a silver knife, and then snatching the vampire's iron sword. He screeched as he ripped the arrow out of his own shoulder before continuing to pull her in the direction of Nicolae's home. Even within the confines of the house, she didn't feel safe.

"Get away from the windows!" Dracula shouted in a commanding tone. He overturned the table and those in their group that hadn't gotten separated in their attempt to flee huddled behind it while chaos ensued just outside. She counted and realized they were missing Ilona, Lucian, and his brothers.

Her heart beat fast, terrified out of her wits. Over the course of her life, she had found herself in many sticky situations, but none of them involved a city full of vampires and a large-scale civil war.

The entire house became deadly silent aside from the whimpering escaping a couple of Nicolae's children. Shouts and screams erupted outside, the chaos of death and destruction.

Blood dripped from Dracula's shoulder and soaked his clothing. She swallowed hard when the wound didn't reknit itself. The damage done was permanent.

They remained huddled behind the safety of the table until the screams and shouts from outside ceased. The only one who dared to stir was Dracula. His massive vampire size shrunk down into a bat. He flew lopsidedly to the window and landed on top of an unlit lantern sitting on a smaller table. One of his wings drooped considerably, as if he were unable to hold it up himself.

"Mama?" one of the children whimpered. "Are we going to die?"

"No, sweet boy," Madeleine replied as she stroked his blond hair. "They only meant to scare us. Nothing more."

Elisabeta released a shaky breath and put her head between her knees. This was supposed to be an easy job. Immoral, but easy. Instead, she couldn't leave the city, a civil war broke out, and there was a big chance she might not make it out of this city alive. Either her potion would wear off and she'd be eaten by a vampire, or she would be killed by a vampire with a sword or an arrow.

Something fluttered through the air, and she raised her head to find Dracula in his bat form, standing on the edge of the upturned table. He looked at her inquisitively, and she had an awful feeling he might be trying to communicate with her in the way only vampires could hear. She should have told him she was a human long ago.

"I am fine, Dracula," she said quietly. "I am just realizing I came to Ichor Knell at a horrible time."

He continued to look piercingly at her, his ears moving as if with the sounds she was unable to hear.

She looked to Nicolae with pleading eyes.

"I agree with you, Dracula," Nicolae cut in, though not without a frown for her for obviously not having told Dracula her secret yet. "Trying to flee again will prove to be too dangerous. But so is staying. I cannot allow them to pick apart my family one by one. What are we to do?"

Dracula's wing drooped even further.

"Can you escape using your transformations?" Elisabeta asked.

"No," Nicolae shook his head. "They will be expecting it. Besides, Madeleine and I are water animals, and a couple of our children have transformations much too slow for a quick escape. We may look like animals, but we still smell like vampires."

"And what if you smelled like a human instead?" she asked slowly, thinking of using her own blood to mask their scents. She looked from Dracula to Nicolae, who also shared a look with the other.

Once again, Dracula's ears began twitching, and her frustration only grew. Communicating would be much easier if he untransformed.

"If they are hungry," Nicolae finally said, "then we will be in just as much danger. Your idea would only work on the off chance that our enemies already fed."

Madeleine groaned and held a hand to her belly. Nicolae immediately jumped to his feet and hefted his mate into his arms. "You cannot go into labor yet," he said softly. "Just a little bit longer, darling. Just a little bit longer."

They disappeared into their room while the children made their way upstairs to sleep. That left her and Dracula alone together in the darkness. She wrung her hands nervously at simply being alone with him again. The last time they were alone...

Her cheeks blushed crimson, and she found herself unable to maintain eye contact.

"I need to tell you something, Dracula," she

whispered. "It's quite serious, and I would prefer to tell you as a vampire and not as a bat."

Moments later, he transformed from a bat to a vampire, and he glanced once more toward the window before leading her to the sofa where he sat next to her, their knees brushing. A shiver ran up her spine, and she wasn't sure if it stemmed from his touch or her nervous fear.

"What is it?" he asked, his expression severe, though he hissed when he moved his injured arm. She hopped to her feet and fetched a basin of water and clean rags. She helped ease him out of his bloodied shirt only to find his wound looked much more terrible than she had anticipated. Carefully, she dipped a rag into the water and slowly dabbed at the wound, all while he remained stoically still.

Her fingers softly brushed his arm while she cleaned the wound, and she released a slow breath from her lungs. She loved Dracula—how could she hurt him by telling him the truth? The entire truth.

He caught onto her hand, and this forced her to finally look into his eyes. His gaze pierced her, the breath fleeing from her lungs.

"What is so serious?" he asked. "You have been acting strange ever since this morning. All I can think is you are unhappy to be my mate."

"No," she replied, shaking her head insistently. She placed her hand against his bare chest and sighed when she felt his heart pulsing against her hand. "I am quite happy in that regard." *Though guilty*, she added silently. "I need to tell you the reason I came to Ichor Knell in the first place. The real reason."

Nicolae exited his room at that moment, and she

had never seen Dracula appear more cross in the time she had known him. However, his annoyance quickly turned into concern.

"How is Madeleine?" Dracula asked.

"Not good," Nicolae replied with a shake of his head. "I fear she won't last until the end of the week."

"Is there nothing you can do?" she asked, standing. "Nicolae, I am confident I can get her across the border. If you and Dracula worry about everyone else—"

"Still too risky." Nicolae sighed, weariness showing in the dark circles beneath his eyes. "If your plan failed, and if she went into labor, even you aren't enough to protect her from a dozen vampires."

Dracula stood and crossed his arms over his chest. "Why do I feel like I am being left out from pertinent information? What are you two talking about?"

"Elisabeta will talk to you," Nicolae answered. "For now, the immediate danger has passed, and we survived. I think we all need a good night's rest."

Nicolae disappeared into his room once more, and the moment he left, all confidence fled her. She turned to face Dracula, only to find him watching her carefully. She disliked being under his scrutiny.

"You had something you wanted to tell me?"

She shook her head and sank tiredly onto the sofa. It had been a long night. "Nothing that can't wait until tomorrow. I just need to sleep right now."

He grunted but didn't protest as he curled up with her on the sofa, both of them barely able to fit. He placed a soft kiss on her neck before his arms tightened around her, and she fell asleep in his embrace.

Chapter 22

Waking up to Elisabeta's absence was becoming agitating. Dracula wasn't a deep sleeper by any means, so how she managed to slip from beneath his arm baffled him.

He winced as he pushed himself into a sitting position and studied the arrow wound that had scabbed over. If pierced by any other metal, he would have healed long ago. But this injury would remain for far longer before it became a scar.

A frown formed on his face as he studied the two perpendicular scars on his ankle. The only other time an iron weapon had pierced his skin was during his and his mother's escape from his father many years ago. That horrid man. He was the very reason for Dracula's hatred of humans.

"Good, you are finally up," Nicolae said as he walked into the room. He threw a clean shirt at Dracula, who carefully pulled it over his head as to not agitate his wound any further. "I feared iron poisoning."

He shook his head and winced at the effort it took from his sore shoulder. "I am made of tougher nails than that." He glanced around the room to find it disappointingly empty other than the two of them. "What is the damage from last night?"

"Twenty-two deaths, six homes burnt down, and there is no escaping Ichor Knell anymore. Guards are crawling about the city. We are free to go about our day, but the border is heavily patrolled."

"I suspected as much." He ran a hand down his face at this new reality, and then his gaze traveled to the iron sword propped against the wall. Using the unstained parts of his bloodied and discarded shirt, he ripped thin strips from the fabric and tied them around his hands before handling the sword to prevent himself from getting burned by the metal. He swung it through the air, annoyed at how good it felt in his hand.

"I have never killed a vampire before, Nicolae," he whispered as he stared at the lethal metal. "But it will be inevitable. I know it will."

Nicolae placed a hand on his good shoulder and looked at him with pleading eyes. "Please protect my family, Dracula. If I am unable to do so myself... Please."

"They are my family too," he corrected. "I would give my life for them. You have my word that I will do everything in my power."

Finally, Nicolae nodded and dropped his hand. "If you care about Elisabeta, you'd better tell her to leave the city and the rest of us behind while she still can."

He raised an eyebrow. "Why would she be able to leave when the rest of us cannot?"

"She hasn't told you yet?" Nicolae huffed. "Unbelievable. I thought she told you last night."

"She was *trying* to tell me something until you rudely interrupted." He slid the iron sword into his sheath and tied it to his belt. "Will *somebody* please tell me what's going on?"

"It's not my place."

With a roll of his eyes, he said, "So you keep

saying. Well, I better go track down my mate before I lose her altogether."

Nicolae's eyes widened. "Dracula, please tell me you didn't."

"I did. What of it?"

"You don't even know her!" Nicolae paced back and forth across the small space. "Out of all the decisions you have made in your lifetime, this one is the most foolish. Do you even know *why* she is in Ichor Knell? I don't. Do you know what she did yesterday? Or the day before?"

Dracula's eyebrows furrowed. "Wouldn't you know? She spent the entire day here yesterday."

His friend stared at him until he finally shook his head. "Dracula, she never came."

"What?" His head spun as he attempted to wrap his mind around this new bit of information before he decided there had to be a logical explanation. "I asked her to spend the day with me, but she said she wanted to check on Madeleine... Perhaps something came up."

"And does something *come up* a lot? Hmm?" Nicolae raised an eyebrow at him. "You clearly don't even know who your own mate is, Dracula. I fear you have made a horrible mistake."

Shaking his head in denial, he crossed the room to look out the window, only to find guards skulking about. Elisabeta was nowhere in sight. Thoughts swirled in his mind, of all the excuses she had made up. When she had refused to go hunting with him, when she had made him promise not to bite her, when she didn't tell him her secret the other night. She didn't know much about vampire culture, nor had he ever seen her vampire transformation.

However, she smelled like a vampire, and in the end, instincts were never wrong. Elisabeta was his mate for a reason. He believed that, and he refused to give into Nicolae's doubt until he understood everything himself.

"I need to find her," he said suddenly, and before Nicolae had a chance to reply, he transformed into a bat and flew out the window, albeit lopsidedly. The guards gave him wary looks as he flew past, but none of them tried to attack him. It wasn't until he made it to the edge of the city following Elisabeta's scent he slowed his flight. His heart hammered in his chest when her scent led him to the slaughtering house. The human stench attacked his nostrils, almost making him lose her scent. It was nearly imperceptible, but it was there.

He continued forward cautiously, but as he followed the path of blood, no vampires attacked him. Even when the trail of blood ended and opened up into forest, no one followed.

His heart sighed in relief, not because he was safe, but because Elisabeta was likely trying to find a way for all of them to escape the city. Nicolae had no reason to distrust her. No reason at all.

Now that her scent became stronger, he followed it through the forest until he heard a familiar voice.

"Let go!" Elisabeta cried, unaware of Dracula's presence nearby. He flew closer, following her voice until he found two figures down below. "I said let go!"

The second person roughly grabbed Elisabeta and threw her to the ground. "And I said finish what you came here to do. How many times do I have to—"

Dracula released a vampire screech as his protective instincts kicked in. He flew down from the

222

sky and untransformed moments before he slammed the second person against the tree. He pinned him to the tree by the collar and—

He grunted in surprise when he stared back into all-too-familiar green eyes and red hair, freckles dotting the bridge of his nose. He dropped the person and spun to face Elisabeta, who watched with wide eyes from the ground. They were the same. The exact same.

Miles.

When Dracula turned back to Miles, he was scrambling away, but the powerful scent of human hit him full on. Miles was human. Very human.

Trembling, he turned back to face Elisabeta. "You said you were born a vampire." She said nothing, but only stared at the ground where she still remained on her hands and knees. "If Miles is a human, your *twin*, you cannot be a vampire."

"I'm sorry," she said huskily. "I tried to tell you. I tried."

He stared at her, but he no longer knew who she was.

A bag with its contents spilled on the ground caught his attention, and he stooped down to pick up a small leather-bound book.

"Dracula, please," she said. "Don't read that. I beg you."

He ignored her pleading and opened the book, only to freeze as his eyes scanned the page. *How to seduce a vampire.*

His heart twisted painfully as he stared at the page for far too long, going down the list of things Elisabeta had done to *him. Fake an injury. Play cat and mouse.* All this time, he had been her target. But why?

Dread rose inside of him as he realized something awful. He had mated with her. Now he could not choose another mate for as long as he lived.

"Elisabeta," he whispered, "what have you done?"

"It's not what it looks like. I swear! I love you, Dracula. I love you." Tears started flowing down her cheeks, but her words went unheard as he stared in horror. The tears were clear, not red. She had deceived him. Lied to him. Tricked him into mating with her. She was a filthy, lying, deceiving *human being*.

He skipped to the final page where he noticed a bulge in the pages, and his heart stopped completely when he found a familiar key, one he had kept on his person for years. The very key he had lost a couple nights ago. The key to the royal treasury.

He lifted his gaze to Elisabeta, who now stood on shaky feet. "Please allow me to explain, Dracula. Please."

"You are a human," he spat angrily as his heart finally resumed beating again. "I trusted you! I let you in. I...I...*mated* with you." He pocketed the key, slammed the book closed, and threw it to the ground. "What have you done, Elisabeta? What have you done?"

"I am so sorry," she sniffed. "I never wanted you to find out like this. I wanted to tell you myself."

"That would have changed *nothing*!" He angrily punched the nearest tree with all his might, and despite the bones he cracked in the process, he didn't feel it against the roaring pain in his heart. The tree groaned and tipped precariously as some of the roots dislodged from the ground, but in the end, it stayed standing. He was just about to kick the tree to topple it when a loud ringing bell filled the air. His gaze darted to the skies as he felt the fear emanating from Ichor Knell.

That wasn't a mourning toll. It was a warning bell. A frantic warning bell.

His gaze shot back toward Elisabeta, his anger evaporating into worry. Although this woman had tricked him, she was still his mate. Protectiveness surged through him as the bell continued to ring vigorously.

"Get as far away from Ichor Knell as you can," he ordered before turning back toward the city.

"Wait!" she cried, stopping him with a hand to his arm. "Let me prove this is not just a trick. I am going with you."

"You might die."

"You might die too." She produced two knives and held them in either hand. They were made of steel, hardly a match for a vampire. "We need to find the others."

His nostrils flared, but he said nothing more as he ran ahead, Elisabeta barely keeping pace at his heels. His worry for his mate remained constant, even above his worry for the rest of his family, much to his annoyance. He feared he had made a terrible mistake by mating with her, but that only mattered if he lived through the next day.

Upon arriving in the city, his eyes widened as fear took hold of his heart. Vampires scattered with screams stuck in their throats as they ran from church guards, many getting cut down before reaching safety.

This wasn't the standard terror runs. This was the purge.

Without thinking, he pulled his iron sword from its

sheath and rammed it through the chest of the nearest church guard. He killed one after the other, his limbs working reflexively all while keeping an eye on Elisabeta at all times. She had picked up an iron sword for herself and managed to injure one guard. He finished the next guard off by swinging his sword and slicing the male's head clean off his shoulders.

Terror seized his throat as he glanced at the dead bodies of the innocent scattered at his feet. He had to do something. He knew he did.

"Everyone to the caves!" Dracula barked to the remaining living vampires. "Now!"

They scrambled up the slope that led to the lake and the surrounding caves with entrances hardly large enough for two vampires to stand shoulder to shoulder. He spun on his heel and charged in the opposite direction, striking down any enemy that stood in his path. The church had strength in numbers. They had iron weapons. But they were no match for the skill he had accumulated over the years. He barreled straight through them, attempting to save as many lives as possible.

The warning bell ceased suddenly as a church guard shot an arrow straight through the bellringer's neck. The vampire slumped forward and fell a hundred feet before smashing into the ground below.

Where was his family? Sheer panic threatened to take control when they were nowhere to be seen.

He turned to Elisabeta who had managed to follow him through the slaughter. "Get to the caves. If you don't, then so help me, Elisabeta."

She paused for a moment as if daring to defy him, but finally she whispered, "Be safe. Please."

Without another word, she ran after the vampires fleeing for the caves, but he didn't have time to watch her find safety. He ducked as someone swung a sword at him and then he ran his own sword straight through his attacker.

Screams and blood filled the skies, the overpowering smell clawing at his nose and weakening his senses. He glanced wildly around for mops of blond hair, and to his relief, he found them cowering behind a mop of black hair.

Raw determination drove him forward, blow after blow. He ignored his protesting injured shoulder. He ignored the vampires he could not save. He knew he couldn't save everyone, but every life counted.

"Lucian," he gasped when he finally reached his side. The Covaci children were all here, safe, and unharmed. "Where are Nicolae and Madeleine?"

Red spattered Lucian's face, and it was then he noticed Lucian's brothers lying lifeless on the ground as if they had given their lives to protect the children. He feared the worst for his friends.

"Nicolae went to search for her," Lucian replied just before Dracula spun and smote another head off, not bothering to spare the terrified children of the gore. "The baby... Madeleine's not doing well. She can hardly stand. She needs help."

Dracula frowned as another wave of panic and screams permeated the air. He couldn't go after Madeleine himself with the defenseless children to protect.

"Go," he ordered. "I will take the children to the caves. Tell any survivors to do the same."

Lucian nodded and hurried away, and he grit his

227

teeth with concentration as three vampires charged at him. He ran his sword through the first one, only to quickly kick the dying body off his weapon to impale another. He was covered in blood, though he wasn't sure if it was his enemies' or his own.

The third vampire approached cautiously as if he warred between fleeing and fighting. The coward turned to flee, but Dracula quickly reached out and grabbed him by the collar, choking him until he dropped his weapon. He didn't spare even one vampire. He killed this one and tossed his body aside before turning to the terrified children who stared at him with wide eyes.

"Follow closely, and whatever you do, don't fall behind."

The children nodded and held onto each other's hands while following him to the caves. The road to their destination was not nearly as treacherous as the city, but the enemy followed. He increased his pace and ushered the children in front of him. Only when they were safely inside the cave did he turn around and continue the fight. He didn't dare leave the caves defenseless now. For the vampires hidden inside, he was their only hope.

He fought until his entire body ached. He fought with every ounce of energy he possessed. Only a few more stragglers made it to the caves, and when one in particular stumbled up the path, he couldn't stop a relieved smile from forming.

However, his smile quickly fell when Madeleine tripped onto her hands and knees, revealing the iron dagger protruding from her back.

The entire world spun sickeningly as he rushed

forward, hardly able to find his footing. He reached her and cradled her in his arms only to see the truth of the situation for himself. His eyes widened when he placed a hand on her shoulder and took in the blood that soaked her dress. Madeleine's skin was beyond pale, her chin quivering with pain.

"I-I'm not g-going to m-make it," she stuttered as tears trailed down her cheeks. "S-save my b-baby. T-tell Nicolae I love h-him."

Madeleine's chin ceased quivering, and her arm fell limp to her side as her eyes stared blankly up at the sky. For a single moment, Ichor Knell fell deadly silent as he stared down at her face, and for the first time since his mother had died, he shed a tear.

"No," he whispered as he cradled her face in his hands, but the word came out strangled in his throat. "W-w-why did it have to be you?"

His tears blurred his vision red, and in a momentary flash, his grief turned to anger. Somehow, he found the willpower to get to his feet as a chorus of battle cries rang in the air. Somehow, he found the strength to put one foot in front of the other as he climbed the hill to the cave. And then his heart broke when he set Madeleine's lifeless body on the ground and turned back to the entrance of the cave just in time to run his sword through a vampire who almost slipped inside.

"Cut the child out!" he cried to Elisabeta, only sparing a brief glance toward the refugees before he turned back to the mouth of the cave to stab another vampire straight through the heart. He could no longer feel his hand. His own iron weapon had burned it so badly through the tattered strips of fabric he'd wrapped around his hand that he worried he might never be able to feel anything again.

"Cut it out?" Elisabeta shrieked. "I can't! I'm not...I'm not..."

A vampire.

Yes, he knew all too well. The knowledge created an intense ache in his heart. Her nails would be dull like a human's, not able to slice open the skin like a vampire could. He tossed her a knife, but even then, she stared at the weapon with wide, uncertain eyes.

With a strong kick to the next attacker's chest, he shoved his sword straight through him as well, and then all was quiet. At least from where he stood. He only had a short time. Perhaps a minute at best.

He spun toward the cowering group and laid his eyes upon Nicolae's still mate. Madeline's heart had stopped. She was most certainly dead.

He dropped to his hands and knees and tore open her dress, her round belly protruding for all to see. If his laceration missed its mark, the child could die. But if he did nothing, the child would most certainly die. This was the babe's only chance at survival. It was the only way. It was her last wish.

Thankfully, several females had enough sense to turn the Covaci children's eyes away.

Using one of his razor-sharp fingernails, he created a long laceration across the bottom of her belly—right where the child's head should be—that stretched from one hip to the other. Everything that had been inside gushed right out in a river of red, and he only just barely managed to catch the unmoving child before he—no, *she*—hit the ground. She was so still he feared she might be dead. But then he caught the faint sound of a small heartbeat. The child was still alive.

After cutting and tying the babe's cord, he pulled his own shirt from his back and swaddled the baby tightly, handing her to Elisabeta in a bloody mess.

"Get her breathing," he ordered as he turned back to the mouth of the cave just in time to impale the next intruder who dared attempt to kill the survivors. He was all too aware he was the only thing standing between the innocent and the attackers.

Sweat dripped from his face, from his neck, from his bare back. He had never fought so hard in his life, but he had also never had so much he needed to protect. He fought with all the energy he could muster. He fought without a care for himself, but all the care in the world for the vampires behind him. He fought with a passionate intensity until every last one of the attackers in the vicinity were vanquished.

His lungs struggled to suck in air as he threw down his sword and leaned heavily against the cave's rocky wall. His breathing came in gasps. His hand throbbed painfully where the iron had touched him, his skin raw and blistered. And he was so slick with sweat and blood that even the waters of the Brendall river would cry with shame. The only thing that brought him out of his labored rest was the sound of a newborn babe crying.

He turned with wide eyes to find the child swaddled tightly in Elisabeta's arms. Tears streamed down her face, though he wasn't sure if she cried because of fear or joy.

"Thank Ylios," he sighed as he slunk to the floor, his back to the wall as he positioned himself to give him a clear view of both the outside of the cave and the inside. Just because the immediate danger was gone didn't mean a new danger wouldn't arise.

Elisabeta quickly soothed the baby girl with rocking and a sweet lullaby. He sighed as he listened to her words, a solace when the world around them felt dark and dreary. Her lullaby helped to dispel the darkness from his heart and replaced it with hope. Hope for the dying. Hope for the fallen. Hope for the living.

She didn't stop singing as she approached him while rocking the baby in her arms. He should have looked at the child, but he was looking at *her*. At Elisabeta. Her expression appeared serene despite the tragedy, her green eyes alight with such beauty.

Human or not…he loved her.

"Would you like to hold her?" she asked as she crouched to his level.

"Nicolae should be the one to hold her," he whispered. "He is the father."

"And you look so despaired that I fear you might fall apart completely."

He swallowed as he stared back into her eyes before he finally nodded and took the child from her, cradling her in his arms. Her eyes were closed but she breathed without difficulty. She was certainly a beautiful babe. She had the characteristic Covaci blonde hair, and he had no doubt that once the color of her eyes came in, they would be blue. Her cheeks were plump and rosy, and she looked content in his arms. Child number six.

But Madeline didn't survive. She never even stood a chance.

"Hello, little one," he whispered when the babe yawned and opened her eyes the slightest bit. "You have a very brave mother. What a lucky little babe you are."

Emotion stole across him and he didn't try to stop it. His shoulders shook as he buried his face into the child's side. He cried for Nicolae. He cried for Madeleine. And he especially cried for this innocent little child who would grow up without a mother.

Elisabeta wrapped her arms around him and he turned his face into her shoulder, grateful for the comfort she brought him with her touch. Although he was still angry with her, he couldn't bring himself to waste the precious little energy that remained to despise her. At least not today.

She continued to sit beside him and hold him even when his shoulders stopped shaking and his tears dried. He felt...numb. He had seen bloodshed before, but never on this scale. How many vampires had he killed? It wasn't something he could recall, as he had struck down a great number.

A high-pitched vampire cry rose into the air and his eyes shot open. Nicolae.

He returned the cry with his own high-pitched noise as he rose to his feet, trepidation filling every inch of him as he held the baby close to his chest. His hand still throbbed from the burn of iron, but the pain was nothing compared to that of what his dearest friend would soon face.

Nicolae and Lucian came into view, both bloody and disheveled, but they were otherwise intact. Nicolae started to rush forward, but his steps slowed as if noticing the despair on Dracula's face.

"Madeleine," Nicolae whispered, his eyes wide.

He clutched one hand over his mouth as he started to run, darting past him and into the cave. He froze when he found the bloody mess surrounding his mate.

Dracula wished he didn't have to watch as Nicolae sank to the ground beside Madeleine and clutched her lifeless hand, pressing it to his forehead. He didn't weep openly—he wasn't one to show his emotions in front of others, but rather behind closed doors. However, the grief on his friend's face was almost too much for him to bear.

Nicolae touched Madeleine's hair, his fingers trailing across her overly pale face, but then his fingers froze when he saw the deep cut across her belly.

"My child," Nicolae said frantically.

"Here," Dracula answered quickly. "She is a healthy baby girl."

Nicolae swept the child into his arms, holding her tightly to his chest. Tears glistened in his eyes, but he still didn't weep. Not yet at least. "Has she a name?"

"No."

Letting out a strained breath, Nicolae nodded. "Then I will name her Madeleine. To be named after her mother seems appropriate."

He used his fang to prick his finger, spilling a droplet of his own blood onto the babe's forehead as a name-giving ceremony. Dracula watched as he drew an eight-pointed star, a symbol of hope.

Hope he did not feel.

Yet, this wasn't over.

He tore his gaze away from his happy but grieving friend and scanned the vampires in the room, counting heads. Two hundred and five in all, including the new babe. He desperately hoped there were more survivors out there, otherwise what they had just witnessed hadn't just been a massacre, but a near-annihilation.

"What of the others?" Dracula asked Lucian, who looked to be more level-headed than Nicolae at the moment. Understandably so.

"Heavy losses," Lucian replied as he wiped blood from his cheek. "I only hoped some survived. There are other pockets we found. Three others. Those in this cave are not the only survivors."

"Good," he murmured. "And what of the enemy?"

"Heavy losses on their side as well. Not enough survived the coup."

That meant they had run for the hills, but their retreat didn't mean they would stay away.

"Release me!" a voice cried. "I am your shah and I order you to unhand me."

Two vampires dragged Jorin into the cave, his crown lopsided on his head. Anger rose within him, and no one stopped him as he picked up an iron sword and pointed the tip at Jorin's throat. The iron burned his hand with a renewed intensity, but the external pain was nothing compared to the pain of loss.

"You started this," Dracula spat, digging the tip of the sword into Jorin's skin, enough to make him screech with the burn of the iron. "What do you have to say for yourself?"

"I am your shah," Jorin spat back. "On your knees. All of you!"

He wrenched the crown off Jorin's head and threw it to the ground, the metal clattering against stone until it lay still in a pool of blood. He squeezed Jorin's shoulder until he winced in pain and collapsed to his knees. "You are no one's shah, and this is your trial. What defense do you have for yourself?"

"You are all wicked! Impure! Every last one of

you. You deserved Ylios' judgement."

An eerie calm took hold of him as he stared at the pathetic fool before him. "The only judgement today is yours." He lifted his sword, well aware of everyone's gazes glued to the scene. "I, Dracula Ardelean, Captain of the Ichor Knell Guard, sentence you, Jorin Leonte, to death. May Ylios rightly judge your soul."

Jorin's eyes widened. "No, you cannot—"

With one powerful swing of his iron sword, Dracula smote off Jorin's head before he dropped the weapon and forced himself to take a deep, calming breath. Killing Jorin did nothing to erase his grief. In fact, he was overly aware of the vast amount of vampire blood on his hands today. But he had done what needed to be done.

And he would keep doing what needed to be done.

He turned and faced the survivors, some silent, others weeping for loved ones lost. Not a soul grieved over Jorin's death.

He spotted a familiar face in the crowd. "Frederick."

"Yes, Dracula?"

Frederick bowed, and if Dracula wasn't exhausted to the bone, he would have corrected him. Just because he killed the former shah didn't mean he wanted to be in power.

"You seem to know a lot about our religion and the correctness thereof. You will be our new Diviner." He raised his voice. "If anyone finds fault with his new position, speak up now."

No one spoke up, except one.

"D-d-diviner?" Frederick stuttered. "I cannot. I am only thirteen years old."

"And wiser than us all. Someone needs to lead the church."

Frederick didn't protest again, but rather stared after Dracula with a shocked expression. Thankfully, no further arguing ensued. He didn't have time for it.

Raising his voice again to the survivors, he said, "Gather your dead. Prepare their bodies. Tomorrow, we will mourn as a people and see them to the spirit world."

The moment he ceased speaking, the weeping started anew and echoed throughout the cavern, and when he turned around, Nicolae and his new daughter were nowhere to be seen.

Dracula knelt beside Madeleine and held tightly onto her cold hand. His friend was gone, killed unjustly, and he didn't know how to accept it.

Chapter 23

Elisabeta's vampire scent was beginning to wear off and others were starting to notice. One vampire had tried to attack her, and she would have been its next meal if it wasn't for Dracula, who fought her off. Although he stayed near her, he refused to speak to her, let alone look at her.

The group of survivors spent the night and most of the next day in the caves in case danger still lurked within the city. But when Dracula deemed it safe to leave their haven, people left the cave to collect the bodies of their loved ones. As night descended upon the city, Dracula led the procession of mourners to the lake, where everyone proceeded to lay their dead on a large raft before pushing it into the water to drift toward the middle of the lake. There were too many deceased to bury.

"Dracula," Frederick said, bowing as he approached. His gaze flickered to Elisabeta briefly, confusion in his eyes when he likely picked up her human scent. He continued to speak anyway. "Everything is ready to send them off. Will you provide the light?"

Dracula silently took a bow and arrow from Frederick and stuck the cloth-covered tip of the arrow into the lantern Lucian held. Immediately, it burst to life, bathed in fire. Elisabeta watched as he drew back the arrow and released it with perfect precision, the arrow arching into the air before it *thunked* into the wood of the raft. The fire licked quickly at the wood, and within seconds, the entire raft was in flames.

Frederick lifted his hands to the sky and shouted, "*Odihneasca-se in pace!*"

One by one, each vampire took each other's hands until they formed one long, continuous line. Elisabeta held Lucian and Nicolae's hands, as Dracula still refused to acknowledge her existence.

She deserved his shunning—she knew she did. But it hurt all the same.

The space around her filled with a low hum, and then the hum grew louder and louder until it resembled a tune, a short tune that repeated itself again and again. She glanced to her right and then her left, only to find everyone closing their eyes as they hummed.

Although she didn't understand vampire mourning rituals, she allowed herself to close her eyes as well and think of Madeleine. In the brief time she had known her, they had become friends, and all too soon, she was ripped away from this life, leaving behind Nicolae and their six children to raise himself. Her heart had never broken for anyone as much as it did for Nicolae.

And Dracula.

She opened her eyes to watch him as he hummed along with the others. He had lost a good friend. He had likely lost many friends yesterday. She wanted to comfort him, but how?

The humming continued well into the night until the flames finally died, giving way to the stars above and sporadic dark patches of Ichor Knell clouds.

One after the other, vampires returned to the city

until only she, Dracula, Lucian, Nicolae, and his children remained.

"Nicolae," Dracula said quietly. "I will take your children tonight."

Nicolae nodded without protest, a hollow being of what he once was.

"Come, children," Dracula said as he gathered the little ones around him and took the newborn from Nicolae's arms. "We get to sleep in the castle tonight. I've heard the beds are quite cozy."

Elisabeta caught onto his arm. "Dracula, can we please talk?"

He wrenched his arm out of her grip and continued toward the castle, not speaking a single word to her. She watched his retreating back become smaller and smaller, a single tear escaping her eye. Deceiving him had been the biggest mistake of her life.

"Dracula has ordered me to lock you in your room," Lucian said as he gently took a hold of her elbow and steered her down the path.

"Of course he did," she muttered miserably. She was exhausted. She was hungry. And the vampire she loved with all her heart hated her guts. "It's any wonder he doesn't throw me into the dungeon."

"Oh, he's considered it. Believe me."

They walked in silence the rest of the way to the castle, up the stone steps, and into the empty corridors. The castle was large—a city within a city. And it was far too quiet, save for the noises Nicolae's children made just down the hall.

Lucian led her up a flight of stairs and to an empty bedroom. He gave her a sorrowful, apologetic look before he locked her inside.

Tears trailed down her cheeks, and she didn't know whether they stemmed from her growing hunger or from Dracula's behavior toward her. Death suddenly felt far too close for comfort, and she waited to find out what would be the ultimate cause of her death—hunger or a broken heart. She loved Dracula, and her mistakes had hurt him. She didn't deserve his forgiveness.

Not able to bear the heaviness in her heart any longer, she curled into a ball beside the unlit hearth, quietly sobbing onto the marble floor. She had ruined everything, and she didn't know how to fix it. What had she done?

Chapter 24

"Dracula!" a female cried from the throng of vampires surrounding the castle. He turned just in time to find her picking up her skirts as she shoved her way through the crowd. "Dracula! How will you protect us from future threats? What will come of Ichor Knell?"

"My Shah!" a male shouted, his voice overpowering the female's. "What do we do next?"

Unable to help himself, Dracula scowled at the mention of Shah. Their ruler was the last thing he ever wanted to be.

Before he could agitatedly correct the male, Lucian pushed him inside the castle and ordered the appointed guards standing in front to keep anyone from entering. Once inside, he could finally breathe again, as well as hear his own thoughts. The palace was much quieter than the chaos ensuing in the square. These vampires needed direction, and fast.

"What in the—" he started, but Nicolae cut him off.

"Not here," Nicolae said as he cast a cautious glance toward the front doors. As the former advisor to the former shah, he knew his way around the palace, and he led them up a flight of stairs and into an expansive library. Dracula had never seen so many books in his life.

"I thought Jorin burned every book in the city," he

commented as he picked up a thick volume that must have been centuries old. It was written in the Old Language, and although he was well-versed, this proved to be difficult to read.

Nicolae shook his head as he locked the library door behind them. "Jorin wanted power. To burn his own knowledge was to throw away some of his power."

Dark circles had long since formed beneath Nicolae's eyes, a haunted look in his expression. Everyone in Ichor Knell had lost someone they cared for, and Nicolae was no exception. Dracula felt Madeleine's loss acutely, but Nicolae had been mated to her for many years. He couldn't imagine what it must feel like to lose a mate.

His nostrils flared as his thoughts shifted to Elisabeta.

There was not enough time in the day to release his anger for what she had done. But the longer he pushed the issue aside, the hotter his anger flared.

"The people want you as their shah, Dracula," Lucian said, getting straight to the point as he took up a spot beside the window that overlooked the river.

"No." He slammed the book in his hands down onto the table, making Nicolae jump in his seat as if he had been sucked into his own haunted mind only moments earlier. "That is the worst idea anyone has come up with in the past forty-eight hours."

"You forgot the mason's idea to construct a heroic statue of you," Lucian pointed out in a humorous tone as he glanced toward Nicolae, but Nicolae's mouth didn't even twitch in amusement.

He rolled his eyes as he clearly remembered the ludicrous idea. As if he would let *anyone* erect a statue of him in any city.

"Who will do it if not for you?" Nicolae asked.

"You will, Nicolae," he said, placing his palms flat on the table between them. "You have experience working in the palace. You know everything there is to know about what it takes to rule a nation."

Nicolae sighed and lifted his gaze. The hollowness in his eyes startled him. He would do anything to take his pain away. "I am broken, my friend. I cannot be the shah, not after what...what happened. I can hardly...hardly take care of my new daughter."

Another pang of grief flashed through him as thoughts of Madeleine entered his mind. He knew it wasn't fair to place such a heavy burden on Nicolae's shoulders. Not now. Not ever.

"Lucian?" he asked with desperate hope lining his voice. "It must be you to step up to the position. The people will listen to you. They must."

Lucian didn't answer but continued to stare out the window as if considering the proposition.

Continuing in hopes to sway Lucian, he said, "I don't want to rule. I *cannot* rule. With Elisabeta as my mate." He spat her name. "She is...is...a *human*! She is not fit to rule beside me, nor is she safe in Ichor Knell."

"You cannot leave your people," Nicolae said exhaustedly. "Leaving Ichor Knell with Elisabeta is a mistake. She will need to stay regardless of whether you take up your position as shah or not."

With clenched fists, he replied, "Nicolae, she is a *human*. Did you not catch that?"

"I have known for a while. And I also know being away from your mate is heart-wrenching. Betrayal or not, you *will* feel an intense desire to stay by her side."

He wanted to punch the wall. He wanted to shove every book to the floor until his anger had nothing left to topple. And he just might have done it if Nicolae hadn't been watching him carefully. Now was not the time to let his anger control his actions. Not while his friend was in deep mourning.

"Lucian, please," he begged.

Finally, Lucian slowly walked away from the window and steepled his fingers together. His violet eyes bore a hole straight through him. "Nicolae is right. You are the best fit as Shah. You protected what is left of the citizens of Ichor Knell when no one else could. You fought off the danger, and if I remember correctly, it was *you* who smote off Jorin's head with an iron sword. To choose anyone else to become the shah would be ill-advised."

Lucian's words were the final blow. He sank into a chair, his head falling into his hands. For the longest time, he said nothing. He was still unsure of what to do with Elisabeta. Of course, he was a natural-born leader, but to become the shah? He was not the kind, benevolent ruler Nicolae would be. He was not the thoughtful, careful ruler Lucian would be. He was brash. He was dominating. He was ruthless. How could someone like him be a good ruler?

His lips pressed together in a thin line as his thoughts continued to swirl in his mind. There was no other type of person fit to take charge after the mass destruction that had befallen Ichor Knell. These people needed someone who was resilient. They needed someone who knew how to take charge. They needed someone who could protect them from future threats, someone who could provide structure.

He was that someone.

It felt as if an eternity had passed before he finally lifted his head only to find the other two watching him. He stood and placed his hands on top of the table as he made his decision.

"Our people are in ruins," he said quietly. "We have all lost so much. We need to rebuild this kingdom, and we need to do it together. The three of us, with me at the head. I will do this with the two of you as my trusted advisors, or I will not do it at all."

"I cannot do much in my state," Nicolae warned.

"Then you will join us when you are ready."

Nicolae nodded and clasped Dracula's wrist. Although he said nothing more, he knew he had Nicolae's loyalty to the crown.

Lucian stepped forward and he, too, clasped his wrist. "I will stand by you, Shah Dracula. From now and until the end of time."

He took a deep breath and let it out slowly. Gone was the brash captain of the guard. He was now the shah, and he would do his best to lead his people out of the ruins that had become of Ichor Knell.

"First, we will hold the coronation," he said. "After, we will take this one day at a time."

Chapter 25

When Elisabeta had first arrived in Ichor Knell, she had been in search of an army captain. That vampire was now the king of all vampires, or Shah, as the vampires called him. She wasn't sure whether to feel intimidated or downright guilty. What she had done to him... It was unforgivable.

"Dracula is still not speaking to me," she whispered hurtfully to Lucian as she watched Dracula on the other side of the cathedral, standing tall next to Ilona while they spoke to several vampire subjects. The two were complete opposites. Whereas Dracula was easy to spot, tall and foreboding in the room, Ilona was small and timid, easily overlooked.

"But he allowed you to attend the coronation," Lucian commented. "His invitation was more than generous."

She rolled her eyes as she gave him a pointed look. "Do you think I don't know what he's doing? Do you think I haven't noticed you and Nicolae fastened to my side at all times? He doesn't want me to escape."

"He's protecting you."

"Being locked inside an empty room with hardly a thing to eat and nothing to keep me warm but a meager fireplace is protection? It's torture."

"Dracula has been...busy."

She ran her hands up and down her arms in an

attempt to ward off the chill that had seeped into her bones. "You needn't make excuses for him."

Lucian fell quiet, and so did she. She was overly aware she was a human in a room full of vampires, those who could obviously smell her human scent now that Miles's potion wore off completely. Even then, her concern was for Dracula, not herself. His father, a human, had hurt him and now she had done the exact same thing. She was deeply ashamed of herself. It would have been better if she hadn't come to Ichor Knell at all.

"You are relieved of your duty for the night," Nicolae said to Lucian upon approaching. "Dracula is bored out of his mind. Why not save him before he strangles Frederick?"

Lucian chuckled before heading in Dracula's direction. Although she liked Lucian just fine, she was much more comfortable in Nicolae's presence.

"He does not look happy," she commented after several moments of easy silence.

Nicolae shook his head and watched Dracula as she did. "He does not find joy in taking the throne. He fought us over the idea, but in the end, he decided it was necessary to take the position for the good of what remains of our people."

"He is incredibly selfless," she said with a frown. *Unlike me.*

"Yes. He has always been that way. I knew he would become the shah the moment he finished Jorin. He always does the right thing, no matter how difficult."

If only she could do the same. She hadn't realized how blurred the line between black and white had become until the moment she had met Dracula at the training grounds. She was a thief. A traitor. She did not at all like the person she had become, but she did not know how to change. He was too good for her and she knew it.

"Nicolae?" she asked suddenly. "What is it like for a vampire to find a mate?"

He nodded his head sagely as if he knew exactly why she asked. "Finding the right mate can take a long time—decades, and even centuries for some vampires. Vampires are selective when choosing their mates. It is a basal instinct we have deep inside us, to know when we find the right one."

"And what does it *feel* like?"

For a moment, he paused in thought as he clasped his hands behind his back. Although he appeared calm, she couldn't help but wonder what happened when he was alone after losing Madeleine.

"I am not quite sure how to explain," he said at last. "It is a deep connection. It is always being aware of where the other is in the room. It is needing the other so desperately it hurts. It is feeling a festering, aching pain when they are away."

She glanced at Dracula, and her curiosity got the better of her. She moved closer to the stained-glass windows of the cathedral with Nicolae trailing behind and watched as Dracula's body shifted with her movement. Nicolae was right. Dracula *was* aware of her, though he clearly was not about to admit it.

A low-pitched growl broke her out of her thoughts, and she turned, startled to find a nearby vampire with deep red eyes staring back at her. She recognized the red eyes for what they were—the vampire was hungry, and he smelled her blood.

Dracula's posture instantly turned rigid and he stepped in the space between her and the hungry vampire. Though he said nothing, didn't even turn to speak to her nor look her way, she knew he was protecting her.

"I think we should leave," Nicolae said quietly.

He gripped her arm tightly and steered her out of the cathedral. She struggled to keep up with his long, quick strides, and it wasn't until they entered the palace, climbed a set of stairs, and stepped into the spacious room she called her prison did they stop their flight.

"It is not safe for you in Ichor Knell," Nicolae said.

She watched as he threw back the curtains to look down below and then paused for a few moments as if to listen before he closed the drapery once more.

"Why do you care?" she asked, her throat closing up around her words. "I betrayed your friend."

Nicolae sighed and shook his head. His expression looked increasingly haggard the longer they were away from the public eye. "Remember what I told you about vampires choosing a mate? You may have deceived him, but his instincts still whispered for him to choose you. You were mine and Madeleine's friend long before any of this happened. You will forever be my friend."

It was a rare occasion when her emotions became so raw they inspired tears. Her eyes watered up, and she gratefully stepped into Nicolae's embrace. Oh, how she needed a friend right now. When her world had suddenly fallen apart, she would give anything for a stable hand to help her to her feet.

Wiping her tears away and stepping away from him, she took a turn by the window and looked outside. It was amazing that such a dark and seemingly foreboding place had begun to feel like home. She had never had a home before. And now she needed to leave it behind.

"I need to leave," she whispered quietly, though she knew Nicolae heard her words. "I have no place here."

"Good luck," Nicolae said as he made his way toward the door. "You won't make it past the border before Dracula finds you and drags you back. He may be angry now, but you are still his mate. He will not allow you to leave."

"But I must. I am a human, and I will not become a vampire for him, for anyone."

The mere thought of becoming a vampire caused her to shudder. The strength, the immortality, the culture... None of it enticed her enough to change her mind.

He gave her an empathetic look before taking his leave. She stared after him with a lump forming in her throat. Leaving was her only option, as she had certainly made a muddle of things. She broke a vampire's heart. She had done unspeakable things. She would leave without the dragon egg. And she was ashamed of herself. For all her efforts in Ichor Knell, she had nothing to show for it.

And the one thing she would miss the most was Dracula.

Chapter 26

The heaviness on Dracula's heart had not lifted. He mourned for the loss of Madeleine. He mourned for the heavy loss of his people. And he mourned for himself and the fact that he had unknowingly chosen a human as his mate. A thief. A fraud.

He twisted the ring on his finger, gazing down at the royal crest etched into the metal. He had destroyed the crown once belonging to Jorin, as it had represented malice, terror, and cruelty. This ring represented a new beginning, a fresh start, a kingdom rebirthed. And it felt heavier than life itself.

He walked away from the cathedral, away from the burden of his new role, away from the people who looked at him expectantly, as if he could fix all their problems and heartache overnight.

It would take time. It would take *a lot* of time. But someday, their kingdom would prosper again.

"Dracula," Nicolae said, startling him from his thoughts. He hadn't even heard his friend approach in the empty hallway.

"Elisabeta is safe?"

He mentally kicked himself that his concern had immediately leaped to her. But after the bloodbond, he couldn't help himself. His thoughts, his heart, *everything* about him had altered, making far too much room for the woman who had hurt him deeply.

"Yes and no..." Nicolae answered with a frown. "Dracula, she is going to leave. And I suspect she will do it tonight."

Crossing his arms, he turned away from Nicolae. "And I should care *why*?" Truthfully, he *did* care if she left. Quite a bit. A pulsing ache formed in his heart at the very thought of her leaving him and Ichor Knell behind. After what she had done to him, his devotion to her made no sense.

"You should convince her to stay," Nicolae spoke plainly. "Give her a reason to."

He snarled, his fist striking the wall. "She took something from me."

"I believe you freely gave it. You are both to blame, so stop your whining and do something about it."

One thing he hated more than anything was when Nicolae was right. He preferred to stay in his own confinement of pride and stubbornness. But a human? How on earth was he supposed to make things work with a human? Elisabeta would never agree to being turned, which meant he would constantly have to look out for her and keep her safe. Besides, he doubted his own capability to bite her and watch as she underwent a painful transition.

"A human?" he whispered, mostly to himself.

"We have begun a new era in history," Nicolae said as he continued on his way down the hall. "As Shah, you can mold it into what you wish."

Nicolae's words echoed in the hallway long after his departure. He had feelings for Elisabeta. Plenty of feelings, most of them good. He loved her despite her betrayal. Although she was the only mate he would ever get in his lifetime, he wanted her by his side.

Forever and always.

He muttered an oath under his breath. The blasted woman had far too great of a hold on him.

After retrieving a couple items from his chambers and somehow managing to prepare a decent meal for a human, he found himself in front of Elisabeta's door. He took a deep breath and braced himself as he knocked.

At first, he heard nothing on the other end, but then someone stirred. He almost bolted in the other direction, but he was no coward. Not today. Not ever.

Elisabeta opened the door, shock registering on her face. "Dracula? I…I…"

"Am I allowed inside?" he grumbled, looking at a spot just over her shoulder rather than daring to meet her gaze. "Or will I get burned if I step forward?"

"That surely is just a myth."

"Is it? Do you dare test that *myth*?"

She bit her lip as if truly considering it. Finally, a sly grin pulled up on one side of her lips. "No, you are not allowed inside."

Despite himself, he couldn't help it when his mouth twitched in amusement. It seemed as if *this* side of her was real, and he took heart in it. Perhaps not all of her act was actually an act.

"You must really like to hurt me," he smirked as he leaned on the doorframe, keeping just out of reach of the barely shimmering barrier only vampires could detect. "Like the sunlight, these burns take a while to heal."

"How long is a while?" she asked. "Considering this myth is actually true."

"It depends on how long I am exposed. It could kill me if exposed too long. Otherwise, a minor burn could take a little less than an hour to heal."

She lifted an eyebrow in a challenge. His smirk lingered as he folded the sleeve of his shirt up to expose his forearm. The burn would fade, but his satisfaction of being right would last forever.

He crossed his arm over the threshold of the room, and immediately, an intense burn seared his skin. He hissed as he retracted it, holding his wounded arm close to his side. He'd forgotten how much these wounds hurt.

Alarm flitted across her features as she snatched his arm and turned it over to expose the glaring red mark on his forearm.

"Oh, Dracula," she whispered, her fingers lightly brushing against his skin. "I am deeply sorry. I genuinely thought it was a myth."

When she glanced up to meet his gaze, his stomach rolled pleasantly over itself. All week, he had been trying to fight these feelings, but now they hit him at full force. This was his mate. Elisabeta was his mate. And he could not deny the strong emotional pull he had to her.

"Now may I come inside?" he asked, not bothering to roll his sleeve back down. "I brought food—human food—and a truce. I do not wish to fight any longer."

"Fight?" she laughed as she ushered him inside. "If that is how you become when you are truly angry, then fighting with you is not all bad if all I have to suffer through is a bit of hunger and being locked inside."

Dracula frowned. "You think I am locking you in? What I am doing is locking the population of Ichor

Knell *out*. The smell of your blood is…tantalizing. I do not doubt for a single second others think the same thing."

To admit his lust for her blood shamed him. Warm and undoubtedly delicious. He wanted to sink his fangs into her neck and taste the very thing that had tortured him all week. But it would either kill her or turn her, and he could not do either one of those things to his mate.

Not giving her a chance to reply to his comment, he reached into his pocket and held her well-read notebook out to her. She took it hesitantly, her eyes wide. When he lifted his hand to simply touch her arm, she flinched.

His fingers paused mid-air, a hurt encompassing him. "I am saddened you even think me capable of hurting you." He turned away from her in an attempt to gather his emotions. "I am not your brother. I would never hurt you."

"Are you not…are you not angry?"

"Not anymore." He gestured to the tray he had left on the table. "I'm sure you are famished. Eat. And then if you will, meet me on the upstairs balcony. I have something I wish to speak to you about."

Without another word, he climbed the stairs and didn't look back as he stepped out onto the balcony. A light nighttime breeze touched him gently, and with it the faint, lingering scent of ash. Plenty of buildings had been burned down under Jorin's final week of reign, all of which would be rebuilt in time. There was plenty to do, and hopefully, they would have many years to do it. Once word reached the other races of what happened in Ichor Knell, he hoped it would inspire fear instead of opportunity. He had taken down an army of vampires. He would do the same to an army of humans or elves or dwarves if necessary.

He looked down at the city below. It looked much smaller from up here, but much of it was now uninhabited. He would need to find a way to encourage foreign vampires to migrate to Ichor Knell, to make this place a thriving land again.

Footsteps behind him alerted him to Elisabeta's presence. He turned around slowly, only to find her wringing her hands nervously and staring at the ground. Did she think he came here to punish her?

"I assure you I have no ill intentions toward you, Elisabeta," he said. This was a side of her he had never seen before, the side that expected to be beaten for doing wrong. He disliked it very much, and it only made him want to beat the life out of Miles for instilling it in her.

She relaxed, but only marginally.

He reached inside his pocket and held a ring in his enclosed fist, his heart beating wildly. He was taking a chance on her, and he was not yet sure if it was a wise move.

"I'm not entirely sure how to approach the subject," he said as he shuffled his feet uncertainly, "so I will just say it. You are my mate, and however it happened, it still happened. And...I don't regret it. Even if you are a human. I hope we can make it work still."

At last, he opened his fist to reveal the ring. Unlike the shah's ring that bore the seal of royalty, the kumari's ring was a deep emerald. He liked it especially because it reminded him of her eyes.

Her mouth hung open in disbelief as she looked from the ring, to him, and back to the ring. "You are asking me to marry you?"

He had been living in Ichor Knell for so long that he had almost forgotten what the human term meant. He shook his head, then nodded, then shook his head again. Human terms were incredibly confusing.

"We are already bonded. Or at least I am bonded to you. You are my mate already." He shook his head and blew out a long breath while pinching the bridge of his nose. He wouldn't have to explain this to another vampire. "What I am asking of you is to stay in Ichor Knell. Become our kumari. Rule by my side. Frederick, the Diviner, can perform our union ceremony and your coronation at the same time."

As he had feared, she shook her head, withdrawing from him and taking several steps back.

"I am a human." She clutched her hands to her heart. "I don't belong here, Dracula, in this world full of vampires. I should not have come in the first place. I have done something unforgivable to you."

Stubborn woman. Did she not realize how much of a chance he was taking on her?

"If you are willing to stay, if you are willing to try to make this work, then all is forgiven. As I said, I don't regret it now, and I hope you will not make me regret it in the future. Stay with me."

"I don't...I don't know if I can," she replied breathlessly.

He reached for her hand, and she let him have it. He slid the ring onto her finger, his hope flaring alive once more when she didn't resist.

"I *want* you to choose me as I have chosen you,"

he said quietly. "Which is why I must give you this."

He produced the key to the treasury and placed it in her palm. Her eyes widened as she glanced up at him, a trace of fear in her eyes.

"Please don't give me this choice," she whispered. "I beg you."

"I must." A whisper of nervousness fluttered in his heart. "Whatever is in the treasury is yours. I will not stop you from taking anything. But if you take anything at all, don't bother coming back here again."

"Dracula…" Her voice shook as she spoke his name. "Please. Don't do this."

He didn't listen, but rather placed a gentle, lingering kiss on her forehead. "I hope to have your answer soon."

Leaving her alone on the balcony, he descended the stairs and exited the room. A sick feeling entered his toes and crawled up his body until distress consumed him. She might very well choose the dragon egg.

After all, that was exactly why she had come to Ichor Knell in the first place—to seduce the key from him and take the egg behind his back. But perhaps there was a chance she would choose him instead. He had given her a reason to stay. Would she take it?

Chapter 27

Elisabeta knew her answer the moment Dracula had placed the key into her hand. The entire reason she had come to Ichor Knell was for the petrified dragon egg. Miles was counting on her to deliver the egg to him, and she couldn't bear to disappoint him. He was counting on her to do this. No one had ever needed her help like he did.

As midnight crept closer, she awoke more fully as her heart pounded furiously in her chest. She sat quietly by the window as she watched the sky become increasingly darker until hardly a shadow remained outside.

It was time.

She located her knives, her sword, and she packed up what little she owned into her knapsack. When she shrouded her face with the hood of her cloak, the flash of deep green on her finger caught her attention. The kumari's ring was beautiful with rich color and a brilliant sparkle when caught under just the right lighting. It was the only thing she would have of Dracula, and although she knew she should return it, she couldn't bring herself to give it up.

"You should never have given me this key," she whispered to the darkness. "I have no choice but to finish what I started."

Pushing down her growing feelings of heartache

and regret, she quietly exited the room and closed the door behind her, the handle making a soft *click*. She froze in her tracks and listened to the still castle, not a sound to be heard within the vicinity. In any normal circumstance, she wouldn't have fretted over such a small sound, but knowing vampires had excellent hearing, she needed to take every precaution to remain quiet.

Her shoes soundlessly traversed the darkened hallways, each footfall as silent as the last. Although Dracula said he would not stop her from taking anything from the treasury, she didn't want him to know of her activity. She could not bear to see the hurt and disappointment on his face.

A barely audible *whoosh* rushed past behind her, and she spun around, her heart beating wildly as she glanced every which way, only to find the hallway empty and void of creatures and vampires alike. The window must have had a crack in it to let in the wind. That's all it was.

Letting out the breath she had been holding, she continued on her way down the hallway, quicker this time, until she stood in front of the treasury door she had scouted earlier.

Her fingers shook as she produced the key from her pocket. Every fiber of her screamed this was wrong. Every piece of her shouted for her to throw away the key and rush into Dracula's arms instead.

But Miles needed her. Kin came first before anything else.

After several attempts, she turned the key in the keyhole, the door clicking open. Although the room was dark, she marveled at what she *could* see. Precious gemstones, gold coins, priceless heirlooms... She and Miles could live like royalty for the rest of their lives with this wealth.

A prick of guilt stabbed her gut at the thought. She *could* live as royalty by Dracula's side. Real royalty, a queen who helped others instead of took from them.

But Miles would never live in Ichor Knell, no matter how much she might try to convince him. He was counting on her to do this. She must do this!

She carefully sifted through the items in the treasury until she spotted the silhouette of an oval, larger than any egg she had ever seen. Her breath fled her lungs, and she suddenly felt entrapped in a dream as she approached slowly and laid her hand atop the egg. The dark blue, petrified scales were pointed and rough, whatever life inside having died a long time ago. She picked up the beautiful egg and held it in her arms. This dragon egg was worth more than she could possibly comprehend.

It was real. It was valuable. It was beautiful.

And it was time to leave, lest she get caught before she managed to escape.

She took only the dragon egg and locked the door behind her. Instead of absconding through the front doors of the castle, she crouched in the window and weaseled it open until chirping crickets greeted her ears. However, no wind rushed to the window. It was a still night, not a wisp of wind to be found.

It wasn't until she hopped down from the window and landed on agile feet did she realize the wind she had felt earlier in the castle hadn't been wind at all.

She had been followed.

She spun around, her throat constricting as she

caught a pair of dark eyes watching her from the shadows. Dracula didn't move. He just watched with a pained expression, and the hurt she had been afraid to face hit her at full force. Once again, she had betrayed the vampire who had trusted in her again and again. She was not worth his trust. She was not worth anyone's trust.

"I am so sorry," she whispered, knowing he would hear her.

Tears formed in her eyes and she forced herself to tear her gaze away as she spun on her heel and disappeared into the darkness of the night. Her tears refused to cease as she continued to run, wanting to be as far away from Ichor Knell as was physically possible. She was leaving the only home she had ever known. The only male she had ever loved.

When there were no sounds of pursuit, she finally slowed. She didn't know if Miles would be waiting for her at their rendezvous point, but it was the first place she needed to look.

As she had suspected, a dim fire burned ahead. She recognized Miles's red hair despite most of it being hidden beneath the hood of his cloak. A twig snapped beneath her shoe, and he immediately launched to his feet and pulled out a lethal dagger.

"Elisabeta?" Miles gasped upon seeing her face.

"Miles." Relief flooded through her at seeing him alive and well. She had a sudden urge to rush into his arms, but she refrained. Their relationship was not like that. Not at all.

He first peered over her shoulder as if expecting Dracula to show his face, but when he was satisfied the vampire shah was nowhere to be seen, he sheathed his weapon and rested his gaze on the dragon egg she held in her arms.

"Is this…?" he asked, his eyes widening. "How did you… I thought our ruse was found out."

"It doesn't matter," she shook her head. "The important thing is I got it, and we need to leave immediately."

Ever the cautious one, he furrowed his eyebrows and asked, "Where is Dracula?"

"He won't come after us. There was a civil war… He has too many other vampires to worry about to chase after the egg." It was a half-truth. After all, she didn't want to tell him the real reason—that Dracula made her choose between becoming the vampire queen and taking the dragon egg. Somehow, Miles would exploit the opportunity and find a way to make her use Dracula all over again.

She would never do it again.

Ever.

He held out his hands. "Give it here."

She hesitated.

"I said give it here," he repeated impatiently.

She glanced longingly behind her toward the direction of Ichor Knell. If she returned now with the dragon egg and begged Dracula for his forgiveness, she might be able to fix this. But if she handed her brother the egg, there was no going back.

Turning back to her brother, she bit her lip and asked, "What are you planning on doing with it?"

"Does it matter?"

"Yes, it does."

He scowled and took a step toward her. She held her ground despite her desperate need to grovel. Being away from her brother all these weeks had given her courage she didn't know she had.

"I have given this plenty of thought," he said. Although he was taller than her, his height was nothing compared to Dracula. "I want to keep it. Whoever holds the dragon egg holds the most power. Why sell it when I can keep it for myself?"

Dread overcame her like a sheet of rain falling suddenly from the sky. "We will be a target. You will kill us all."

He grabbed her roughly by the arm, a new hunger for power in his eyes she had not seen to this degree before. When she didn't relinquish the egg, he made a grab for it, but she still didn't release it.

"No!" she cried. "This will be the death of us, Miles! The *death* of us!"

They grappled for the egg until they were both on the ground, the dirt turning into a cloud that choked and suffocated and clawed. Miles kicked her in the shin once, twice, and then the third time, the pain was too unbearable for her to continue to hold tight to the egg. Her grip failed her, and he triumphantly snatched it away.

"Don't, I beg you!" she cried again. She launched to her feet and threw herself at him, but he was much quicker than her. He wrapped his arm around her neck and squeezed, blocking most of her air flow.

"Dracula!" she wheezed. "Dracula!"

No answer came except the faintest of breezes blowing in from the north. Dracula had not followed her this time. There would be no one to help her.

Miles started dragging her in the other direction, and it was all she could do to keep her feet beneath her.

"You will return to the ship with me, and that is final. You retrieved the petrified egg for me, so I think I can overlook your recent disobedience. But try it again, and you will find I won't be so forgiving a second time."

A tear of regret trailed down her cheek as she watched Ichor Knell become smaller by the second. She had made a terrible mistake, and there was nothing she could do to reconcile what she had done.

****

Dracula returned to the castle with a heavy heart, his shoulders drooping as he veered toward the library rather than his bedchambers. How could he possibly sleep when his mate ran away with the egg?

A light from a candle flickered in the library, and when he turned the corner, he found Nicolae seated at one of the tables, his nose in a book. Though, from the empty look in his eyes, he wasn't sure whether Nicolae was reading the page or staring into nothingness.

"You couldn't sleep either?" Nicolae asked. When he glanced up, his haggard expression sharpened into worry.

"She's gone," he whispered. He slumped into the chair across from the other vampire when his legs could no longer bear his weight. "Nicolae, Elisabeta is gone."

Nicolae closed his book, and although he said nothing, he gave Dracula his complete attention.

The memory of Elisabeta sneaking out of her room and into the treasury squeezed his heart painfully. And she didn't just take the dragon egg, she took the ring as well. Was he really nothing more to her than a quest? Someone to cheat? He felt as if his entire being had torn apart, his heartache fierce, battered against an unforgiving tempest. Elisabeta had used him. She had taken from him his mating bond, something he could never have again. She had left him to face the rest of eternity alone. A lonely, painful eternity.

"I really thought she would choose me," he said quietly. "I clearly don't know her as well as I thought I did."

"Perhaps she will return."

He shook his head. "She will not. She made that abundantly clear."

Nicolae reached across the table and rested a hand on his shoulder. There was a world of empathy in his eyes. He knew exactly how it felt to lose a mate, and he could understand better than anyone else. Although Elisabeta was not dead, she might as well be.

Closing his eyes and releasing a shuddering breath, he asked, "Who else knows Elisabeta is my mate?"

"No one," Nicolae answered. "Lucian is the only other privy to that information."

"Good. Let's keep it that way."

Chapter 28

Months passed since Elisabeta had left Ichor Knell. The pain of leaving Dracula lingered fresh in her heart as if it had only happened yesterday. Not a day passed that she didn't regret what she had done, and now there was nothing she could do about her trespasses. They had been at sea ever since their departure, and short of jumping overboard and swimming to a land nowhere within sight, she had no choice but to stay on the ship.

Besides, if she jumped overboard, she would not just be risking her own life, but another's as well.

She placed a trembling hand over her belly, feeling a light kick in response to her touch. Leaving Dracula had been a grave mistake indeed, especially now that she carried his child. She stayed as far away from the ocean water as possible in the instance that the child she carried was a vampire and not a human. Should the child be exposed to salt in any way, it could die.

A knock sounded on the door, and she hurriedly snatched a blanket to cover herself. "Yes?" she called, making sure the blanket hid her belly.

Someone sighed heavily on the other side of the door. "Are you still pouting in there?" Miles asked, his voice muffled. "I haven't seen you in ages. Come out here or I will drag you out."

She panicked. She might have been able to hide her growing belly several weeks ago, but now her roundness was all too noticeable.

With a nervously pounding heart, she opened the door enough to only show her face. "I am feeling under the weather," she lied. However adept she was at lying, Miles was much better. He saw through her immediately.

"What are you about?" He peered at her suspiciously. "Is somebody in there?"

"No!" she gasped, appalled at the idea of letting *any* of the crew members pass the threshold into her room. "No one is in here, Miles."

Still, his brows furrowed with doubt. He nudged the door open wider and pushed past her. She scrambled to catch the door to stop him from barging in, but in the process, she lost her grip on the blanket around her shoulders and it fell to the floor. Her brother froze, staring at her belly with wide, shocked eyes. He said nothing for what felt like an eternity, and she waited for him to either strike her or yell at her.

Surprisingly, he did neither.

He closed the door and turned to face her. Slowly, his shock turned into anger, though the anger was not directed at her. "Which one of the crew members did this? I swear I will—"

"It's...it's Dracula's," she whispered.

Silence filled the room, at least until Miles began pacing the length of the small cabin, running a hand over his mouth. Finally, he stopped in front of her, clearly distressed. "I didn't mean for this to happen."

"Well, it did!" she snapped.

"What are we going to do?" he snapped back. "This is a *baby*, Elisabeta. A ship is no place for a baby." He began pacing again, and when he stopped, he said, "I cannot take you back there. To Ichor Knell."

"And why not? I want to be with Dracula. I never should have left."

Miles laughed hysterically and shook his head. "You want to be with a *vampire* over your own *brother*? It has been you and me all our lives. You cannot leave me behind now. We can put the baby up for adoption."

Tears threatened to escape her eyes. She was not usually emotional, but since being with child, her emotions now had a mind of their own.

"But what if the baby is a vampire?" she argued. "No human will want to adopt a vampire, Miles. You and I grew up without our parents. I cannot force my baby to suffer through the same thing."

He lifted a hand and she flinched as she braced herself for the pain, but he paused mid-air as if thinking better of it, and slowly lowered it again. He opened his mouth as if to argue further, but the frantic sharp toll of a bell interrupted him.

Both their eyes widened, and she followed him as he raced out onto the deck. The bright sunset alarmed her, and she instinctively turned away to shield the baby from the sunlight. However, nothing happened from the exposure. Her posture relaxed, at least until she saw why the crew had sounded the alarm in the first place. A ship was headed straight for them, and it did not appear friendly. The other crew hoisted their flag. The red and black colors filled her with dread.

The Sea Devil.

It was the pirate ship with one of the most ferocious captains to sail the waters. Like Miles, they left no survivors, but they often attacked ships for the pure enjoyment of it. In this case, she knew what they were after—the petrified dragon egg.

She didn't want to die, especially when she had not yet met her child. While Miles shouted out orders to a frantic crew, she retrieved her sword and returned to the deck, watching as the ship drew nearer.

Miles proudly hoisted their own flag for *The Scarlet Dawn*, a scarlet and yellow depiction of a snake with blood dripping from its mouth.

"You fool!" she cried as Miles rushed past. She grabbed his arm and glared at him. "I told you that you would kill us all. Get rid of the egg. Get rid of it!"

A grin split across his face as he jerked his arm out of her grip. "Oh, don't you worry, dear sister. *The Sea Devil* is not as fast as *The Scarlet Dawn*. Today, we will outrun them, make them work for what they want. And when they finally catch up, we will have a little surprise waiting for them."

He gleefully took up his place at the helm, continuing to sail straight toward the enemy ship. Elisabeta was terrified. Not for herself, but for her unborn child.

Her grip on the hilt of her sword tightened, and she was suddenly glad it wasn't made of iron. Human or not, she wanted to protect her baby with everything she had.

Her heart pounded harder and harder, sweat glistening on her brow the closer they sailed toward *The Sea Devil*. Soon, they were close enough that she could make out faces on board. Their weapons were drawn. They were ready for a fight.

Miles steered the ship closer and closer, and at the last moment, he turned the ship sharply, completely changing their course. The action took the other ship by surprise, and they hurried to follow after them, but by the time they turned their ship, *The Scarlet Dawn* had already overtaken them.

When they were far enough away from the other ship, her grip relaxed on her sword. She hoped Miles was wise enough to stop this before it turned into bloodshed.

Wearing a confident grin, her brother hopped down from the stern and saluted to *The Sea Devil*, which was much too far for anyone to have seen the gesture.

"Please," she begged, rubbing her belly for emphasis. "Dock the ship and allow me to disembark. This is too dangerous for the both of us."

"So you can run off to your vampire beau?" he laughed. "There is no time to dock. The game has already begun."

She paled as he left her side, and she once again turned her attention to the ship following them much further behind. She'd had enough of games in the past year to last her a lifetime. There had to be a way to convince her brother to dock. If he didn't, she and her unborn child were in grave danger.

****

Elisabeta woke abruptly as the ship jolted violently. At first, she thought nothing of it other than it was a deep-sea creature brushing against the vessel, but when the jolt happened a second time, she flew out of bed and threw her door open. The light of late afternoon smashed into her, and she shielded her eyes against the brightness. Chaos erupted in a flurry of activity on deck, men running to and fro as they attempted to put out a fire at the stern.

Dizziness threatened to collapse her knees, a feeling of sick dread tightening its grip on her now fully rounded stomach. It took a minute for the dread to pass before she found her head again. Miles. She needed to find Miles.

However, when she turned to locate him, her eyes widened when she found something else altogether. *The Sea Devil* had caught up to them after months of pursuit, and the ship looked much more formidable up close.

They were under attack.

A second wave of dread clutched at her midsection, stealing the breath right from her lungs. Her knees buckled and it was all she could do to catch herself on the railing. She was going to die. They were all going to die.

The Sea Devil shot another cannon, and it struck a hole straight through the middle of the ship. The ship jerked roughly, causing her to stumble to her knees. Fire at the stern spread even further, consuming a fourth of the ship within minutes.

Despite fear the size of a mountain, she struggled to her feet and rushed toward the flames. Many of the crewmen attempted to douse the flames with what remained of their drinking water. She took up a spot beside them and scooped a bucketful of water before tossing it toward the burning wood. The fire fizzled and hissed when the water hit it, but it continued to grow despite their efforts.

Still, she didn't give up.

Pain squeezed her midsection, and she gasped as if she had been struck by a cannonball itself. She bent over and nearly lost her lunch, and it wasn't until the pain faded when she continued to douse the flames.

It did no good.

The flames crawled up to the main mast, leaving half of the ship free of flames, and the other half doomed to a quick and sudden death. The sailor beside her threw his bucket down and ran in the opposite direction.

"Abandon ship!" he cried. "Abandon ship!"

But it was no longer the flames they need fear. The second ship had placed a platform between the two ships, and their crew began to board what was left of *The Scarlet Dawn,* striking down anyone in their path. Several of their sailors attempted to rescue the cockboat from the flames, but when their own clothes caught fire, they screamed and jumped overboard.

Once more, agony ripped through her abdomen, but she pushed through it with gritted teeth. Where was Miles? She needed to find Miles!

She frantically moved through the heavy smoke that filled the air, suffocating every breath she struggled to take. Enemy sailors ran right past her, likely not finding her a threat when she was both with child and unarmed. Her first instinct was to find a safe place to hide to protect her baby, but as the flames grew and the smoke thickened, the entire ship was dangerous. She needed to find Miles and escape to safety.

At last, she spotted him on the main deck, deep in combat with the captain of *The Sea Devil*. She watched in horror as the other captain disarmed Miles and produced a club, beating him on the head. Her own scream filled the air as Miles's limp body fell over the side of the ship and splashed into the water below.

The captain turned his attention in her direction,

and it was only then she noticed his missing eye, blood spurting down his face. He started toward her, but the ship jolted and groaned as wood splintered. In a single heave, it split right down the middle, throwing her from the deck and into the icy ocean water.

Violent water dragged her downward, further into its depths. No matter how hard she kicked, the ocean was determined to claim her.

Her head unexpectedly broke the surface of the water, and she gasped in a breath of air but only breathed in smoke. She coughed and spluttered, turning frantically in the water as she attempted to find help. A piece of splintered wood drifted by and she threw herself on it just in time for a wave of horrendous pain to rip and claw at her.

Her eyes widened with horror as she spat out a mouthful of salt water. No, no, no! Her baby was in danger, but as she glanced around frantically for a way to pull herself out of the ocean, she spotted land nearby. If she could only manage the swim…

However, she gasped when she spotted wet, red hair floating in the water. "Miles!" She couldn't leave him to the mercy of the unforgiving ocean.

She started to swim toward her brother, ignoring the screams of death and destruction behind her. With all her might, she heaved Miles onto the wooden plank, which dipped with their combined weight.

"Just hold on," she sputtered through her efforts to both propel them toward land while at the same time keeping Miles on the plank.

The effort proved to be too much, and Miles ended up rolling right off the wood. She dove for him but as a result, the wood floated away from them. She hadn't the strength to chase after it.

To her horror, blood began to spread through the water around her. Dark red blood. Her own.

"No!" she gasped as fear for her child consumed her, but the moment she opened her mouth, salty water entered, and she choked, hardly able to draw breath as she struggled to keep herself and Miles afloat. The shore was so close, but she didn't have the strength to reach it.

"Help!" she half-shouted, half-sobbed. "Someone, please!"

She continued to swim toward the shore, Miles unmoving and unresponsive. Keeping his head above water took every ounce of strength she possessed, and all the while, the blood continued to darken the water around her. Her abdomen constricted painfully, and she screamed in agony. Her grip on Miles slackened, and she nearly lost him to the sea. Somehow, she pushed through the pain until it ebbed. She didn't need to have experienced this pain before to know she was in labor.

"Please help!" she sobbed again. Another wave of agony ripped across her midsection, a horrendous pain that hit her like the attack on the ship earlier.

Just when her body was about to give up, she heard a pair of legs splash through the water, and moments later, strong hands heaved her from the ocean and cradled her in his arms.

"Miles," she sobbed. She struggled in the man's grip, but her attempts were so weak it did nothing at all.

"My son is seeing to him," the man reassured.

Another contraction clutched her abdomen with such ferocity that she could not help but to cry out. Her breathing quickened, her fists tightening against the man. She hardly noticed when they entered a house and he laid her down on a cot.

"Anna!" he shouted, and moments later, a woman with straight brunette hair and wide brown eyes entered the room. She must have been his wife. "I think she's in labor. Tell me what to do."

"Oh dear," Anna breathed. She rested her hand over Elisabeta's belly and frowned. Worry engulfed her, but she didn't get the chance to inquire over Anna's look when a contraction hit her at full force, this one much stronger than the last.

She screamed, tears trailing down her face. No more thoughts entered her mind other than getting this baby out of her. The pain was too much to bear.

"Fetch some fresh linen and a bowl of water, Clive," she ordered. "And fast. This baby is on its way."

Anna lifted her sopping wet skirts, soaked with both ocean water and blood. The next moments passed in a blur. She was hardly aware of who came in and out of the room when the pain was so great, and her only objective was to get the baby out. Breathing heavily, she pushed several times until she felt the baby slide out of her, but there were no cries to accompany the birth. The baby was not crying. There was no sound at all.

She knew the truth when Anna said nothing as she swaddled the baby in a clean blanket. Silent tears escaped her eyes. The tears, the heartache… They were more painful than all the contractions in the world.

"It is a boy," Anna said finally. "Would you like to hold him?"

Not trusting her voice, she nodded and took the bundle from Anna's arms. Indeed, the baby was stillborn, his face peaceful in death. Her tears came faster and hotter as she stroked the boy's hair, a full head of dark brown hair—just like Dracula's. She lifted his upper lip to find a pair of fangs sprouted from the baby's gums, no other teeth beside those in his mouth.

A sob escaped her, and then another. "I killed him. I killed my baby."

"You were in a shipwreck, dear," Anna said while squeezing her hand comfortingly. "You could not have prevented what happened."

Hugging her boy close, she shook her head. If only Anna knew. If Elisabeta hadn't taken the petrified dragon egg, she would not have been stuck on Miles's ship, and the ship would not have been attacked. The baby died from salt exposure in the ocean. She knew it without a doubt.

"He will never forgive me," she sobbed. "He will never take me back now. I have killed his son. I have killed him." Her head shot up as she suddenly remembered Miles. "What of my brother?"

Clive must have heard her question, because he stepped into the doorway, wearing a grave expression. "It appears he suffered a heavy blow to the head. Your brother—Miles—it seems he passed away when he received the blow. I am sorry. I am so very sorry."

In a single moment, her entire world shattered into a thousand pieces, broken shards of an irreparable mirror. She lost Dracula. She lost Miles. She lost her beautiful, precious baby. She lost everything.

Night fell, and she still hadn't set her baby down. Dracula's baby. She held tight to him, knowing the moment she put him down, his death would become all too real. She kissed his smooth forehead. She kissed his cold, plump cheeks.

"Alucard," she whispered into the darkness. "I will name you Alucard. May your soul rest in peace knowing you had the bravest, most selfless father in the entire kingdom."

One final tear rolled down her cheek before the dark nightmares of sleep claimed her.

Chapter 29

Four years later

Dracula stared out the window of the library as he often did, watching the border of the city carefully. His eyes scanned the edge of the trees, the visible parts of the city, and he even watched the front steps of the castle in case he might have missed something.

But there was still no sign of what he had hoped to see for years now.

"I have waited years for her to return," he whispered discouragingly. "She is not coming back."

He still loved Elisabeta to the same degree as when she had left—even more, perhaps, as the ache in his heart festered and burned. Memories of her lingered in his mind as if he had seen her only yesterday. Losing her felt like someone ripped a piece of his heart right out of his chest. A mate's bond lasted forever. And it was painful.

"I had hoped Elisabeta might return as well," Nicolae sighed, flipping the page of his book. "If she has not returned yet, then it's not likely she will return at all."

"But what if something happened to her?" he asked worriedly. "What if she got caught in a vampire trap? Or another thief took her life to obtain the dragon egg?"

Nicolae pushed his book away and looked directly at him. "This is the same Elisabeta who walked knowingly into a city of vampires as a human and made it back out safely. It's not likely an unfortunate death has befallen her. It's more likely she and her twin brother are living luxurious lives in a beautiful country far away."

Although Nicolae's reasoning made much more sense than his own distressing thoughts, he didn't want to believe it. To believe it meant to accept she didn't want him, and she was never coming back.

His friend came to stand by the window with him. His coloring appeared brighter than it had five years ago, his posture didn't droop quite as much, and his eyes didn't contain the torturous look over Madeleine's death.

"There comes a time," Nicolae said quietly, "when you have to accept your mate is gone forever. You can spend the rest of your life waiting for her, searching for her, even, or you can let her go. Elisabeta made her choice. Now you have to make yours."

He gripped the windowsill tightly as pain flashed across his heart like a bolt of lightning. To be rejected so soundly... He couldn't imagine a worser pain.

Slowly, his grip on the sill slackened until the rigidness in his entire body melted into acceptance. Five years had passed since Elisabeta left Ichor Knell. Nicolae was right. If she hadn't come back already, it meant she didn't want to.

"Then I suppose I will have to move forward," he said as he started toward the door. "Where is Ilona?"

"Dracula," Nicolae warned. "You don't know what you are doing."

"I do," he said coldly. "I have contemplated it for several years now. It's my only other chance, Nicolae. I have to try."

He turned back to Nicolae, heaviness in his expression. He had been weighed down by Elisabeta's absence for too long now. The nothingness he felt for Ilona was much preferable to the knife in his heart every single moment of every day from Elisabeta. He would welcome a lack of spark, a lack of love, if it meant he no longer had to feel this horrible ache.

Nodding with understanding, Nicolae replied, "Ilona is on the upstairs terrace."

He nodded his thanks and started toward the stairs. The castle had only begun to feel like home after a long period of adjustment. He knew every room, every nook and cranny, but perhaps that was just the captain in him talking. If he left any corner of the castle unturned, it meant potential places for invaders to hide.

Indeed, he found Ilona alone outside on the terrace. She hummed to herself while she watered plants she had planted herself. They were a species able to thrive without sunlight.

Clearing his throat in an attempt to not startle her, he walked out onto the terrace. "Ilona," he greeted. He was painfully aware that his heart felt as muted as a dull sword in her presence, but then he reminded himself it was better than a constant knife. "I like what you have done out here."

She looked to the ground and blushed. The blush made her curly brown hair appear darker. "Thank you, Dracula. Ichor Knell is finally looking like a city not crumbling to pieces. Do you not agree?"

"It will still be a while longer before we can call ourselves prosperous, but I do think we have made great progress."

He rested his arms on the stone wall and looked down below at the city. The near recent attack had made many vampires cautious. Some had left the city entirely. Others from the outside made Ichor Knell their home. Perhaps in another hundred years, they would be born from the ashes like a phoenix rising in the new generation.

"How are you?" she asked with a bright smile. "I have not seen you around lately."

"I have been busy is all."

He cringed at the way he sounded short with her. That was not the approach he was going for at all.

In an attempt to rescue his muddled attempt at conversation, he decided to get straight to the point. He had never been good at small talk.

"Actually," he said, turning to face her head on, "I wanted to see you specifically."

"Oh?" Her eyebrows furrowed, and she set her watering tin down to give him her full attention. "Is something wrong? Do you need me to do something for you?"

"I did not come as your shah."

He took a deep breath and contemplated if he really wanted to do this. There was still time to walk away. But then he dwelled on the aching pain that squeezed his chest with fierce talons, and he realized he *did* need to do this. If not for anybody else, then just for himself.

He pulled out a simple white handkerchief from his pocket and handed it to her. He watched as her eyes widened, her gaze drifting from the handkerchief in her hands to him.

She searched his eyes as if suspicious this was a trick. He should have done this from the beginning rather than allow himself to get caught in Elisabeta's guile. Life would be a sliver less complicated than it already was.

"Are you in earnest?" she finally asked.

"I am," he affirmed. "I should have done this long ago."

Her face turned beet red, and she couldn't even look at him as her timidity seemed to hit her at full force. One of her hands flew to her cheek as if she thought she could hide her blush. It was far too late.

"Oh," she whispered as her thumb almost reverently brushed the fabric of the handkerchief. She reached into a pocket hidden in the skirts of her dress and pulled out her own handkerchief, the very one she had given him years earlier. Her blush deepened as she pressed it into his hand. "I do not usually carry it around with me. An impulse, perhaps."

He swallowed the lump in his throat as he closed his fingers around her handkerchief. He hoped more than anything that Ilona could yank this knife out of his heart. He didn't know how to survive otherwise.

"Join me for a carriage ride tonight," he said. He planned to court her like a female was meant to be courted, not the whirlwind tryst he had with Elisabeta.

"I would love to."

He released a shaky breath. It did not stem from nervousness, but from malady. His stomach churned sickly at the thought of courting someone who was not his mate. But he could get past this. He *needed* to get past this.

"Then I will see you tonight," he said. He kissed her cheek and turned away quickly when bile rose up suddenly. This was wrong. This went against every vampiristic instinct he possessed.

But he had to try.

Giving her a nod of his head, he turned and walked in the other direction. If he took this one day at a time, then surely he could see this to the end.

****

Dracula and Ilona had been publicly courting for a couple weeks now, and although he found the distraction helped keep his thoughts off Elisabeta, it didn't take the knife out of his heart. But tonight, he hoped to change that.

His stomach churned unpleasantly at the thought of kissing someone who was not his mate. He dreaded it, but he hoped somehow, it would dispel the uneasiness and discomfort he felt as he spent time with Ilona.

Thoughts of stolen moments with Elisabeta and the kisses they had shared entered his mind, but he forced the thoughts away when the pain of her absence threatened to overcome him. If he didn't make this work with Ilona, then he would be alone for the rest of his life.

"Are you coming?" She smiled as she turned back to face him. "You seem a bit distracted today."

"Right," he said quietly, reminding his feet to move forward through the spacious Ichor Knell gardens.

The more steps he took forward, the sicker he became. He was overly aware of the perspiration gathering on his forehead. The bile rising in his throat once again reminded him this was not his mate. But he pushed through these uncomfortable sensations.

It was now or never. If he waited any longer to do this, he feared he wouldn't be able to pull through.

Ilona's hand was surprisingly soft as he took her fingers in his. Her breath hitched as he cupped the side of her face with his other hand. And then he leaned in slowly until his lips brushed against hers—

His stomach heaved violently, and he quickly jerked away from her before he doubled over. By some miracle, the bile didn't escape his mouth. The last thing he wanted to do was hurt her feelings by retching on her shoes moments after he kissed her.

"I am so sorry," he murmured. He straightened and rested his hand against the trunk of a tree, though he still clutched his stomach as if bile might escape at any moment.

"Are you ill?" she asked worriedly. She touched his arm, and the mere contact made his stomach heave once more. It was all he could do to force the bile down.

Ashamed of himself, he slid down with his back resting against the tree, his head between his knees. He felt ill. So very ill.

Emotion pricked his eyes when he realized this would never work. A relationship with Ilona could not exist when he had already mated with another female.

"Forgive me," he said, his voice cracking with emotion. "I had hoped this would not happen."

Ilona sat beside him, and thankfully, she didn't touch him this time. "Dracula, will you tell me what's going on? Did I do something wrong?"

He shook his head between his knees. He rarely shed tears, but he had never been this broken before. And there was nothing he could do to fix it. "No, you did nothing wrong, Ilona. It was me who made the mistake." He covered his eyes with his hand to hide the moisture gathered there.

"I made the mistake of mating with Elisabeta five years ago. I hadn't realized she was a human at the time. And then she left me behind. It seems as if my instincts will not allow me to find another mate. Please forgive me. It was never my intention to hurt you."

Several long moments passed in silence before she spoke. "I was unaware you mated with Elisabeta. It is me who should be forgiven of my trespasses. You have not seen her since? Do you know where she is?"

Again, he shook his head. "No."

"Do you want to talk about it?" she asked quietly. "As friends. I know now I can never be more to you."

He lifted his head to find a sad understanding in her eyes. He hated that he had put the sadness there, but he was sure his own expression mimicked hers. How lonely his future was destined to be...

"I wish I could hate Elisabeta for what she has done," he started, desperately needing to tell this to someone other than Nicolae. "But I have found I miss her terribly. I love her and I miss her, and I am angry and hurt that she left me. I don't understand why I wasn't enough to convince her to stay. Perhaps she doesn't love me as I love her."

She lifted her hand as if to rub his back comfortingly, but she seemed to think better of it and dropped it into her lap. "Did she tell you why she left?"

"She did not need to. She got what she had initially come to Ichor Knell for."

Silence fell between them, and the knife in his heart dug deeper. The space around them became darker, signaling dusk. Instead of happiness and relief he had hoped to find, he discovered quite the opposite.

His future looked bleak. Sure, he was the shah, and he could help rebuild this kingdom. Sure, he had great friends. But he no longer had his mate. He would never have the opportunity to have children. Grandchildren.

"If Elisabeta showed up tomorrow," she said hesitantly, "would you be happy to see her?"

"I don't know," he answered honestly. "I think I would be furious. My pride would be hurt."

She nodded and said nothing more on the subject. "Come on. Let's get you back to the castle. I think any longer in my presence and you might actually retch."

Dracula couldn't help himself—he laughed. He hadn't laughed in what felt like years. He was grateful for her understanding. For as bleak as his future might look, he was glad he was surrounded by great friends.

Chapter 30

Ilona pulled the hood of her cloak over her head and set out into the night. Her heart hurt far more than she cared to admit. She had waited so long to court Dracula, only to find out he could never be hers. Vampires mated for life, and he already had a mate. One who did not seem to care about how much he suffered without her.

But he deserved to be happy. More than anyone. And there was no better tracker in the entire kingdom than her. No matter how long it took her, she would find Elisabeta, and she wouldn't return to Ichor Knell until she did.

She paused mid-step on the bridge and took out the silky blue handkerchief she had stolen from Dracula's room. Gaining admittance to his chambers without alerting him of her activity was difficult. But she had her ways, and the moment she caught a whiff of the handkerchief, she knew it had belonged to Elisabeta. It still contained her faint scent.

Lifting the handkerchief to her nose, she closed her eyes and took a deep breath. Finding someone using a five-year-old scent would be next to impossible, but she had to try.

The scent stuck to her memory like stubborn pieces of lint. She shrank down into her bobcat transformation and wandered through the forest just outside Ichor

Knell. She wandered for hours, and she was just about to try another location when she caught Elisabeta's scent embedded in the ground. She lowered her nose to the forest floor and sniffed carefully, following the scent. It was almost imperceptible. Following it would not be easy.

She caught a more distinct trail of the scent and followed, weaving through trees, crossing the river, until finally the path she traveled became straight. When she reached another well-traveled path, her scent became lost among dozens of other scents, only to peek to the surface occasionally. Still, she followed the trail for hours until it led her to the great city of Ironfell.

Swallowing hard, she continued forward. Ironfell was a dangerous place for vampires. She would be risking her life if she stepped foot in the city.

But she continued forward anyway. For Dracula. She would do anything for the male she loved.

The skies started to lighten as early morning yawned and stretched upward. She quickened her pace and followed Elisabeta's scent until it stopped right at the edge of the docks.

"Drat," she whispered to herself as she untransformed in the shadows. She could not follow a scent over the sea, nor would she want to risk her life by traveling by boat.

It was time to ask around.

Chapter 31

Elisabeta had quickly learned life was much more difficult when choosing to live honestly. Five years had passed since she had stolen anything, since she had lied and cheated. But dishonesty had gotten her into this mess in the first place. Turning her life around had been the only other option. She had found herself a decent living working as a laborer in the wheat fields. She stayed with an old widow desperate for company in her lonely house, and it was just as well because she was lonely too.

She quickly suppressed her thoughts of the ones she loved before they overcame her. She did not want to cry in front of Alba.

"Are you headed to the gravesite?" Alba hummed from her rocking chair beside the glowing fire. The weather was only beginning to turn cold as autumn approached, but the old widow still wrapped herself in a blanket while she knitted gloves for winter.

"Yes," she nodded while lacing her boots, casting a mournful glance through the crack in her bedroom door at the petrified dragon egg she kept on her nightstand. She had found it washed up on the shore after the shipwreck, and although she had wanted to throw it back out to sea, she couldn't bring herself to part with it. It reminded her of everyone she had lost. "Don't wait up for me."

Grabbing the bouquet of wildflowers she had picked earlier, she wrapped a shawl around her shoulders and headed out the door. Her feet knew the path to the gravesite like the back of her hand. She visited every week—more if she found the time.

The afternoon turned into dusk, and she trekked onward until she reached a small, grassy grove bearing two headstones. *Alucard Ardelean* and *Miles Trelles* with their respective dates. It had taken years to save up for the headstones, but it had been worth it.

She lay half of the bouquet on Miles's grave and the other half on Alucard's before she knelt in the grass in front of her baby boy's headstone. She lightly trailed her fingers across his engraved name. The action was enough to undo her. Tears trailed ceaselessly down her cheeks as the memories of holding him in her arms one last time surfaced.

"I love you," she whispered to the air. The headstone blurred through the tears in her eyes, but she had memorized every bump and groove. She loved her dear boy with all her heart.

A twig snapped behind her, and she instinctively leaped to her feet and reached for her knife. To her dismay, it no longer rested on her hip. She had sold it two winters ago to pay for food.

She scanned the trees and saw nothing, but the sound had been too loud to have just been a small animal. Something or *someone* was here.

"Alba, is that you?" she asked as she scanned the trees once more. The elderly woman wouldn't have been able to make it up the steep slope.

Another twig snapped, and she spun around. Immediately, her eyes widened, and the air rushed from her lungs as she found herself staring back at familiar light brown eyes, a familiar soft, round face, and recognizable curly brown hair.

"Ilona?" she gasped. Despite Ilona having been competition for Dracula's affection five years ago, she wanted to throw her arms around her and hold her tight. Seeing her filled her with vigor she thought she had lost.

Ilona's posture relaxed considerably. "So you *are* alive," she sighed in relief. "After all the tales I had heard about the shipwreck, I all but lost hope."

"You were looking for me?" Her heart pounded fiercely as she glanced up at the boughs as if she might find a bat watching her from above.

"I have been looking for you for weeks," Ilona said. "But I am alone. Dracula does not know I left in search of you."

Disappointment pulled her heart into watery depths, but she didn't know what she had expected. Of course Dracula wouldn't come to find her. He had told her to never come back to Ichor Knell. He certainly would not want to see her still.

When she didn't answer, Ilona approached the grave, sadness passing over her face. "Dracula does not know, does he?" she asked. "Did he die in the shipwreck?"

"Yes." Another wave of tears pricked at her eyes. "The salt from the ocean killed him shortly before he was born."

"Then the boy was a vampire."

She nodded. Her heart ripped open as she relived the memories of that day. The fire. The screams. The death. The blood. What she wouldn't give to go back and make different choices to change the outcome of what had happened.

"Why are you here?" she asked when the sadness dragged on for far too long. "You of all people would want me to stay away so you could court Dracula."

"We tried that," Ilona muttered, inspiring a spike of jealousy in Elisabeta's heart. "He kissed me moments before nearly vomiting on my shoes. And then he broke down in tears, telling me how much he still loved you and missed you."

"What?" she whispered as she tried to comprehend Ilona's words. She wasn't sure what surprised her most—Dracula becoming sick over courting Ilona or him giving into tears or him still loving her. "How long ago did he say those things?"

"Three weeks ago. We ended the courtship before Dracula became too ill to stand, and I left that very night to find you and bring you home."

Home...

Her heart pounded with hope, but she turned her back to face away from Ilona as she tried to gather her thoughts. "Dracula told me to never return to Ichor Knell. He would be furious if I showed my face. And if he found out about Alucard..."

"Then he would drag you back himself," Ilona said. "If you don't return with me, I will tell him about his son. I am sure he would be furious with you either way." She lightly touched Elisabeta's elbow, turning her to face her. "What happened to the woman who was not afraid of the big, bad vampire?"

"She lost everything," she whispered, glancing toward the two graves. "I cannot leave Alucard. I...I need him."

"Dracula needs you. Even if he would never admit it to your face."

She wiped a tear away, and then another. She missed Dracula with all her heart. But what if she returned to Ichor Knell and he would have nothing to do with her? She would be risking her life by returning.

As if sensing she was on the verge of agreeing, Ilona said, "You can come back and visit Alucard often, and I am positive Dracula will want to come with you. Elisabeta, you cannot stay here and live in the past. You must move forward. You must make amends with Dracula." She reached out and took her hand to display the ring she wore on her finger. "You still have the kumari's ring. I don't believe you would have kept it if you didn't have the desire to return."

Cradling her hand to her heart, she shed yet another tear. Ilona was right. She needed to move forward, and she certainly wasn't doing that by staying here. But did she have the strength to leave her brother and her son?

Finally, she nodded. Facing Dracula would be difficult, but at the very least, she needed to make amends. Even if it meant risking her life in a city full of vampires.

"Just let me say goodbye," she whispered.

"Take all the time you need." Ilona gave her a sympathetic look. "I need to hunt anyway."

Her eyes widened in alarm. "You can't hunt here. I care about these people."

Ilona smiled and shook her head. "Dracula has passed plenty of laws since you've been away. I won't hunt anyone of consequence. Don't you worry."

With that, she disappeared, and Elisabeta turned back to the graves. First, she would say all her goodbyes, and then she would return to Ichor Knell with Ilona.

She didn't have the least idea of what to expect.

Chapter 32

Dracula rubbed his hand down his face as he poured over the documents before him while several of his advisors spoke in hushed tones around the table. However, they didn't sound hushed when he could make out every word and syllable. What he needed was peace and quiet. And to get out of this blasted chair.

"If I may," Ivar said, clearing his throat. "Trade with the humans is our best option."

"And the part about where we like to drink their blood?" Gabriel threw out there. "They would never accept our terms, and quite frankly, I don't think we should accept theirs either."

The entire room erupted into chaos as each vampire tried to make themselves heard above the others. Dracula wanted to slam his head against the wall. Or jump out the window. Whichever would make the arguing disappear quickest.

Not able to stand the noise any longer, he slammed his fist against the table. "Quiet!" he roared.

Immediately, the room hushed, each vampire clamping their mouth shut. Everyone looked to him, and once again, the weight of his position felt heavy on his shoulders. "What we need is an intermediary. Someone who appears non-threatening. Someone who can make this work. Someone who is—" The door opened right then, a head of long blond hair appearing moments later. "Nicolae?"

"Your Highness," Nicolae said with a bow. Thankfully, he only used formalities when around other people. "There is something you will want to see…"

He waved him away with a hand. "I am busy. After the meeting, perhaps."

Nicolae's lips pressed together, and he shook his head. "You will want to come immediately."

He resisted the urge to roll his eyes. Everybody wanted something of him all the time. When would he get two moments of peace to himself?

Adjourning the meeting for the time being, he followed Nicolae out of the room and down the hall. "What is so urgent that you needed to pull me from my meeting?"

"Ilona has returned," Nicolae answered, his expression serious. Dracula had only seen his friend this serious a number of times. His guard instantly shot up.

"Is she all right?" he asked worriedly. "She left suddenly. I had assumed she went hunting. But she's been gone for over a month…"

"She is fine. It is something else I think you need to see."

Their footsteps hurried down the hallway, and the more seconds that passed, the more worried he became. And drat this castle! If it wasn't so large, they would have arrived at their destination already.

Finally, they reached the great hall through the back entrance, and his eyes darted around the room until he found Ilona. She appeared unhurt, but the guilt on her face…

He glanced at the person at her side. He inhaled a

sharp breath and lost his step. He might have taken a tumble if he didn't quickly catch himself. His mouth fell open in disbelief as his gaze raked up and down the newcomer. She looked familiar but oh so different. Five years had aged her nicely, her face more feminine with a few more freckles across the bridge of her nose, her green eyes bright in the dim room, her curves more pronounced. She wore her red hair up in a neat but plain bun, and she wore a *dress*. He had never seen her wear a dress before.

And she smelled human.

"Elisabeta," he choked.

He wanted to pull her into his arms and weep. He wanted to shout at her and storm out of the room. But he stood frozen to the spot, such was his shock at seeing her again. He'd thought she would never return.

Remembering why she had left in the first place kindled his anger, pushing and pushing at him until he snapped his finger in the direction of the door. "Get. Out."

Her chin quivered, but she stood her ground. "No."

This was the Elisabeta he remembered. He'd always admired her stubborn side, but he didn't particularly like it just then.

"What part of 'never come back here' did you not understand?"

"The part where you made it sound like a rule," she answered with her head held high. "I don't like rules. Never have." She took a step toward him, and he took a step backward. "I am here to stay. For good."

Although she put up a brave front, her body trembled. She was terrified to be here. As she should be.

But he could put up a brave front too. He took a step forward and towered menacingly over her, his lip curling into a snarl. "You lost your right to be here long ago. If you want to stay, I recommend you find a place with the other humans. The ones we eat."

"You don't mean that."

"These humans are criminals. You will fit in nicely." He turned away, but she grabbed onto his hand.

"If you just let me explain—"

He jerked his hand out of hers, hating the way her touch upended him. It burned a fire within his chest. It slashed a knife across his heart. He needed to be alone, otherwise he feared he would fall apart. "I said... *Get. Out.* Of my castle. Of my city. Leave now!"

"Dracula," Nicolae said quietly. "You cannot toss her out. She has come a long way to get here."

"Watch me."

Nicolae glared at him and took Elisabeta by the elbow. "This is my castle too. She will be my guest. And until you can calm down enough to talk peaceably, she will stay with me."

They walked right past him, and he returned his friend's glare until they disappeared from the room. Only then did his shoulders slump. Elisabeta was here. After all these years, she was here, and he did not at all have the reaction he thought he would.

He turned around and stared at Ilona accusingly. "Why did you bring her here?" He paced back and forth across the room before finally stopping in front of her. "Why is she here?"

Ilona took his hand and looked at him earnestly. "Because you are my dear friend, and it hurts me to see you unhappy. At least now you have a chance to find the happiness you rightly deserve." She smiled, but the action didn't quite reach her eyes. "Elisabeta... She came willingly. I think she has been lonely too."

He shook his head, still unable to take in all the events of the last five minutes. Before he could reply, Ilona stood on her toes and kissed his cheek.

"Goodbye, Dracula."

His eyebrows furrowed worriedly. "Where are you going?"

"Somewhere I can find my own happiness. I don't think I can stay here and watch you find yours."

A pang hit his chest as he realized he was losing yet another friend. Not to death this time, but because she was going away. But still, he nodded. If this was what she thought was best for her, then he would support her. "You are welcome back anytime."

"Thank you," she smiled. "And perhaps when I come back someday, I will have a mate of my own." She gave his hand a squeeze and smiled one last time before exiting the great hall.

His frown deepened as his inner turmoil peaked. Elisabeta was here. After all these years, she had returned. And it hurt deeply to see her face again. What did she want this time? Jewels? Gold? The shah's ring circling his very finger? She would betray him again. He just knew it.

He kicked a chair in frustration and stomped out to the castle's training grounds. It had been a while since he'd felt the need to vent his frustration, but as he picked out a sword and dueled the new Captain of the Guard, he found that each parry, each blow helped lessen his anger, if only just a little bit.

The captain swung his weapon in a circular arc,

and he easily parried and returned with a swing of his own. They fought well into the hour, and he relished in the distraction from each and every one of his problems. The issues continued to pile up, and this most recent one outshined all the rest.

At last, he managed to disarm his opponent and called an end to the skirmish. He nodded his head to the captain, and the captain bowed while breathing heavily. It hadn't been easy finding his own replacement, but so far, he was satisfied with his choice—an outsider from a small coven of vampires from the north. Although the male wasn't quite fluent in Dracula's own language, he would get there someday.

Just as dusk rolled into Ichor Knell, he entered the castle, running a hand down his face as he finally faced the truth—Elisabeta had returned. She was here in the city, in the castle, even. And she was his mate.

"What am I supposed to do?" he asked himself under his breath.

He very well knew he couldn't possibly throw her out of the city, even if his anger demanded such a thing. He would *never* allow another vampire to feed on her, despite his threat. And after everything she had done to him, he still loved her.

Then why couldn't he trust her?

Once again, he lashed out at an inanimate object, kicking the wall as he passed by. Why had Elisabeta agreed to return with Ilona? Where had Ilona found Elisabeta in the first place? Had she been living in wealth like Nicolae had suggested not long ago?

He shook his head. The state of Elisabeta's dress and hair told him she lived in poverty unless it was a ruse.

What was a lie, and what was the truth?

He stopped short at his bedchambers, his eyebrows shooting up in surprise when he found a large sack sitting at the foot of his door. Glancing cautiously from one end of the hallway to the other and seeing no one within sight, he approached slowly and lifted the flap of the sack. His heart stopped momentarily as he picked up the petrified dragon egg, its scales just as pointed as he remembered them being five years ago.

"Elisabeta," he whispered to himself as he ran his fingers over the rough surface of the egg. "What happened to you since you left?"

Now he didn't know *what* to believe.

He clenched his jaw as he entered his room, set the egg aside, and replaced it with a quill and ink. If Elisabeta wanted to stay in Ichor Knell, he'd make sure she knew exactly what came with the package.

Chapter 33

Elisabeta stared out the window of the library as morning approached in Ichor Knell. She had forgotten how dark mornings in the vampire city were when sunlight didn't exist. Still, the lack of light comforted her, making her feel like she had finally returned home.

Nicolae entered the library holding a stack of letters in one hand and a book in the other. She knew she was cowardly for sticking close to his side over the past couple of days, but a part of her feared Dracula would make good on his threat to feed her to the vampires.

"A messenger asked me to deliver this to you," Nicolae said, his expression full of uncertainty. He handed her a letter, and she immediately recognized Dracula's handwriting. Her stomach tumbled nervously, her palms sweating as she broke the seal. The letter was short and to the point.

Elisabeta,

I am holding a feast tonight at dusk. I expect you to attend. Do not be late.

Dracula

"I would be careful if I were you," Nicolae cautioned as he read the invitation over her shoulder. "Dracula is still angry. Be prepared for anything."

She read the short letter again and frowned before absently running a hand through her hair, which a castle servant had pulled up into a more fashionable style. Her dress was borrowed as well from one of Nicolae's acquaintances. Five years ago, she might not have been able to fit in the frock two sizes smaller than her usual size, but she had lost weight since she'd last been in Ichor Knell. Poverty did that to a person.

"By feast, he means…"

Nicolae nodded. "A vampire feast."

Without her consent, her heart started beating rapidly, and an urge to flee the city overcame her. She stood, but her legs refused to obey her when she told them to run. Since when had she become a coward?

"I cannot attend," she whispered in fear. "He will eat me. Or feed me to someone else."

Surprisingly, Nicolae laughed out loud while he crossed the room and stood by the very window she left moments earlier.

"I think you need to become more acquainted with vampire culture," he smiled, his expression much lighter than it had been five years ago after losing Madeleine. "Dracula, furious or not, will defend his mate to his very last breath. You will be in no physical danger at the feast. Come here, Elisabeta. What do you see?"

She joined him at the window and looked out at the same scenery she had admired not even a minute earlier. "The entire city. Everyone looks miniscule from here."

Nodding, he said, "Vampire eyesight is better than a human's. I can see all the way to the border, and Dracula could too. Over the past five years, he stood in this very spot every day, watching for you to return. Make what you will of that information."

Heat blossomed in her cheeks as she envisioned Dracula watching for her. Hope returned to her at full force.

"Should I hunt for my own food for the feast?" she asked.

"Knowing Dracula's temperament, it would be wise."

She took a deep breath and let it out slowly. She knew Dracula respected courage, boldness, and a bit of flirtatious fun. But could she be that person again, even after she had lost so much of her light?

From the looks of it, Dracula had lost his light too. They were both broken, and she was here to fix the damage she had caused.

"Do you have a weapon I can borrow?" she asked, though she knew Nicolae was the last person in Ichor Knell she should ask.

"I do not, but I believe you will find what you need at the training grounds."

She swallowed hard at the thought of going back there again. "What if I run into Dracula?"

"Is that not what you came to Ichor Knell for? Consider it another opportunity to earn back his favor."

Earning back his favor sounded much easier than it actually was.

Pushing back her fear and uncertainty, she held her head high and walked through the castle, past vampires who watched her in confusion, and padded across the training grounds currently in use by vampire males. She smirked. It seemed as if Dracula still wouldn't allow females into his army.

Her smirk died instantly when several pairs of eyes flashed red as they watched her pass, and suddenly, she didn't feel quite so brave anymore.

Please spare me, she prayed to no god in particular. She had never been religious and being caught between a world of humans and a world of vampires made that aspect all the more confusing.

She took a deep breath and let it out slowly as she continued forward, expecting to get attacked at any moment, but no attack came. Instead, she received more curious stares as vampires ceased practicing just to watch her walk across the field and enter the armory.

The armory itself looked exactly as she remembered it to be, and the sense of familiarity brought her back to a time that changed her life. It had changed *her* and made her yearn for it again. She wanted to spar with Dracula, in more ways than one. She wanted to sit and listen to Nicolae droll on about philosophy and other subjects she didn't quite understand. She wanted to witness Lucian's odd behavior and hear his odd theories.

But first she needed to earn Dracula's trust.

A large vampire with long brown hair pulled back at the nape of his neck approached her and said something in a language she didn't understand. She stared blankly at him until he spoke again, this time slower and in her own tongue.

"Human," he said, pointing to her.

Elisabeta pointed to herself. "Dracula's mate. Elisabeta. I need to borrow weapons." She then pointed to a rack of knives only a few feet away.

The vampire's eyebrows furrowed as he looked her up and down before a dawn of understanding filled his expression. His gaze darted to the kumari's ring she still wore on her finger before he dipped into the briefest of bows.

"Apologies, Mrs. Dracula," he said, carefully choosing his words. "Shah say you come."

Dracula knew she would come to the armory? Then this must be one of his games.

Not wanting to linger any longer than necessary, she borrowed a belt to strap around her dress and located a couple of knives, tucking them into the belt. Then she found a bow and a quiver of arrows before setting off toward the woods. The hairs on the back of her neck stood up, and she glanced over her shoulder to find one of the vampires with red eyes watching her closely. She shuddered and quickened her pace until she was safely concealed within the trees where she breathed easier.

These trees...this forest...she was home.

"Alucard," she whispered to the skies. "If only you could see this, I know you would love it here."

Her son would have been four years old had he lived.

She placed her hand to her heart and closed her eyes as she remembered the baby boy she had held in her arms only years ago. She and Dracula had created something beautiful together, and she liked to believe that somewhere, Alucard was laughing and playing in the afterlife. If Ylios and Iqris truly did exist, she hoped they watched over her little boy until she someday joined him in the heavens.

A twig snapped behind her and her eyes flew open as she spun around while drawing her knife. She pointed it menacingly in the direction of the sound, but there wasn't a soul in sight.

"It's just an animal," she tried to reassure herself,

but then a sick feeling of dread overcame her when she remembered vampires could turn into animals.

She needed to travel further away from Ichor Knell to hunt.

Once again, she quickened her pace but forced herself not to run. The sound was nothing more than her imagination playing tricks on her.

A rustle in the bushes to her left set her heart to panicking. She sprinted forward now with both knives drawn. The bushes rustled louder, and a flash of gray pounded after her as she ran. It was then she knew the truth.

Someone was hunting her.

Her breath quickened in rhythm with her frantic feet. She sprinted over rocks and protruding roots. She splashed through the river, soaking the hem of her dress, and losing both her shoes at the same time. And then she glanced over her shoulder just in time for a large gray wolf to pounce.

Her scream echoed through the forest as the creature knocked her to the ground. When it opened its massive jaws, she shoved her knife into its neck. The creature released a pained whine, distracting it long enough for her to escape from beneath it. She scrambled to her feet and dashed in the opposite direction, but when she looked back again, it wasn't a wolf chasing her but the same vampire who had been watching her with hunger in his eyes.

And he was fast—much faster than her.

The vampire tackled her to the ground once more, and when he sprouted his fangs, she swiped her other knife at him, only managing to graze his cheek with the tip. He wrenched her weapon away with a strong hand.

She attempted to clamber away, but the vampire grabbed onto her ankle.

He sank his fangs into her skin.

She cried out in pain when the vampire sucked a mouthful of her blood. She kicked at him, but her attempts were feeble at best compared to a vampire much stronger than her.

She reached for her bow and an arrow, but before she could string the arrow, a blur of black soared down from the skies and turned into a burly vampire before her eyes. He grabbed the vampire around the throat and yanked him off her, only to slam him against the nearest tree with his feet dangling a foot above the ground.

"Are you aware of who she is?" Dracula growled, squeezing his fingers tighter around the vampire's throat until he clawed desperately at his hand. When the vampire shook his head, Dracula's lip curled into a snarl. "She is my mate. The punishment for feeding on my mate is a long, torturous death. You would be wise to remember that."

He dropped her attacker who scrambled away with her blood still dripping from his mouth and a knife still lodged in his neck.

Never in the time she had known him had Elisabeta seen Dracula this furious, not even when he learned she was a human. His fists curled and uncurled, his lip still pulled into a snarl as he watched the vampire flee back toward the city. Only when he disappeared from sight did he turn to face her.

Immediately, his expression softened, and although he said nothing, the tender way he looked at her confirmed what Ilona had told her about his feelings.

He still loved her. She could see it now.

His gaze darted to her ankle, and his nose twitched as he sniffed the air. She knew he was searching for venom in her blood, but he seemed satisfied that there was none when he transformed back into a bat and flapped toward the boughs of trees.

She released a tense breath. If he had arrived any later, the vampire would have killed her.

She brushed her fingers over the two puncture wounds in her ankle, and her heart leaped as a terrifying thought crossed her mind. If she wanted to earn back Dracula's trust, she needed to become a vampire. Then he would understand the depth of her sincerity.

Swallowing the fear lodged in her throat, she reached for a sturdy branch to help support her weight and stood on shaky feet. Once, she told herself she would never become a vampire. Not for anything or anyone.

But now she would do it for Dracula.

****

Taking Nicolae's advice very seriously, Elisabeta entered the great hall cautiously, mentally preparing herself for anything Dracula might throw her way. When she walked inside the vast room, she found an entire table full of vampires already sitting with Dracula at the head. Every pair of eyes turned in her direction, and all at once, chairs scraped against the floor as everyone stood in her presence, including Dracula.

The great hall erupted into whispers, and she didn't need vampire hearing to know they were all talking about her. Likely, everyone now knew she was Dracula's mate and obviously had something to say about it.

"I wasn't sure you had the guts to join us tonight," Dracula said, which effectively silenced every whisper in the room.

"Then I would be a poor mate indeed to the infamous Dracula the Impaler." She stood tall and stared him down, reminding him who she was to him and that she was aware of exactly who he was as well.

Another wave of murmuring filled the room, at least until he silenced everyone with the raise of his hand. He continued to glare at her, but she would not be cowed. If he wanted to play this game, then she would play.

And she would win.

She ignored the pain flaring in her ankle as she took the only empty seat at the end of the table, directly across from Dracula with a couple dozen vampires between them. When she sat, everyone else followed. Nicolae sat on Dracula's right and Lucian on his left. They both wore cautious expressions, as if they expected something to happen very soon.

Dracula clapped his hands, and moments later, servants dragged in several humans who looked terrified out of their minds. She swallowed hard when she realized where his game was headed, but she forced herself not to react.

"This man right here," he said as he grabbed a human man by the back of his shirt and looked directly at her, "targeted innocent women and children and performed unspeakable acts."

Without warning, he snapped the man's neck and tossed him aside, all while carefully watching her reaction. A long time had passed since she'd seen someone die in a brutal manner, but she forced her facial muscles to relax and held her head high as she watched.

He grabbed the next human, who tried but failed to struggle away from him. "This man is a thief. He stole directly from the Emperor himself."

This time, he grabbed a knife and rammed it into the man's throat, never taking his eyes off her as he did it. The man gagged on his own blood and struggled to breathe, and then finally he lay still.

Her expression remained impassive.

"And this man…" he said as he grabbed the final human and slammed his face down on the table. The man whimpered, but it didn't sound quite right. It was then she realized these criminals previously had their tongues cut out. "He killed a ten-year-old vampire child. We show vampire killers no mercy."

He didn't kill this one, but rather held out a knife to her.

She clenched her jaw as she stared back at him, searching for the jest, but there was none. He was completely serious from the hardness of his eyes to his rigid posture as he waited on her answer.

"Killing and feeding on humans is at the core of being a vampire," he continued. "If you want to stay in Ichor Knell as a human, then you have to act like us, you have to accept us, and sometimes you will have to get your hands dirty."

Images of red flashed across her mind as the shipwreck came unbidden to her mind. She saw Miles bleeding and lifeless in the water. She saw her own blood staining the dark water red as she lost her child. And she remembered her vow to herself to turn her life around. Killing her own kind was not turning her life around.

But she would become a vampire. If not today, then soon.

She attempted to stand, but the pain of the punctures in her ankle caught her off guard and collapsed her back to her chair. Did Dracula see her as weak? For years, she had felt weak. After losing the ones she loved, she had felt beyond weak.

She clenched her teeth as she bore the pain and forced herself to her feet once more. She was *not* weak. This man had killed a child, vampire or not. Thoughts of someone killing her own son should he have been but four years old or ten caused her anger to grow hot.

Instead of walking around the table, she drew her own knife, one she had kept from the armory. It felt good to have a weapon on her person at all times again.

Dracula roughly grabbed the murderer by the hair and lifted his head to give her a clear shot. It was the fear in the man's eyes that gave her pause. Who was she to take a life?

But then she remembered the emerald kumari ring on her finger. If she was to rule by Dracula's side, there would undoubtedly be times she would need to enact the law and bring justice to those who had been wronged. This was exactly what he was testing her for. He didn't care if she killed a human or not. What he cared about was to see if she could do what was necessary.

It seemed as if everyone in the room held their breath, even her. She drew back her arm to take aim, and then she threw the knife, the sharp point going straight through the man's eye.

Dracula dropped the man back to the table and

looked at her with surprise. He clearly hadn't thought she would do it.

She quietly returned to her seat as everyone resumed talking and whispering. The servants filled goblets with the blood from the dead humans, and when Dracula received his goblet, he seemed to finally gather his bearings. The scowl returned to his face as he glared at her, and she glared right back, showing him she wasn't afraid of him.

He sprouted his fangs as if he meant to intimidate her. She took off the lid from her tray of food and made a show of wafting the smell toward her nose, taking a deep breath, and releasing pure satisfaction.

Two could play at this game.

Peering at her over the rim of his goblet, he took a long swig of the blood and licked his lips while never taking his gaze off her. She played along and dug her fork into her meat, giving him a coy look as she lifted her utensil to her mouth. She might have smiled at the way this took her back to the days when she had only just met him, but his expression was anything but jovial, which effectively held her back.

Who will lose the game first, Dracula? her eyes asked him. He answered with a resounding glare.

She lifted another forkful of meat to her mouth and made a show of savoring the bite. He did not appear amused.

She lifted her own goblet of water to her lips and broke eye contact with him as thoughts of the deceased ten-year-old boy filled her mind. To die at such a young age... It broke her heart.

Finally, she raised her gaze and her voice as she asked, "Whose child was the one that got killed? No one should ever go through such loss."

"And what do you know of loss?" he scoffed as he waved his goblet of blood in the air. "All you have ever done is take and steal."

Anger flashed through her, and her chair nearly toppled to the ground as she stood abruptly. The room fell into yet another awkward hush. She ignored the protesting pain in her ankle. "What do I know of loss?" Before she could stop them, tears rolled down her cheeks as she finally broke—surely, exactly what he had been hoping for. Although they had an audience, she glared back at him as if he was the only person in the room. "Miles is dead." Her voice quivered, and she almost couldn't say the next part. "My baby...your baby...he is dead as well. And yet, you sit there and mock me."

His goblet *thunked* to the table as he stared back at her in disbelief. Gone was the anger, the glare, replaced by complete and utter shock.

She continued vehemently, "Don't you *dare* speak to me of loss as if you know the meaning of the word. There is nothing more painful in this world than losing your child."

She swiped a hand across her eyes and felt his gaze bore into her as she rushed from the room with a slight limp. She ran up the stairs, across the hallway, and she didn't stop until she reached her bedchamber. She grabbed the first of her belongings within reach and stuffed it into a knapsack, not caring if everything ended up in a wadded lump. If he didn't want her here, then she wouldn't stay.

Perhaps returning to Ichor Knell had been a mistake after all.

Chapter 34

Dracula stared down at the table with wide eyes as he tried to wrap his mind around Elisabeta's words. *Baby? He?*

"By the nine," he whispered, running a hand over his face. He felt like such a fool. Such an utter fool. He had been holding fast to his stubborn pride, all while she was suffering through this loss on her own. They had a child? How had he died? What happened?

"You were a father?" Nicolae asked with the same disbelief that stood out on his own face. "Did you know?"

He shook his head. "No, but I think I finally understand why she never came back until now. I am a complete fool."

When he stood abruptly from the table, he ignored the stares and whispers directed at him. Court would have gossip to fuel the entire city for months or even years to come at this rate.

He followed after her wildflower scent, which led him right to her bedchamber. He needed answers, and perhaps he needed to apologize as well.

He swallowed hard and shook his head in shame. How could he not have known? True, she had left before the baby's heartbeat would have started, so he wouldn't have been able to hear it. But still, how could he not have known about his own son?

Taking a deep breath, he dared to knock on her door. The flurry of activity within stopped for a moment before the door opened to him. She did not appear surprised in the least to see him, as if she had been expecting him to show up at her door.

His gaze drifted from her face to her packed bag. Panic shot through him as if an arrow struck him in the heart. "You are leaving?"

She left the door open and continued to pack what few belongings she had brought with her. "You clearly don't want me here, and I can't keep up this battle with you. If the time comes that you *do* want me here, come find me."

He silently watched her from the doorway, sensing the barrier that prevented him from entering the room. How could he have let his pride come between him and the woman he loved? It was tearing them apart. Again.

"I don't want you to leave," he said quietly.

"Really?" She stopped to raise a skeptical eyebrow. "That is the exact opposite of what you have been telling me since I arrived." She sighed, her shoulders drooping dejectedly. "I want you to want me, Dracula. For who I am, despite what I have done. And I don't want you to want me just because you have learned of our child. You refused to listen to me when I first arrived, and you don't deserve to listen to me now."

He nodded, noticing he was calm. Completely calm. She had successfully reined in his overbearing pride. "That's fair," he agreed. "But it's obvious I have misjudged the situation. Please. Give me another chance. I am listening now."

She wavered, pausing her packing. She bit her lip and looked at him with uncertainty, all while he held his breath. Finally, he felt the invisible barrier drop on the door even though she said nothing to confirm it. He entered the room and closed the door behind them. For the first time since he had learned she was a human, he was glad she wasn't a vampire and couldn't hear the way his heart pounded loudly in his chest. He hadn't been alone with her in a very long time. Not since he had asked her to become his kumari.

As he approached, she watched him cautiously, distrustfully. He sat at the table in hopes his lack of intimidating height might put her more at ease.

And daggers, she looked more beautiful than he remembered, especially as the soft candlelight flickered off her red hair. He had a sudden urge to touch it, to feel the soft tendrils between his fingers, but he refrained, if only just.

"I suppose I should start with that night," she began. She took up the space beside the window and looked out, facing away from him. She didn't say anything for the longest time, as if it hurt her to relive the past.

"Go on," he said encouragingly, and he watched as the faintest of shimmers reflected in her eyes.

"I was more loyal to Miles than you gave me credit for," she continued finally. "I took the egg and delivered it to my brother, but I realized it was a mistake. We grappled for the egg after I told him of my intention to bring it back to you that very night. He was stronger than I was, and he dragged me all the way back to Ironfell and onto his blasted ship."

When she turned to face him, tears streamed down her face. He wanted to reach out and wipe her tears away, but he refrained. He needed to hear the rest of the story.

"It was on the ship when I learned I was with child," she continued in a husky whisper. "I begged Miles to let me off the ship in fear that my child was a vampire. He refused to listen to me. Miles kept the egg. He would not sell it. Our ship got attacked."

He stood and moved closer to her—as close as she would allow.

"What happened after?" he asked quietly, though he could venture a wild guess.

"The pirate captain killed Miles and I went into labor. They set fire to the ship. I…" Her chin quivered, and this time he couldn't resist the urge to reach out and place his hands on her shoulders, gently caressing her neck with his thumbs. Thankfully, she didn't oppose.

"I fell into the sea. A kind couple helped me and Miles's body out of the water, and the woman delivered the baby… Alucard was stillborn. A vampire. The salty sea had killed him." Her tears came unceasingly now. "Before the wreck, I had been confident you might have taken me back. But after Alucard's death… I couldn't bring myself to return. I returned to ask for your forgiveness. For all my many mistakes."

"Alucard," he whispered. "It's my name spelled backward."

"Yes."

"I was a father." He dropped his hands and leaned heavily against the wall as the information rushed over him. Disbelief turned into guilt as he realized he had a hand in all of this too. "If I had gone after you, Alucard would still be alive."

"There are too many 'ifs' to beat yourself up about it. I have gone through every 'if' in the book, but I cannot change what happened. Neither can you."

Shock stabbed him with a hundred icy needles. Elisabeta, his mate, had given birth to his child. The child was now gone, and although he had never met him, he felt an acute ache beginning to form in his chest for what could have been. He should have fought harder for her. He should have stopped her from leaving.

She touched his hand, startling him out of his somber thoughts. Her eyes were alight with hope, the tears now gone from her face.

"Will you take me back, Dracula?" she whispered. "Or is it too late?"

Honestly, he didn't know what to think anymore. He was confused and learning about his deceased son confused him even more.

"You are a human," he replied before turning his back to her. "As long as you are a human, you can still betray me. You can still leave me again. You can still hurt me. I can't...I can't give you that power."

"And what if I wasn't a human?" She stepped around him, so they faced one another again. She stood on her toes, her breath tickling his ear as she whispered her next words. "Bite me, Dracula. Turn me into a vampire like you."

His heart skipped involuntarily with surprise as he stared back at the sincerity in her fiery eyes. For a moment, he was at a loss for words. She used to detest the idea of becoming a vampire. What changed her mind?

"I want this," she continued in a whisper, and this time, her lips grazed his ear. A shudder ran up his spine, and he released a shaky breath. He threaded his fingers through her hair, finally giving into the temptation to touch those beautiful locks.

He turned her head to expose her neck, her scent overpowering him and making him lose his mind. He needed her so badly. He needed her in his life, by his side. He needed to feel her lips against his.

She kissed his jaw, and then right below his ear. "And then you can be my mate as I am yours."

He breathed in sharply as he mentally dumped cold water on his self-control and pushed her away.

"No," he shook his head with finality. Although he had never turned anyone before, he had seen firsthand the pain of transitioning. "I cannot put you through such pain, Elisabeta. Besides, I made you a promise years ago that I would never bite you."

The light, the hope, the life drained from her eyes, and he hated for being the one to do it. She shouldered her pack and nodded to him. "Then I believe we have nothing more to discuss. Goodbye, Dracula."

Before he could wrap his mind around her words, she slipped from the room, leaving no trace but her intoxicating scent of wildflowers. He wanted to follow after her—he *knew* he should follow after her—but his confused heart tripped over itself. Instead of dashing from the room and enveloping her in his arms, he fell to his knees as a wave of heartache and confusion overcame him. Everything he had assumed in the past five years had been a lie.

Chapter 35

Elisabeta had no intention of leaving Ichor Knell just yet.

She dashed down the corridor of the castle as fast as her wounded ankle allowed. Instead of taking a right that led to the entrance of the castle, she took a left, hurrying down the hallway leading to Nicolae's chambers. This needed to happen now, before she lost her nerve. If Dracula wouldn't turn her, she knew Nicolae would.

Her knuckles rapped urgently on the door, and she glanced behind her to make sure no one had followed, especially not Dracula. When Nicolae didn't answer immediately, she rapped on the door again. This time, he opened it, surprise lifting his eyebrows.

"Elisabeta," Nicolae said. "What are you doing here? It's getting late."

"I need to ask a favor of you," she said, moving past him into his room. The room was spacious and filled with books, from the large volumes resting on his desk, to stacks of manuscripts filling his bookcase. The room opened up into a smaller study, also filled to the brim with books.

"And what is this favor, may I ask?"

Turning to him, she took a deep breath and said, "I want you to turn me into a vampire. Dracula refuses to do it, but he is still refusing me because I am a human."

Nicolae's expression hardened, and instead of replying immediately, he strolled to the opposite side of the room where his books sat on his desk. He rested his hand on top of one, but he didn't open it.

"What you are asking of me..." he finally started slowly as he turned his gaze to her. "I am not sure you understand what it implies."

"Please, Nicolae," she whispered as she approached and tugged on his billowing sleeve. "I beg you. This is my only chance."

He studied her for a long moment as if contemplating the feat in his mind. What didn't she understand? She knew it would be painful. She knew she would only wish for death during the transition. But she would be just like Dracula, and maybe he would want her again.

"Are you sure you want to do this?" he asked, wearing a hesitant expression. "It comes with...implications."

She swallowed hard, fear creeping into her heart. "What implications?"

"As you are probably familiar with, vampires are born not very fertile to begin with. It takes many years, even decades to conceive a child. But..." He took a deep breath and let it out slowly. "If you are a human female and a vampire bites you... The venom will kill many of your eggs, giving you an even lower chance of ever conceiving. Of course, there is always a chance, but it is not very likely you will have another child if I turn you."

Her eyes started to water as she fought back tears. After losing Alucard, she wanted another child to help fill the gaping hole in her heart. But Dracula wouldn't have her as a human, and she didn't want anyone else but him. Her only chance to ever have another child with him was if she became a vampire.

A tear slipped down her cheek, but she nodded. "I am sure."

He released a shuddering breath despite his calm demeanor, as if he were remembering Madeleine's transitioning. He gently took her elbow and led her to the bed. "Make yourself comfortable, Elisabeta. It will not help much, but it is something at least. I warn you that this will be excruciating, and it will be slow."

"I am prepared."

He gave her a regretful look as she laid down on the bed. Her heart pounded wildly as he sprouted his fangs. Yellowish venom dripped from their pearly white luster. Each of her breaths came out as fearful shudders, but she had lost so much already. She refused to lose Dracula too.

Nicolae moved her hair away from her neck, and she braced herself when she felt his breath on her skin. In a flash, his sharp fangs dug into her neck, and she gasped at the pain alone. It was instantaneous. A blinding, hot sensation filled her neck, excruciating as if her blood burst into flames.

She could not stop herself—she screamed.

Chapter 36

Dracula bolted upright from his knees. He would recognize that cry anywhere.

Elisabeta.

He had never moved faster in his life as he ran after the sound of her cries of pain, a thousand scenarios flashing across his mind—mostly about a vampire attacking her and consuming her blood. The thought made him run faster until he burst into Nicolae's room only to find Elisabeta on the bed thrashing in pain while Nicolae held her hand. One look and he knew exactly what had happened.

"What have you done?" he thundered, marching through the door, no barrier of permission to stop him this time.

"I did what you couldn't," Nicolae answered calmly as he stepped aside.

He pushed past him and stopped short beside the bed where Elisabeta lay, her hair splayed out around her as she writhed in pain. Every negative emotion connected with her fled from him. Betrayal. Hurt. Sadness. Heartache. They all disappeared as he knelt beside her. She breathed heavily, her face contorting with agony. Sweat beaded her entire body as if fire burned her from the inside.

He took her hand and trailed his fingers through her hair again and again as if his touch alone could take away her pain. It didn't.

She screamed again, but this time it didn't sound quite human. It sounded like a mix between a human scream and a vampire screech. She was already transitioning.

"My sweet Elisabeta," he whispered. "I'm here. You won't have to go through this alone." And then turning to Nicolae with a snarl, he ordered, "Fetch fresh cloth and cold water. And while you're at it, a goblet of blood. She will need it when the transition is complete."

Nicolae nodded and disappeared, leaving him alone with Elisabeta, who appeared delirious and hardly aware of his presence. She thrashed and screeched and wheezed. He watched helplessly. There was nothing he could do to ease the pain of the vampire transition. Although he had never experienced it himself, he had seen firsthand the horrific pain that followed a vampire bite. He wished he could take it away.

Finally, Nicolae returned with the cloth and water, and Dracula dipped the cloth into the basin and placed it on Elisabeta's hot, sweating forehead. Her writhing stopped for a few moments, and he was relieved at least something helped.

"Why, Nicolae?"

With a sigh, his friend pulled up a chair to sit beside them, but Dracula preferred to stay kneeling on the ground where he could remain as close to Elisabeta as possible.

"She came to you first," Nicolae answered. "She asked you first, but you wouldn't bite her. Elisabeta thought it was the only way you would want her again."

He was a fool.

She was his mate, despite the bitter sting of her

betrayal. He should have opened his arms to her when she returned to Ichor Knell. He should have been beside himself with happiness that she had returned at all. Instead, he wasted precious moments with anger and resentment. He had pushed her away to the point where she thought the only way she could be with him was to turn into a vampire.

"Foolish female," he whispered as he stroked her long red tresses once more. Truthfully, he had missed her beyond imagination. Bond or no bond. He missed their little games. He missed their deep conversations. He missed everything about her, and dare he say it, he almost missed those ugly trousers she used to wear.

Almost.

He spent long hours beside her during the painful process of transitioning. She writhed. She perspired. She screamed. And it tortured him. This was his fault. If he had been forgiving from the beginning, this wouldn't have been necessary. Right then, he vowed to himself he would love her no matter what. He would forget the heartache of the past and love her because her mere presence filled him with joy. He hoped one day, she might feel the same way about him too.

He felt a movement beneath his head, and he hadn't realized he had fallen asleep until he heard Elisabeta say his name.

His head shot up and relief spread through him when he noticed the lack of perspiration on her skin, the nonexistent writhing and screaming. Her skin looked a shade paler, and he couldn't tell if her transition caused it or if she looked pale because of the ordeal she just endured. But what took him aback most were her red eyes. She was thirsty.

"Elisabeta," he whispered. He kissed her hand. Her arm. Her cheek. Her head. "Please forgive me. I wish you hadn't felt the need to do this. This is my fault."

She opened her mouth to speak, but her voice came out raspy and indecipherable. "Water," she finally managed to say. "Please, I'm so thirsty."

Instead of fetching water, he reached for the goblet of blood Nicolae had brought earlier and held it to her lips. She drank thirstily like a human who had been trapped in the desert for weeks. When she finished, her eyes flashed back to green. The transition created a hollow ache inside of him.

"There is nothing to forgive," she said, handing the goblet back to him. She hadn't grimaced over drinking human blood, which brought him a small amount of relief. "It is I who needs your forgiveness. I did something to you that was downright cruel."

Yes, it had been downright cruel. But he had never felt more alive than in those weeks of knowing her.

"Was there any point—" He paused as he contemplated his next words. But he was no coward, and he needed to know the answer. "At any point, did you love me? Or was it all just tricks and games?"

She nodded weakly. "I realized I loved you when you kissed me for the first time."

"In the forest during the Game?"

She smirked, which eased the tension inside of him. He remembered the look well. "Wasn't it you who told me those weren't real kisses? Now you finally admit it?"

"I admit nothing," he replied as he crossed his arms, but his grin bellied his stubborn display.

When she placed her hand on top of his, a deep

gratitude filled him just from her mere presence. He had missed her terribly, and now that she was here, he never planned on letting her go again.

"I still love you, Dracula," she said quietly. "You didn't have to be my mate for me to remain completely loyal to you. I hope you will take me back. But if you want me to leave, then I will."

He rested his forehead against hers and whispered, "Never again, draga mea. I am yours."

They remained silent for several minutes, and he hungrily drank in her new scent. No longer did she smell like a human, but she smelled distinctly vampiristic, although she still retained the scent of wildflowers. It was far too arousing for her own good.

She pushed him gently away and trailed her fingers along the features of his face before she played with the ends of his hair. "Alucard looked just like you, Dracula. He had my ears, but that was all."

"Really?" he chuckled as he tried to envision what Alucard would have looked like now should he have survived. "He must have been handsome then."

"Very," she laughed. "He had your very image."

It felt good to laugh together, even over something terribly heartbreaking. He would mourn his son another day. Right now, he had to keep his Elisabeta happy. He couldn't allow sadness to come between them.

She reached for the ring on her finger and held it out to him, and he swallowed his rising emotions. The kumari's ring. She had kept it all this time?

"I believe this is yours. I should have returned it long ago. It was not mine to take."

"It is absolutely yours to take." He closed her fist around the ring and kissed her knuckles. "I want you as my kumari. If you will have me." Her eyes widened in surprise, and he continued, "If you refuse, I will remain on my knees until you yield."

Her gentle fingers touched his face, and he sighed into her touch. "I am sure that would be breaking one of your many courting rules," she teased.

"Oh, it definitely is. At least two."

"When I am Kumari, the first thing I will abolish are your silly rules. I don't like rules."

"I've noticed." Still, he smiled joyously. She had agreed to stay with him. For the first time in five years, his future didn't look so bleak. Quite the opposite, in fact.

She sobered, and for the first time since her transition, she reached up to her mouth and touched the place where her gums concealed her new fangs. "I don't know how to be a vampire."

"Of course you do. You pretended to be one for weeks and no one was the wiser. You even drank blood as a human to keep up your pretense. Besides, Nicolae, Lucian, and I will be here to help." He grinned wickedly as he caressed her smooth neck. "Now I can finally give you that love bite."

She returned his grin with a coy look. "I made you promise to never bite me."

He shrugged. "But now you are a vampire, the promise is obsolete. Shall we practice?"

He had only been half-serious, which was why it took him by surprise when she wrapped an arm around his neck and pulled him down to kiss him. A spark he hadn't felt in years came to life inside of him, and he was powerless against it. He gave in all too easily as he returned her kiss, deepening it with the passion growing inside of him. He threaded his fingers through her hair, breathing out fiery passion. It felt bloody good to kiss his mate again.

Running his fingertips up her arms, he pinned them above her head and kissed her neck, but then he froze. He had forgotten about one very crucial detail.

Much to her confusion, he stood, tromped to the opposite side of the room, and threw open the door that led to Nicolae's study to find him immersed in one of his books. He didn't even flinch at Dracula's glower.

"Get out," he growled.

"These are my chambers," Nicolae said, flipping the page.

His nose twitched as he intensified his glare. "Get. Out."

Nicolae sighed and finally closed his book. "And here I was enjoying a peaceful morning." He stood and sighed again dramatically. "I have a feeling I will not want these chambers anymore once you are done here. Therefore, I hope you will take the liberty of moving all my things to the chambers down the hallway."

Before leaving, Nicolae grinned knowingly, and it wasn't until he left completely that Dracula crawled onto the bed with Elisabeta and resumed the fiery kiss. He poured every lost moment, every missed day into the kiss. He tangled his fingers into her hair, he pressed his body more firmly against hers.

He yelped as her fangs sprouted from her gums and pierced his lip. He instinctively jerked away and pressed his hand to his bleeding lip.

"I am so sorry," she gasped. "I didn't mean to—I didn't realize—"

He couldn't stop himself from laughing at her

fluster while his small puncture wound started to close up. "Young vampires cannot easily control their fangs nor their venom. It will come with time, I promise."

"Then you aren't angry?"

Grinning wickedly, he shook his head and placed feather kisses on her neck. "Though, it isn't fair Nicolae got to bite you first. I want a turn as well."

She returned his grin and whispered in his ear, "Gladly."

Chapter 37

After hundreds of years had passed, Dracula had finally eased into his role as Shah. They'd experienced a few hiccups near the beginning as other vampire covens outside the city challenged them over the opportunity to rule Ichor Knell themselves, but he had quickly put a stop to the violence. Times were much more peaceful now, and he did everything in his power to keep it that way.

"Trade with the humans is going well," Nicolae said in a meeting with a dozen other vampires in attendance. "They give us human criminals in exchange for the peace we bring to their people."

"Can't say I don't miss the chaos at least a little bit," Ivar chuckled under his breath.

"But at least humans aren't quite as afraid of us," Gabriel threw out there. "This trading deal has saved a lot of lives on both ends."

He leaned back in his chair, overcome with satisfaction. The fruits of his labors were paying off. He'd been in rule longer than Jorin now, and the ideas he'd once dreamed of for their city were now a reality. These trades, these laws, were working, and his people were seeing prosperity once again.

The sound of rushing feet on carpet caught his attention, and he cocked his ears as he listened to it getting closer and closer. Now, who would be running through the halls like a maniac?

His question was answered as Elisabeta burst through the door, her red hair a mess as if it had fallen out during her sprint. She said nothing as she breathed heavily, her eyes wide. Everyone's attention was on her, including his own.

"Elisabeta, what the blazes—"

He stopped short when his words became strangled inside his throat, the ice of shock shooting through his veins. His legs turned wobbly and he hardly managed to push himself to his feet as he listened.

Amongst every heartbeat within the room, he detected another one. A fast but small rhythm emanated from Elisabeta's belly. Moisture collected in his eyes, but he didn't bother to hide it as he ran a hand over his mouth. Finally, he spoke.

"Meeting adjourned," he said in a husky voice.

He took one step toward Elisabeta and then another, until he grabbed her hand and pulled her down the hallway. He didn't release it until they entered the gardens. They burst into joyous laughter as he picked her up by the waist and spun her around in circles.

"I thought we'd never be able to have another child," he laughed again, kissing both cheeks, her nose, and finally lingering on her mouth where he poured every single emotion he felt over this new discovery. When he pulled away, she was breathless yet again.

"I thought so as well. It's been centuries."

With a gentle hand, he placed his fingers over her belly. He closed his eyes as he rested his head against hers and listened to the child growing within her. Their child.

"What will we name the baby?" he asked, opening

his eyes to find her smiling at him. She had never looked more beautiful than she did in that moment. Wild red hair, bright, lively green eyes, red lips he planned to kiss thoroughly later tonight, and freckles he felt sure he had each one memorized by heart.

Her smile widened as she took his hand and led him toward the river. They ducked beneath their willow tree, the one they had carved their initials into centuries ago. They remained etched into the bark, as if the tree refused to grow over their declaration of love.

"I will let you name the child if it's a boy," she said, reverently tracing their initials with a finger. "But if it's a girl, I want to call her Willow."

He arched a single eyebrow. "You want to name her after a tree?"

"*Especially* after a tree," she laughed, and the sound alone drew a smile from him.

He wrapped his arms around her waist and pulled her close enough to breathe in her tantalizing scent. "I am so happy, Elisabeta."

"Me too, Dracula," she whispered against his lips. "Me too."

A word about the author...

Sydney Winward is a multi-published author born with an artistic brain and a love of discovery for new talents. From drawing to sewing to music, she has loved to explore every opportunity that comes her way.

At a young age, Sydney discovered her love of writing, and she hasn't been able to stop writing since. Her active imagination and artistic mind take her away to different worlds and time periods, making every new story a fantastic adventure.

When she is not writing (or fawning over animals in the neighborhood) she spends time with her husband and children at home in Utah.

Visit her at:

www.sydneywinward.com

Thank you for purchasing
this publication of The Wild Rose Press, Inc.

For questions or more information
contact us at
info@thewildrosepress.com.

The Wild Rose Press, Inc.
www.thewildrosepress.com

CPSIA information can be obtained
at www.ICGtesting.com
Printed in the USA
BVHW041750250221
601131BV00007B/40

9 781509 235070